BILLY BUNTER'S POSTAL ORDER

FROM A POCKET OF HER APRON, MARY PRODUCED A
CRUMPLED, DUSTY STRIP OF PAPER

Page 239

BILLY BUNTER'S POSTAL ORDER

By
FRANK RICHARDS

Illustrated by
R. J. MACDONALD

First published 1951 by Skilton Ltd

This facsimile edition published 1994 by:
HAWK BOOKS
Suite 309
Canalot Studios
222 Kensal Road
London W10 5BN

© 1994 Una Hamilton-Wright

ISBN 1 899441 00 X

Printed and Bound by Professional Book Supplies Ltd. England

CONTENTS

CONTENTS

CHAPTER I

BUNTER IN A JAM

MR. QUELCH frowned.

His frown was directed towards the fattest member of his form.

Several times, during second school that morning, Mr. Quelch had glanced at Billy Bunter, severely.

Now he frowned at him—thunderously.

Every fellow in the Greyfriars Remove—excepting Billy Bunter !—noted that frown on the form-master's severe brow, and sat up and took notice accordingly.

A frown on Quelch's brow indicated that he was getting " shirty ". It portended trouble.

Quelch's frown, in that form-room, had almost the effect of Jove's nod on Olympus. If it did not exactly shake the heavens, at least it warned all concerned that the thunder was about to roll.

In which circumstances, nobody in the Remove wanted to draw Quelch's special attention to himself.

Harry Wharton, who had a football list under his desk, dismissed it from mind. Bob Cherry, who had been thinking of projecting an ink-ball at Lord Mauleverer, just to wake old Mauly up, abandoned the idea. Frank Nugent, who had been whispering to Johnny Bull and Hurree Jamset Ram Singh, became as dumb as an oyster. Lord Mauleverer, about to yawn—that being the effect of Virgil's deathless verse on his lordship !—suppressed that yawn. The Bounder, who had been lounging, sat up. Other fellows reacted to Quelch's frown in more or less the same way. Not one was anxious to catch his gimlet-eye.

Only Billy Bunter remained regardless. Bunter, apparently, couldn't care less.

That was not because Billy Bunter was a fellow of

7

tremendous nerve, reckless of his form-master's frowns. Quelch's frowns, when he saw them, were wont to make the fat Owl of the Remove quake. It was because Billy Bunter didn't see the signs of gathering wrath.

There were two reasons for that. The first was, that the Owl of the Remove couldn't see very far, anyway, even with the aid of his big spectacles. The second was, that Bunter's attention was fixed, not on Quelch, or on the lesson, but on the form-room clock.

That was why Quelch frowned.

Often and often, fellows in form were interested in the clock. Even Quelch hardly expected them to feel sorry when the hand drew nearer and nearer to 10.45, the welcome signal for break.

But still less did he expect them to devote their whole attention to the clock, just as if the valuable instruction they were receiving from him had been something weary, stale, flat and unprofitable, of which they were anxious only to hear the end !

Any fellow but Bunter could glance at the clock, note the time, and have done with it. Not so Bunter. Bunter had to concentrate his eyes and spectacles on the clock, and even then he was not quite sure. This performance irritated Quelch.

Once, or even twice, he could have pardoned. But every four or five minutes, at least, Bunter's eyes and spectacles swivelled round to the clock. For some reason, known only to himself, Billy Bunter was unusually and particularly anxious that morning for break to arrive. The clock seemed to draw him like a magnet.

Now, once more, those eyes and spectacles were concentrated on the clock, while the thunder grew and intensified in Quelch's brow, unheeded by Bunter, though warily heeded by every other fellow in the Remove.

And then, as if to add the finishing touch to Quelch's wrath, Bunter, still happily unconscious of the signs of stormy weather, whispered to Skinner.

" I say, Skinner ! What's the time ? "

Skinner made no reply. He, if not Bunter, was aware of the frown, and the glint in the gimlet-eye.

" I can't quite make out the beastly thing from here," whispered Bunter, " I say, is it twenty to ? "

Skinner was still dumb. Bunter gave him an irritated blink, and then turned his spectacles on Snoop.

" I say, Snoopey ! You can see that beastly clock ! Has it stopped ? "

Snoop was as dumb as Skinner.

Mark Linley was on " con ". He went on : but Quelch's attention was no longer fixed on the best scholar in his form, whose translation always gave him satisfaction. It had wandered to Bunter—and stayed there !

" I say, Stott, is it nearly a quarter to ? " whispered Bunter.

Stott, like Skinner and Snoop, seemed both deaf and dumb. Peter Todd, though well aware of Quelch's gorgon-like stare, ventured upon a warning whisper.

" Shurrup, you fat ass."

" Oh, really, Toddy ! I say, what's the time ? "

Mr. Quelch breathed hard, and he breathed deep. Not only was Bunter giving no attention whatever to the lesson, and whole and entire attention to the form-room clock, but he was actually whispering in class, right under the glare of the gimlet-eyes.

" That will do, Linley," said Mr. Quelch.

Mark sat down.

" BUNTER ! "

" Oh ! Yes, sir ! " Bunter, thus reminded of the irritating existence of his form-master, turned his spectacles on Mr. Quelch, and became aware of a thunderous frown. " Oh ! I—I wasn't talking, sir ! I only said to Toddy——"

" During this lesson," said Mr. Quelch, " you have given no attention whatever, Bunter."

" Oh, yes, sir ! I—I——"

" You have been continually looking at the clock, Bunter."

" Oh, no, sir ! I—I haven't looked at it at all, sir, and—and I only looked to see whether it had stopped——"

" The clock has not stopped, Bunter. It is exactly twenty minutes to eleven," said Mr. Quelch.

" Oh ! Thank you, sir ! " Bunter's fat face brightened. Only five minutes more of Quelch's tosh, and then——

" You appear very anxious about the time, Bunter."

" Yes, sir ! I mean, no, sir ! Not at all, sir. I—I was only wondering whether there was a letter for me in the rack, sir—I—I—I'm expecting a postal order, sir——" stammered Bunter.

" Oh, my hat ! " murmured Bob Cherry.

There was a general grin, and even a sound of chuckling, in the Remove.

It was no time, with that expressive expression on Quelch's countenance, either to grin or to chuckle. But the Remove fellows could hardly help it.

Every fellow in the Remove, if not every fellow at Greyfriars School, had heard of the postal order Bunter expected. Bunter lived in a perpetual state of expecting a postal order, which seldom or never materialised. Apparently, on this particular morning, Bunter had some particular reason for supposing that that long-felt expectation was to be realised at last—at long last ! So it was, perhaps, no wonder that Bunter was much more interested in the clock than in P. Vergilius Maro and the adventures of the ' pius Aeneas '. If that celebrated and long-expected postal order really was waiting for him in the letter-rack, it was almost cruelty to animals to keep Bunter away from it.

Mr. Quelch gave his form a glance, which checked every sign of merriment on the spot. Every face became serious at once.

" Bunter ! " Quelch seemed rather to bite off the name than utter it. " Bunter ! Such matters should be entirely dismissed from mind during class."

" Oh, really, sir—I—I mean, oh, yes, sir ! Certainly !

I—I wasn't thinking about that postal order from my Uncle Carter, sir——"

" You will now construe, Bunter," said Mr. Quelch in a voice like the grinding of a saw, " and if your construe is not satisfactory, Bunter, you will remain in the form-room during break, and write out the lesson."

" Oh, crikey ! " gasped Bunter.

He gazed at his form-master in horror.

Billy Bunter had been counting the minutes, and even the seconds, till break. At the word of dismissal, he was ready to bound out of the form-room like a fat rabbit, and hurtle to the letter-rack, and clutch down the letter which, he believed at least, contained that long-expected postal order ! And now——

" Do you hear me, Bunter ? "

" Oh, scissors ! "

" Construe ! " rapped Mr. Quelch.

Billy Bunter could have groaned aloud. So far from being prepared to hand out a satisfactory ' con ', he was more unprepared than usual to perform that difficult feat. His fat mind was on other things—more important things, though Quelch of course couldn't understand that. Neither had he given much attention to prep the previous evening : hoping—Bunter's perpetual hope !—not to be called on in form. And as he had not been listening, he did not even know where to go on. And now all depended on a good ' con '—if he failed to satisfy Quelch, that postal order—if any !—had to remain in the rack, till after third school ! Which was practically eternity, to the fat Owl who had expected that postal order so long and so hopefully.

But there was no help for Bunter ! He could only make up his fat mind to do his best to extract the meaning from Virgil to the satisfaction of Mr. Quelch—supposing that the brute had any meaning, which Bunter sometimes doubted !

" If you do not immediately construe, Bunter—— ! " said Mr. Quelch, in a deep, deep voice.

"Oh! Yes, sir! I—I've just missed the place——" stammered Bunter.

"You should not miss the place, Bunter."

"Oh! No! Yes! I——"

"You will go on from ' fragrantia mella '."

"Oh! Yes! Thank you, sir." Billy Bunter blinked at his book, and found that ' fragrantia mella ' was followed by an ejaculation of the pius Aeneas, ' O fortunati quorum jam moenia surgunt ! '

Even Billy Bunter must have known that ' jam ' did not mean the same thing in Latin as in English. In English it was a noun dear to Bunter, denoting an article to which he was deeply and sincerely attached. In Latin it was an adverb of time, denoting earliness, and should have been translated ' already '. But William George Bunter's fat mind was in a state of confusion, and as the sentence, simple as it was, presented no meaning to him, he plunged recklessly, hit or miss.

"O happy ones, whose jam—— ! "

Bunter was interrupted.

"Whose WHAT ? " Quelch almost roared.

"Whose jam——"

"Ha, ha, ha ! " howled nearly all the Remove. Billy Bunter's howlers often added to the gaiety of existence in the Remove form-room. But this was a remarkable effort, even for Bunter.

"Silence ! Bunter, you will stay in during break and write out the lesson. You will go on, Wharton."

Harry Wharton went on. A few moments more, and Billy Bunter was aware that that baffling sentence meant ' Oh happy ones, whose ramparts already rise ! ' But that knowledge came too late to be of any use to the hapless Owl. Neither was he interested. He sat overwhelmed with dismay : thinking of the postal order in that letter in the rack, of the attractive edibles in the tuck-shop—so near and yet so far !

CHAPTER II

IN SUSPENSE

" Oh, lor' ! " breathed Billy Bunter.

There was a happy stirring in the Remove.

The clock, which Billy Bunter had watched so anxiously during that lesson, now indicated 10.45—uselessly to Bunter, though very happily to the rest of the Lower Fourth. Quelch was dismissing the Remove for morning ' break '· in a minute more they would be scampering in the quad, or scanning the rack for letters, while the unhappy Owl sat in his place, occupied with the sayings and doings of the excellent though long-winded Aeneas.

Never had William George Bunter been less interested in the proceedings of that wandering Trojan. Never had the woes of Dido touched him less. Neither for Carthage nor for Rome did he care two hoots, or even one. Whether the ramparts of Carthage rose, or whether they fell, was a matter of supreme indifference to him. In fact, he just hated Aeneas and all his works !

" Rough luck, old fat bean," murmured Bob Cherry, as he passed the dismal and dolorous Owl.

" The roughfulness of the luck is truly terrific, my esteemed idiotic Bunter," murmured Hurree Jamset Ram Singh.

" I say, you fellows," whispered Bunter. He blinked at Quelch, who seemed busy with papers at his desk, " I say, think I could dodge out—— ? "

" I wouldn't risk it, old porpoise," Bob shook his head.

" I—I think I'll chance it."

Bunter heaved himself to his feet.

It was well known in the Remove that Quelch, like an elephant, never forgot. There really was no hope that he might have forgotten telling Bunter, only five minutes ago, to stay in. But if there was the remotest possibility, Bunter was not going to lose it. Surely it was possible, if not probable, that the gimlet-eye might miss him, going out with the crowd !

" BUNTER ! "

The fat Owl had taken two steps, when that dreaded voice fell on his fat ears. He gave a startled jump.

" Oh, dear ! I—I mean, yes, sir," groaned Bunter.

" I think I told you to remain in the form-room and write out the lesson, Bunter," said Mr. Quelch, eyeing the fat Owl grimly from his high desk.

" Oh ! Yes, sir ! "

" Yet you appear to have been going out, Bunter."

" Oh ! No, sir ! I—I—I just got up because I had—had cramp in my foot, sir——"

" You will resume your place, Bunter."

" Beast ! " breathed Bunter.

Bunter did not intend Mr. Quelch to hear that. It was not judicious for any fellow to tell his form-master what he thought of him.

But Quelch's ears seemed as sharp as his eyes.

" What ? What did you say, Bunter ? " he exclaimed.

" Oh, crikey ! I never said anything, sir," gasped Bunter, " I—I mean, I—I said 'Thank you ', sir."

Quelch gave him a look. It was such a look as the fabled Gorgon might have bestowed on its victims. Luckily, he let it go at that. Billy Bunter collapsed into his place. Only too evidently, there was no possibility of escaping the gimlet-eye, and going out with the crowd.

Having petrified Bunter with that look, Quelch dropped his eyes again on the papers at his desk.

But Bunter remained petrified only for a moment. The gimlet-eye being off him, he made an almost frantic sign to Bob Cherry, who was heading for the door with the rest, but casting a sympathetic glance at the fat Owl as he went.

Bob good-naturedly turned back.

" I say, can you lend me a nib, Cherry ? " asked Bunter
—for Quelch's benefit if he was heeding.

" Yes, I've got one," answered Bob. " Here you are,
Bunter."

" I say." Bunter was whispering now. " I say, Bob,
old chap, look in the rack and see if there's a letter for me,
will you ? "

" What-ho ! " agreed Bob, also in a whisper, " I'll tell
you when we come in for third school, somehow."

" That's no good ! I say, get it for me, and chuck it
in at the window," breathed Bunter. " Quelch will be
gone in a minute, and it will be all right."

" O.K.," assented Bob.

" Cherry ! " came a grinding voice.

" Oh ! Yes, sir ? "

" You may leave the form-room."

" Oh ! Certainly, sir."

Bob Cherry followed his friends out. The gimlet-eye
followed him to the door, and then fixed on Bunter.

" You will now write out the lesson, Bunter."

" Oh, yes, sir," said Bunter.

He was looking more cheerful now. He dipped his pen
in the ink, and started. Of course it was rotten, in fact
definitely putrid, to have to sit there and write out Virgil,
instead of hurtling rack-wards and grabbing that precious
letter. But there was comfort in the knowledge that Bob
Cherry would get the letter from the rack and ' chuck '
it in at the form-room window. There was, so to speak,
still balm in Gilead !

Quelch would be gone in a minute or two. Bunter
would have the form-room to himself ! For that minute
or two he had to write Latin. But immediately the door
closed after Quelch's lean form, Latin was going to be,
not merely a dead language, but buried too, so far as Billy
Bunter was concerned. That precious letter would come
whizzing in at the open window—Bunter was going to

grab it up—and though he wouldn't be able to expend the
postal order in tuck during break, at least he would know
that it had come, and would have it in his fat hands!
Actually, really and truly, his Uncle Carter had promised
him a pound: for once, if for once only, Billy Bunter's
postal order was not merely a figment of a hopeful imagi-
nation! Billy Bunter's fat soul yearned to feel that postal
order in his fat fingers!—if it had come, and he was sure
that it had!

He wanted to spend it at the tuck-shop. But almost
more, he wanted to let the other fellows see it, just to let
them know that he really did get postal orders from affectionate relatives. If that letter materialised, and if it did
really contain the expected postal order, every fellow in
the Remove was going to know all about it during third
school. Bunter was going to let it be seen, carelessly as
it were. He was going to drop it accidentally, and pick
it up again. He was going to leave it lying negligently
on his desk. He was in fact going to make it quite clear
to everybody who was interested, and to everybody who
wasn't, that he really had a postal order for a pound!

They made jokes in the Remove about Billy Bunter's
postal order. Fellows would ask him whether it was the
same one that he had been expecting when he was in the
Second Form. They would ask him whether it had grown
whiskers in the post, having been so long on the way.
Well, now they would jolly well see!

Bunter scribbled Latin, dropped blots, and added
smudges, impatiently waiting for Quelch to go. Quelch
generally went out after the Remove: 'break' being,
probably, as welcome to the form-master as to the form.
It was unusual, though not unknown, for him to remain
in the form-room. But on this occasion he seemed very
slow in getting a move on.

He sat at his high desk, going through papers—some
rot, no doubt, that he was getting ready for third school.
Bunter, while he scribbled, incessantly cast blinks at Quelch,

just as he had cast blinks at the form-room clock during the lesson. Would the beast never go ?

It looked as if he wouldn't !

Slowly, and with horror, it dawned on Billy Bunter's mind that Quelch wasn't going !

Sometimes he stayed in the form-room in break—not often, but sometimes. Was this one of the times ?

It looked like it !

The unutterable and indescribable beast—such was Bunter's view of his form-master !—seemed to have settled down at the desk. The minutes were passing—and break lasted only fifteen minutes ! If he did not go—— !

Bunter felt quite faint at the awful thought !

Bob Cherry would wait a few minutes, to make sure that Quelch was gone—not knowing that the beast wasn't going ! Then he would ' chuck ' that letter in at the form-room window, for Bunter to field—right under the gimlet-eyes ! What would happen then ?

What would Quelch do, if a letter were thrown in to a fellow under detention, and he saw it ? Bunter didn't know what Quelch would do—but he knew that it would be something frightfully unpleasant.

" Oh, lor ' ! " breathed Bunter.

From the bottom of his fat heart, he wished that he hadn't thought of that astute plan for getting his letter during break after all. He had been yearning for it to whiz in at the window. Now he hoped that it wouldn't ! He even hoped that it hadn't come ! He was prepared to hope for anything, except for that letter to drop into the form-room under Quelch's eyes !

If only he would go—— !

Five minutes had passed ! If that letter had come, and if Bob Cherry kept his word, as he was certain to do, it might come whizzing in at the window any moment now. Would Quelch go ?

The minutes seemed like hours to the hapless Owl. Then, at length, Quelch moved. Bunter's eyes almost

B

popped through his spectacles at him.   Was his luck in—
was the beast really going ?

He was !

Having neatly arranged the papers on his desk—Quelch
was always exact—he turned towards the form-room door.
He gave Bunter a glance—a severe glance—and walked to
the door—actually going !   Another minute—less than a
minute—and all would be serene.   Hardly a minute—— !

Quelch's hand was on the door-handle.

Whiz !

Plop !

Quelch did not open the door he was about to open.
He turned round, in surprise, at that unexpected ' plop '
behind him, to ascertain the cause !

CHAPTER III

THE LETTER FOR BUNTER

" HALLO, hallo, hallo ! "

" What—— ? "

" It's come ! "

A little crowd of fellows were looking at the letters in the rack. Bob Cherry's eyes fell upon one addressed to W. G. Bunter. He picked it out from the rest, and held it up.

Whether that letter contained, or not, the postal order that Billy Bunter was expecting, could not be said. But the letter, at all events, had arrived. But for the un satisfactory nature of Bunter's ' con ', the Owl of the Remove would have been there, to receive it. Really, it was rough luck on Bunter. Generally, in break, he haunted the letter-rack like a fat ghost, with eyes and spectacles eager for a letter that might contain a remittance. And now that, at long last, such a letter had arrived, Bunter was detained in the form-room by a remorseless form-master : and could feast neither his eyes nor his spectacles upon it.

" Poor old Bunter," said Harry Wharton. " If there's a postal order in that letter, it's tough to have to wait for it."

" If ! " said Frank Nugent, laughing.

" The if-fulness is terrific," remarked Hurree Jamset Ram Singh.

" Terrific and preposterous ! " agreed Bob Cherry. " But the old fat man seemed jolly certain about it, and it may have come this time."

" Wonders will never cease ! " remarked Johnny Bull.

" Look here, if Bunter's postal order has come, he

oughtn't to be allowed to spend it," said Vernon-Smith. " It ought to be framed and hung up in hall."

" Ha, ha, ha ! "

" Quelch ought to stretch a point, and let him have his postal order, if it's come ! " said Peter Todd. " It's not a thing that often happens."

" He's going to have it," said Bob. " I told him I'd chuck the letter in at the form-room window if I found it here : and here it is."

" Fathead ! " said Johnny Bull. " You're not allowed to speak to a fellow in detention, let alone to take him letters."

" True, O King ! " admitted Bob, " but poor old Bunter isn't going to wait till after third school for his postal order."

" If any ! " remarked Skinner.

" If you're spotted chucking that letter into the form-room, you'll get into a row, you ass," grunted Johnny Bull. " Quelch would go right off at the deep end—and he's not in the best of tempers, to begin with."

" Well, I said I would," answered Bob, " so it can't be helped. Besides, think of poor old Bunter pining for his postal order : he really thinks it's in this letter, and he will be on tenterhooks."

" Oh, come on," said Harry Wharton. " We'll stroll past the form-room window, and you can chuck it in when nobody's looking."

The Famous Five walked out into the quad, Bob Cherry with Bunter's letter in his hand. It was true that it was a somewhat serious infraction of the rules and regulations, to convey a letter to a fellow in detention : but as Bob had good-naturedly undertaken to do that very thing, it couldn't, as he said, be helped. But it was necessary to be cautious.

The juniors strolled, in a careless, casual sort of way, round by the form-room windows. They had a wary eye open for Mr. Quelch, who often walked in the quad in morning break. But Quelch was not to be seen in the quad, and they concluded that he was in his study, where he was safe out of the way. That this was one of the rare occasions when he stayed on in the form-room naturally did not occur to them.

But though Quelch was not to be seen, two other beaks dawned on them, on the path under the windows—Prout, master of the Fifth, and Capper, master of the Fourth. Prout and Capper were walking along that path, talking as they walked.

" No go ! " murmured Frank Nugent.

" Hang about a bit," said Bob.

The Famous Five hung about a bit. Prout and Capper progressed as far as the corner of the building : and then turned and walked back.

" Bother them ! " murmured Bob. " If they're going to trickle up and down that path all through break——"

" Better chuck it," suggested Johnny Bull.

" Can't chuck it while two beaks stick there."

" Ass ! Chuck it up."

" Prout's got his eye on us," said Nugent.

Mr. Prout glanced round at the five juniors. He gave them a severe glance. There was no law against fellows loitering in the quad, in break, if the spirit moved them so to do. Still, the majestic Prout did not approve of a bunch of juniors standing and staring at him.

" Better clear," murmured Harry Wharton. " Prout will guess that we're up to something, if we stick here."

" The guessfulness will be terrific."

" Bunter's got to have his letter," said Bob.

" Cut off now, and come back when they're gone," said Harry.

" Oh, all right."

The Famous Five strolled off the scene. Prout and Capper walked to and fro on the path under the windows. From a distance, the chums of the Remove had an eye on them.

But it did not seem useful to wait till they were gone, as the captain of the Remove had suggested. They did

not seem to be going. Apparently they were booked for
walking and talking on that path by the form-room windows, so long as the morning interval lasted.

"They're fixtures there," said Johnny Bull, at last.
"What about punting a ball, you fellows ? "

"Bunter's going to have his letter," said Bob, obstinately.
"I told him I'd chuck it in to him."

"You can't, under Prout's eyes and Capper's nose."

"Well, look here, you fellows keep clear, and I'll try it
on," said Bob. "I can chuck that letter into the window,
while they've got their backs turned, see ? "

"If they look round——"

"Oh, rot ! I'll chance it."

"It will be a row with Quelch——"

"Bless Quelch ! "

Bob Cherry settled the matter by leaving his com-
panions, and crossing towards the form-room windows.
They watched him rather anxiously from a distance.

Prout and Capper had passed under the open Remove
window again, and were progressing once more towards
the corner of the building. Bob Cherry strolled on the
path behind them.

He calculated that Prout and Capper would take at
least a minute to reach the corner, where they would
turn again. That was ample time, if they did not
look round before they turned. It was really safe as
houses—or looked so ! Bob made up his mind to it, at
any rate.

He cut across the path, to the open window, which
was well above the level of his head. Up went his hand,
with the letter in it. And then—— !

Perhaps the loitering juniors had made Prout suspicious.
Perhaps he had noted, with the corner of his eye, Bob
cutting across to the path. Anyhow, long before he
reached the corner where he was scheduled to revolve,
Prout looked round.

He looked round at the precise moment that the letter

left Bob's upraised hand and whizzed in at the open
window of the Remove form-room.

"Upon my word!" ejaculated Mr. Prout. "Cherry!"

"Oh!" gasped Bob.

"What are you doing, Cherry?"

"Oh! Nothing, sir."

"Did you throw something in at that window?"

"Um! Yes, sir."

"What prank is this?" exclaimed Mr. Prout, frowning.
"Cherry, I shall report your action to your form-master."

Bob Cherry walked back to rejoin his friends, with deep
feelings.

"Blow Prout, and bother Bunter," he said. "That
means a jaw from Quelch."

"More likely six!" said Johnny Bull: apparently in
the role of Job's comforter. "Quelch will be shirty! I
told you so."

"Fathead!"

"Well, I did tell you so, old chap——"

"You did," agreed Bob, "and if you tell me so again,
I'll jolly well ram your silly head against that tree, see?"

"Come on, and punt a footer," said Harry Wharton,
hastily: and the Famous Five devoted the remainder of
break to punting a ball, and dismissed the matter from
their minds—though there was little doubt that Bob Cherry
was to be reminded of it later.

CHAPTER IV

BEASTLY FOR BUNTER

MR. QUELCH stared.

Billy Bunter groaned.

Mr. Quelch was staring at a letter that had fallen sud-denly into the Remove form-room, and lay on the floor, between the desks and the window. Bunter groaned as he watched Quelch staring at it.

Really, it was cruel luck. A few more moments, and Quelch would have been gone. But Quelch was not gone : he was there, staring at the letter on the floor, in great surprise—which was already turning to wrath.

That letter had been thrown in at the open window, by some fellow unseen below the high sill. Obviously, it must have been thrown in for somebody ! And as there were only Quelch and Bunter in the form-room, and as it was unimaginable that it could have been thrown in for Quelch, obviously it had been thrown in for Bunter. Some reckless and temerarious person, having found a letter for Bunter in the rack, had tossed it in to him, with an utter and absolute disregard of all rules and regulations on the subject of detention ! And if Quelch had not happened to remain in the form-room, the detained junior would have picked up that letter, and read it, instead of con-centrating himself on his task ! No wonder Quelch's brow knitted in a thunderous frown. Quelch was a whale on discipline. This was a serious infraction of discipline.

" Oh, crikey ! " groaned Bunter.

The expected letter had come—evidently ! Bob Cherry had done what he had undertaken to do ! There was the letter ! Everything had gone according to plan—excepting that the letter had dropped into the form-room under Quelch's eyes as well as Bunter's !

Quelch stood staring at the letter: Bunter sat blinking at Quelch! For a few moments there was a dead, indeed a deadly, silence. Then Quelch rapped:

" Bunter ! "

" Oh ! Yes, sir," gasped Bunter.

" What does this mean ? "

" I—I—I don't know, sir," stammered Bunter.

" That is a letter," said Mr. Quelch. " It has been thrown in at the form-room window, Bunter."

" Has—has—has it, sir ? "

" It has, Bunter ! No doubt the boy who threw it in was unaware that I was still in the form-room," said Mr. Quelch, grimly. " I presume that that letter is for you, Bunter !"

" Oh ! Yes ! No ! I——"

" No doubt you arranged this, Bunter, expecting to be alone here."

" I—I—oh—I—ah—I——"

Mr. Quelch gave the fat Owl an expressive look, and walked across to the open window. He passed the letter lying on the floor, apparently more interested in the person who had thrown it in, than in the letter itself.

He put his head out of the window, and discerned Mr. Prout and Mr. Capper peregrinating on the path below. They had reached the corner again, and turned. Quelch waited for them to come nearer. He had no doubt that they must have seen the person who had surreptitiously introduced that letter into the form-room to a junior in detention.

His back was now to Bunter.

Bunter blinked at that lean back, and then at the letter on the floor behind Quelch.

He half-rose.

Quelch, plainly, wasn't going to let him have that letter. But to lose it now was more than flesh and blood could stand.

Bunter was not eager to read the actual letter. What-

ever Uncle Carter might have written to him, could wait,
and it did not matter much how long.   But Billy Bunter
wanted to ascertain whether the postal order was in it.
He was certain—practically certain—as good as sure, but—
there was always a lingering doubt, at least, in the matter
of Billy Bunter's postal orders.   Uncle Carter was going
to send him a postal order for a pound.   Was it in that
letter ?   He had to know !   Quelch or no Quelch, he just
had to know.

" Mr. Prout ! "   Quelch was speaking from the window.
Bunter realised that the Fifth-form master was outside.
Quelch was booked for a minute or two !

The fat Owl rose, and tiptoed towards the letter.

Once he got it open, once he ascertained that there was
the expected postal order in it, it would be all right.   He
did not care whether Quelch let him keep the letter or
not, so long as he had the postal order !   That was the
important thing !

" Oh !   Is that you, Quelch ? " came Prout's boom from
without.

" A letter has been thrown into this form-room, Mr.
Prout, to a boy in detention.   If you saw anyone——"

" I did, sir ! " boomed Prout.   " I certainly saw a boy
of your form throw something in at that window, Mr.
Quelch, only two or three minutes ago.   His name is Cherry.
I warned him that I should report his action to you."

The tiptoeing Owl reached the letter.

He clutched it up.

In an instant, a fat and grubby thumb was inserted into
the envelope, and it was open.

" Thank you, Mr. Prout."

Quelch turned from the window.

No doubt he expected to see Billy Bunter still sitting in
his place, for he gave quite a start, as he perceived the
fat Owl standing only two or three yards from him, the
letter in his fat left hand, the fat thumb of his right jammed
in the envelope, in the very act of slitting it open.

HE PERCEIVED THE FAT OWL IN THE VERY ACT
OF SLITTING IT OPEN

"Bunter!" Quelch fairly thundered.

"Oh!" gasped Bunter.

He jumped, and dropped the letter. It was just like Quelch to spot him at that very moment, before he had had time to see what was in the envelope. There was a folded letter inside—but was there a postal order? Another couple of seconds, and Bunter would have known. Now he was still in ignorance—certainly not an occasion when ignorance was bliss!

"Bunter! How dare you open that letter in detention?" thundered Mr. Quelch.

"Oh! I—I didn't—I—I wasn't—I—I mean, I—I—I never——"

"Pick it up, and hand it to me immediately."

Bunter picked up the letter. But he did not hand it to Mr. Quelch immediately. It seemed glued to his fat fingers. It seemed physically impossible for Bunter to part with that letter—at least until he had looked into it.

"Do you hear me, Bunter?"

"Oh! Yes, sir! But—but——"

"Give me that letter at once."

"I—I—I——"

"At once!" rapped Mr. Quelch, in a voice that made the fat Owl jump almost clear of the form-room floor.

Bunter handed over the letter. There was no help for it. His little round eyes almost bulged through his big round spectacles after it. But it had to go. Quelch's long lean fingers closed on it, vice-like.

"Now, Bunter," said Mr. Quelch, sternly. "You will take a hundred lines for having arranged with Cherry to disregard a very strict rule in this outrageous manner. I shall deal with Cherry later. Now return to your place."

"B-b-but, sir——"

"This letter," continued Mr. Quelch, "I shall take with me to my study. It will be given you after class to-day, Bunter."

"B-b-b-but, sir——"

" I have told you to take your place, Bunter, and resume your task."

" Oh, lor' ! "

The fat Owl took his place. Quelch gave him the grimmest of looks, and walked to the door, with the letter in his hand.

" Beast ! " breathed Bunter, inaudibly.

He shook a clenched fat fist at his form-master's back. He did not expect Quelch to glance round, at the form-room door. But Quelch did !

" Bless my soul ! " ejaculated Mr. Quelch. " What——! "

" Oh, crikey ! I—I—I was only—only scratching my nose, sir——" gasped Bunter.

" You will take two hundred lines, Bunter."

" Oh, scissors ! "

Mr. Quelch left the form-room with that. Not until the door had closed on him, did the fat Owl venture to shake his fat fist again. Then, having brandished that fat fist ferociously at the door, the dismal Owl settled down once more to scribbling Latin.

But he hardly heeded what he scribbled. His fat thoughts followed that letter on its way to Quelch's study : the letter that, ten to one, a hundred to one, contained a postal order for a pound : the long-expected postal order which was, in Bunter's opinion at least, worth all the works of Virgil, with P. Vergilius Maro himself thrown in ! True, he was to receive that letter after class : but how was a fellow to wait till after class for his postal order— especially considering how long Bunter had waited for a postal order already ! That day was going to be the longest Bunter had ever known ! The fat Owl sat and scribbled, scrawled, blotted, and smeared, and like Rachel of old mourned for that which was gone, and could not be comforted.

CHAPTER V

UP TO BOB CHERRY

" I say, you fellows ! "

Billy Bunter rolled up to the Famous Five in the quad after third school. Third school lasted only an hour : but to William George Bunter it had seemed almost endless : dragging its weary length along like a wounded snake. However, it was over at last : all things come to an end : even the weariest river winds somewhere safe to sea ! and such trifling matters as lessons being out of the way, Bunter was free to think of matters of far greater importance : chief among which was the letter now in Quelch's study, which contained—perhaps—a postal order for a pound from his Uncle Carter at Folkestone. From Bunter's point of view, that postal order was the one thing of real importance within the wide limits of the universe : and the stars in their courses were very small beer in comparison.

" You asked for it, Bob, you know," Johnny Bull was saying, as the Owl of the Remove came up. " I told you so——"

" Idiot ! " said Bob Cherry, briefly.

Bob, like Bunter, had been awarded a hundred lines for the episode of the letter at the form-room window. Quelch, as Johnny Bull had predicted, had been ' shirty ' about it. Bob seemed to derive no consolation from the circumstance that Johnny had told him so.

" I say, you fellows——"

" Oh blow away, Bunter," said Bob. " You've got me a hundred lines over your dashed silly letter."

" Oh, really, Cherry——" yapped Bunter, impatiently. It was rather irritating to Bunter, for a fellow to waste

time talking about a trifle that mattered nothing, when
Bunter had affairs of the first importance to discuss.

" Did the jolly old postal order turn up after all ? "
asked Frank Nugent, with a grin.

" Quelch wouldn't let me have the letter," said Bunter,
sorrowfully. " The awful beast was in the form-room, you
know. I got it open while he was burbling to Prout at
the window, but he spotted me before I could take the
letter out——"

" And so the poor dog had none ? "

" Ha, ha, ha ! "

" Blessed if I see anything to cackle at ! " said Bunter
warmly. " Quelch has got that letter, and he says I'm
to have it after class. I know the postal order's in it—
that's practically a certainty. Well, look here, you fellows,
how am I going to get that letter ? "

Five fellows stared at Bunter. If Quelch had taken
possession of the letter, they regarded that as ending the
matter, until Quelch decided to hand it over. Bunter, it
seemed, did not.

"You'll have to wait till Quelch coughs it up, fathead,"
said Harry Wharton.

" Oh, don't be an ass," said Bunter, peevishly. " I want
that postal order ! Think I'm going to wait till after class
for my own postal order ! I say, you fellows, Quelch has
gone out—and he won't be in till tiffin. I heard Prout
ask him if he was going near the post office, and he said yes,
so that means that he's gone as far as Friardale——"

" What about it, ass ? "

" Well, he wouldn't take my letter with him for a walk,"
explained Bunter. " He's left it in his study, of course."
The fat Owl blinked at the Famous Five, through his big
spectacles. " I say, which of you fellows will cut into
Quelch's study and get my postal order ? "

" Echo answers which ! " grinned Bob Cherry.

" Esteemed echo answers that the whichfulness is terrific ! " chuckled Hurree Jamset Ram Singh.

"You fat chump!" said Harry Wharton. "If Quelch has left the letter in his study, you'd better leave it there, too. Quelch would skin a fellow for bagging it."

"'Tain't the letter," explained Bunter. "It's the postal order I want. I don't mind waiting till after class to read Uncle Carter's letter. That doesn't matter at all really. It's the postal order, see? You nip into Quelch's study, Harry, old chap——"

"Do I?"

"Yes, old fellow! Safe as houses, with Quelch gone out, at least as far as Friardale—very likely as far as Courtfield. Besides, if you're copped in his study, you're head boy, you know—you can say you came there about the Form papers, or something, being head boy——"

"Oh, my hat! Can I?"

"Of course you can, old chap! You're not very bright, old fellow, or you'd think of these things yourself! Still, I can do the thinking, if it comes to that," said Bunter. "Ten to one Quelch has left my letter on his table—I don't suppose he'd guess for a minute that any fellow would go there after it——"

"No, I don't think he would!" agreed the captain of the Remove, laughing. "It's not a thing that's likely to happen."

"Easy enough for you, old chap! You can easily pull his leg, if he came in and found you there, being head boy——"

"Head boy isn't appointed for the purpose of pulling his form-master's leg," said Harry Wharton.

"Besides, he won't come in!" urged Bunter. "He's going to a post office for something, and the nearest is a mile away. I don't want you to snoop the letter, you know—Quelch would miss that and kick up a row. But it's open—I got it open before Quelch spotted me. All you've got to do is to take the postal order out. You can leave the letter there for Quelch! He wouldn't look into a fellow's letter—besides, he doesn't know there's a postal order in it, anyway. So you see, it's safe as houses. Cut in, old chap, will you ? "

" Not at all ! "

" O, really, Wharton——"

" Forget all about it, you fat ass ! "

" I say, Nugent, will you cut in and get my postal order out of that letter ? "

" Not in these trousers ! "

" Beast ! I say, Inky—— ? "

" The answer is in the absurd negative, my esteemed idiotic Bunter," said Hurree Jamset Ram Singh. " The waitfulness till after class is the proper caper."

" Oh, don't be a goat ! I say, Bull——"

" Fathead ! " said Johnny Bull.

" Bob, old fellow—— ! "

" Chuck it, you ass," said Bob Cherry. " You've got me a hundred lines already, for pitching that silly letter into the form-room. I don't want six on the bags over and above, for rooting about in Quelch's study."

Billy Bunter blinked at the Famous Five in great exasperation.

" I say, you fellows, don't be mouldy funks," he urged. " I keep on telling you it's safe as houses——"

" Sure it's quite safe ? " asked Frank Nugent.

" Absolutely," declared Bunter. " Couldn't be safer ! Quelch's a mile away. The letter's bound to be on his table. You take out the postal order, leaving the letter there for Quelch when he comes in. He couldn't know a thing. Ain't that absolutely safe ? "

" Looks like it," admitted Nugent.

" You'll go, old chap ? "

" Oh, no ! I won't go ! You go !' "

" Eh ? "

" Safe as houses," said Nugent. " Go in and win."

" Beast ! "

" Ha, ha, ha ! "

Safe as it was, absolutely safe according to Bunter, the

c

fat Owl did not seem disposed to undertake the venture himself.

" Look here, it's up to you, Bob Cherry ! " exclaimed Bunter.

Bob stared at him.

" How is it up to me specially ? " he asked.

" Well, it's all your fault that Quelch has got the letter at all. If you hadn't chucked it in at the window——"

" Why, you fat villain, didn't you ask me to chuck it in at the window and haven't I got a hundred lines for chucking it in ? " roared Bob.

" That's all very well," said Bunter. " But if you'd left it alone——"

" If I'd left it alone ! " repeated Bob, almost dazedly, while his comrades grinned.

" Yes, if you'd left it alone, it would have been in the rack when we came out after third school, and I should have it now," said Bunter, blinking at him. " You've done the whole thing : and now you've landed my postal order in Quelch's study, it's jolly well up to you to go and get it for me, see ? "

" Ha, ha, ha ! " yelled four members of the famous Co., quite entertained by the expression on Bob Cherry's face.

" Why, you—you—you—— ! " gasped Bob. " You—you—you fat octopus—you blithering bandersnatch—you—you——"

" You can call a fellow names," said Bunter, " but you jolly well know that it's up to you to get that postal order out of Quelch's study, after landing it there as you did ! If you'd left it alone, it would be all right. And I can jolly well say—yarooooop ! "

Billy Bunter was interrupted, by a wrathful hand grabbing his collar and slewing him round. Bunter guessed what was coming next : and he roared in anticipation. His anticipation was immediately realised. The largest foot in the Greyfriars Remove landed on the tightest trousers in the county of Kent.

Thud !

" Yooo-hoooop ! "

Thud !

" Whooo-hoo—hooooop ! "

Billy Bunter fled for his fat life. Bob Cherry glared after him, while four members of the Co. howled with laughter.

" You fat villain, come back and have another ! " roared Bob.

" Ha, ha, ha ! "

" Ow ! Beast ! Wow ! "

Billy Bunter did not come back for another. Two seemed enough for him. Bunter vanished into space, leaving Bob Cherry glaring, and the rest of the Co. laughing.

CHAPTER VI

FISHY TRIES IT ÒN

" Fishy, old chap ! "

" Yeah ? "

" I owe you a bob," said Billy Bunter.

Fisher T. Fish fixed his eyes on Bunter. His look was inimical. For more than a whole term, Billy Bunter had owed him that ' bob ', and Fishy had despaired of ever seeing it again. It was a bitter memory. Reminding him of that irreparable loss was sheer cruelty. It was like probing an old wound.

How even Billy Bunter, with all his well-known skill as a borrower, had ever succeeded in borrowing a shilling from Fisher T. Fish, was rather a mystery. Fishy was not the man to lend anybody anything, if he could help it.

Orpheus, with his lute, drew iron tears down Pluto's cheek : but with the aid of a complete orchestra, he could hardly have drawn a loan from Fisher Tarleton Fish. Yet Bunter, on one occasion at least, had done it ! Needless to add, he still owed Fishy that ' bob '. If there was one task more difficult than extracting a loan from Fishy, it was extracting repayment from William George Bunter. The loss of that shilling lingered in Fishy's memory as an abiding sorrow.

" You fat clam ! " said Fisher T. Fish, in measured tones. " You pie-faced piecan, I guess I know you owe me a bob ! You sure do ! You ain't figuring on squaring that bob, I reckon."

" Just that ! " said Bunter. " My postal order's come, Fishy, and I want to settle up that bob I owe you."

Fisher T. Fish almost fell down.

" Wal, whadyer know ! " he gasped.

" Only——" went on Bunter.

" Aw ! There's an ' only ', is there ? " asked Fisher T. Fish. " I sure reckon I might have guessed that one ! Look here, you piecan——"

" It's like this," explained Bunter. " My Uncle Carter sent me a postal order for a pound this morning, and Quelch is keeping the letter till after class, because that fathead Cherry chucked it into the form-room. It's on the table in his study, and he's gone to Courtfield. You cut in——"

" Aw ! can it ! "

" You cut in, and get the postal order out of the letter for me—Quelch won't know, see ?—and I'll square the bob out of the postal order. There ! "

" Oh ! " said Fisher T. Fish, thoughtfully.

Bunter blinked at him anxiously.

He wanted that postal order. He was prepared to sacrifice five per cent of the same, in order to get it into his hands, by ' squaring ' the bob he had owed Fisher T. Fish since the previous term. Bunter did not like paying off old debts—it seemed to him rather reckless extravagance. But it was worth it, as an inducement to Fishy to raid Quelch's study. There would be nineteen shillings left : and even in times of dearth, quite a dazzling quantity of tuck could be obtained for nineteen shillings. Having thought out this new way to pay old debts, Bunter was very anxious for Fishy to close on the offer.

Fisher T. Fish hesitated.

Certainly, he wanted that ' bob '. He wanted the ' bob ' as much as Bunter wanted the postal order. But he did not want the risk of raiding Quelch's study, just as much as Bunter didn't.

" Say, you sure Quelch's gone out ? " he asked.

" I saw him go, after third school," assured Bunter. " And old Prout asked him whether he would be passing the post office, and he said yes. Old Prout walked down to the gates with him—I think he wanted Quelch to do something or other at the post office—anyhow, he's gone——"

" That sure sounds safe," said Fisher T. Fish, slowly.

" Safe as houses, old chap," said Bunter, encouragingly.

" You sure that postal order's in the letter ? " asked Fisher T. Fish, eyeing Bunter with considerable doubt. " I'll tell a man, I've heard a lot about that postal order of yourn, you fat piecan, but I guess I ain't swallowed it a whole lot."

" Absolutely certain," said Bunter. " You see, my Uncle Carter—my rich uncle—promised me a quid, and it's in that letter. I got it open before Quelch took it away, but I hadn't time to get the postal order out——"

" Quelch know it's there ? "

" Of course not ! He wouldn't look into a letter, even if it's open—he just took it away because that idiot Cherry chucked it into the form-room—— "

" Um ! " said Fishy, thoughtfully.

" You leave the letter there—Quelch can keep that till the end of the term if he likes—just nip the postal order out, see ? Safe as houses. You get the postal and hand it over to me——."

" Guess again ! " said Fisher T. Fish, derisively. " I allow I ain't handing that postal order over till it's changed and I get my bob out of it."

" If you can't trust me, Fishy——"

" No further than I can see you, and not quite so far as that," answered Fisher T. Fish. " If I get it, we go straight to the shop and change it with Mrs. Mimble, and I freeze on to that bob you've owed me for dog's ages."

" That's all right, old chap ! Go it," said Bunter, eagerly.

Fisher T. Fish made up his mind.

" It's a cinch," he said.

And Fisher T. Fish went into the House with his jerky steps, leaving Billy Bunter in the quad in a state of happy anticipation. Really it seemed quite a safe enterprise, though Bunter preferred to let some other fellow take what risk there was. That long-expected postal order was as good as in his fat hands !

It did not seem quite so safe to Fishy, going to Quelch's study, as it did to Bunter, staying at a prudent distance from that apartment. Fishy was very cautious in his approach. If Quelch was out of gates, calling at a post office, he was safe off the scene : but other beaks might be about. And it was rather a serious matter to raid a master's study. All depended on Quelch knowing nothing about it—but if all went well, Quelch would know nothing. Fisher T. Fish was very cautious indeed. He stopped at the corner of Masters' passage, and surveyed that passage with a keen watchful eye.

Nobody was in the passage. But one door was open—Prout's. Fishy noted it, but that did not discourage him, as he had seen Prout walking in the quad with Hacker, the master of the Shell. Prout, in the quad, couldn't look out of his doorway, even if it was wide open.

But from Prout's study came a buzzing sound that perplexed Fisher T. Fish for a moment or two. Then he realised that it was the sound of a vacuum-sweeper. No doubt a housemaid was hoovering Prout's carpet.

A housemaid, perhaps, did not matter very much. But Fishy did not want even a housemaid to see him penetrating without leave into his form-master's study. He listened rather uneasily to the buzz of the Hoover plugged in to the electric point in Prout's study. If that housemaid came out——

Still, she seemed busy in Prout's study : and he resolved to chance it. Swiftly, he cut into the passage, and reached Quelch's door.

There was a sudden silence, as the Hoover in Prout's study was shut off. But Fishy had Quelch's door open, and he shot into the study.

He shut the door after him.

All was safe now, even if the housemaid emerged from Prout's quarters. Fisher T. Fish jerked across to Quelch's table, and scanned it swiftly with his keen transatlantic eyes for Bunter's letter.

Bunter had told him that it was on the table. Bunter
had no doubt that it was, which was near enough for
Bunter. There were a good many books and papers on
the table, and Fisher T. Fish gave them a rapid once-over.
If that fat clam had been stringing him along—— !

" Gee-whiz ! " breathed Fishy.

There was the letter. It lay on the table among other
things, with a paper-weight on it. But the paper-weight
did not quite cover the envelope, on which Fisher T. Fish's
sharp eyes discerned part of the name, ' W. G. Bunt——! '
That was enough for Fishy. It was Bunter's letter—open
at one edge where a fat thumb had torn open the envelope.

Fisher T. Fish pounced on it.

He lifted the paper-weight. In another moment, the
letter would have been in his hand, and he would have
been exploring it for a postal order ! But at that moment,
the study door was thrown wide open.

Fisher T. Fish fairly bounded, in his startled surprise.

The paper-weight dropped from his hand, and he spun
round towards the door, in dire terror of seeing a lean form
and a stern countenance there.

Then he gasped with relief.

It was not Quelch. It was Mary, the housemaid, wheeling
in a Hoover.

Evidently, the housemaid had shut off the vacuum-
sweeper in Prout's study because she had finished Prout's
carpet. Now she had wheeled it along to Quelch's study
to give Quelch's carpet similar treatment.

For the moment, she did not observe Fisher T. Fish,
as she wheeled it in. Then she saw him, and stared at
him.

" Aw, wake snakes ! " murmured Fisher T. Fish.

" If you're waiting for Mr. Quelch, sir, perhaps you
wouldn't mind waiting outside," said Mary. " I have to
do the carpet before dinner."

" Oh ! Yep !"' gasped Fisher T. Fish. Under the
housemaid's eyes, he dared not touch the letter on the

table. The game was up! "I—I—I guess I came here to—to speak to Quelch, but he's gone out, I guess."

Fisher T. Fish retreated from the study. The buzz of the Hoover followed him. Mary had plugged in and started. Fisher T. Fish meandered disconsolately out of the House. A pair of little round eyes, behind a pair of big round spectacles, fixed on him eagerly.

"Got it ?" gasped Billy Bunter.

"Nope!" snorted Fisher T. Fish. "There's a pesky help in that dog-goned study hoovering the dog-goned carpet."

"Oh, blow!" grunted Bunter. "I say, Fishy, old chap, just you hang about till she's gone, and try again——"

Billy Bunter broke off. From the direction of the gates, a lean angular figure was coming across to the House. Bunter gave it a dismayed blink.

"Oh, crikey! There's Quelch! He's come back."

"I guess that lets me out!" grunted Fisher T. Fish. "I'll jest mention that I want that bob, when you cinch that postal order, Bunter."

Billy Bunter did not heed. His eyes, and his spectacles, followed Mr. Quelch, with an almost ferocious blink, as the Remove master went into the House. Quelch had returned —and Billy Bunter's postal order was as far from his fat clutches as ever!

CHAPTER VII

SEEING IS BELIEVING

Buzzzzzzzzz !

Mr. Quelch compressed his lips.

He had had quite a pleasant walk after third school. He had walked by the leafy lane down to Friardale : he had called in at the post office there to purchase a postal order for Mr. Prout, who required one to enclose in a letter as a tip for a juvenile nephew : he had walked back through the leafy wood : and he had returned to the school in ample time to prepare a Latin paper for the behoof of the Remove that afternoon. So all was going well, really, and there seemed no reason why Quelch should compress his lips in a tight line, as he came up the passage to his study.

But he did so.

It was the buzz of the Hoover that caused that labial demonstration on the part of Quelch. It was an un-welcome sound to his ears. Quelch had to concentrate on a Latin paper, and with that buzz in the offing, he found it difficult to concentrate. It irritated him. It caused his thoughts to stray.

And it seemed to Quelch that there was a great deal of superfluous and unnecessary hoovering in Masters' studies. Sometimes it seemed to him that he was almost haunted by the humming buzz of the electric vacuum-sweeper. It seemed to happen at all hours. Indeed, he was almost disposed to think that Mrs. Kebble, the House-dame, kept an eye on his study, and jumped at a chance of getting the Hoover into it whenever Quelch got out of it !

Quelch was careful, neat, and tidy : but being a mere man, did not always notice whether his study carpet was dusty or not : and whether it required hoovering—his impression generally being that it didn't !

As he came up the passage, with compressed lips, he hoped that the humming and buzzing was going on in some other master's study, not his own. That would be bad enough : his hearing was keen, and the hum of the Hoover worried him from quite a distance.

But that hope proved delusive. His study door was wide open : the Hoover was humming in that very room : and, looking in, he beheld the trim figure of Mary, the house-maid, steering round the room what Mr. Quelch, in his private opinion, regarded as something like an infernal machine !

With the hum of the Hoover in her ears, Mary naturally did not hear the Remove master coming. Not seeing or hearing Mr. Quelch, Mary took no heed of him : and the Hoover hummed on merrily.

" Upon my word ! " said Mr. Quelch, in great vexation. Hum went the Hoover.

" Mary ! "

Mary did not hear.

" Mary ! My good girl ! Mary ! " hooted Mr. Quelch. Still Mary did not hear.

Quelch's lips, by this time, were set like iron. He gave up the attempt to speak to Mary, whisked across the room, and put his foot to the electric point where the electric sweeper was plugged in. One jab shut off the switch : and silence suddenly descended on Mr. Quelch's study— and never had silence seemed so golden !

" Oh ! " ejaculated Mary, becoming suddenly aware of Quelch.

Quelch breathed hard. He did not want to seem like a cross old gentleman to Mary, whose intentions, after all, were doubtless good. He only wanted to get rid of Mary and the Hoover in the shortest possible space of time. He constrained himself to speak with the courtesy due from an old gentleman to a young housemaid. He did not say, " For mercy's sake drag that horrible thing away ! " He thought that, but did not utter it. What he said was :

"Mary, my good girl, please leave my study for the present. I have some work to do before dinner."

"Yes, sir," said Mary. "But Mrs. Kebble said Hoover the studies, sir——"

"Oh! Quite! quite! Another time——"

"Yes, sir! But I should be finished in ten minutes, sir——"

She might as well have said ten hours, or ten weeks! But Quelch contrived to be patient.

"I am afraid I cannot spare ten minutes, Mary, or even one minute. I have much to do! Another time——"

Mr. Quelch, being a mere man, did not perhaps realise that housemaids, as well as schoolmasters, had much to do! Probably he had never reflected that Mrs. Kebble's staff had their work mapped out, and that to run things smoothly, jobs had to be done at the scheduled times. What was merely an irritating, deafening noise to Mr. Quelch, was to Mary a job of work that had to be done, and that she wanted to get done, and done with.

"I've done the other studies, sir," said Mary.

"Oh! Yes! Quite."

"And if I could finish this room, I could take the Hoover away——"

Mr. Quelch drew a deep, deep breath. He did not expect Mary to understand how very important his work was. But he did expect her to get out of the study with her wretched sweeper, when he told her so to do.

"Please go at once, Mary," he said. There was a perceptible diminution of the courtesy due from an old gentleman to a young housemaid. "At once, please."

Mary, in her turn, drew a deep breath. She did not expect Mr. Quelch to understand that a housemaid's work had to be done, but she did expect to be allowed to finish a room when she had started on it.

"Oh, very well, sir," said Mary. "I shall have to come back later and finish the room, sir."

"Oh! Yes! Quite so."

" May I leave the Hoover here, then, sir ? "

" Eh ?   Oh !   Yes !   Anything !   Please shut the door."

Mary wheeled the Hoover into a corner, leaned the handle there, left the study, and closed the door after her.

Silent and inactive, the Hoover was inoffensive. Quelch did not want it there, but he did not mind, so long as it was not in action. He dismissed it from mind.

Taking a pocket-book from his pocket, he extracted therefrom a postal order for £1, his recent purchase at Friardale Post Office on Mr. Prout's account. Prout, no doubt, would look in some time and ask for it.

In the meantime, Quelch laid it on his table, ready for Prout. Being a very careful gentleman, he picked up the paper-weight that lay on Billy Bunter's letter, placed the postal order on the letter, and replaced the paper-weight on the postal order, thus making it safe from being blown off the table by draught from door or window. Quelch was always very meticulous in such matters.

This done, he sat down at the table to prepare the Latin paper for his form. Such a task was quite congenial to Quelch, and the cloud faded from his brow as he became immersed in it.

Tap !

Mr. Quelch looked up impatiently. If this was Mary, returning in the hope of resuming operations with the Hoover, Quelch was prepared to be exceedingly sharp.

" Come in ! " he rapped.

The door opened.

But it did not reveal the trim figure of Mary the housemaid. It revealed a fat form, a fat face, and a large pair of spectacles.

Mr. Quelch frowned, as thunderously as he had frowned in the form-room that morning. He had, for the time, forgotten the existence of that fat and troublesome member of his form. He seemed to derive no pleasure whatever from being reminded of it.

"Well ?" he rapped. He shot that monosyllable at Bunter like a bullet.

"If you pip-pip-please, sir——" stammered Bunter.

"Be brief ! "

"Oh ! Yes, sir ! I—I—I——"

"If you have anything to say, Bunter, say it at once," rapped Mr. Quelch. "I am busy. What is it ? "

"Mum-mum-my letter, sir—— ! "

"What ? "

"You—you see, sir——"

"I have told you, Bunter, that your letter will be handed to you after class to-day. Leave my study."

"Oh ! Yes, sir ! But—but—but I—I'd like to patch the coast, sir——"

"What ? "

"I—I mean, catch the post," gasped Bunter. "I—I think my postal order's sent me an uncle, sir—I—I mean, I think my uncle's sent me a postal order, sir, and I'd like to write and thank him, and patch the coast—I mean catch the post—if—if—if you don't mum-mum-mind, sir——"

Bunter blinked at his form-master, half in hope and half in terror. Bunter had thought out this one, as a possible chance of getting hold of that letter and its precious contents. He did not feel sure that it was a winner, but it was worth trying on. But the expression on Quelch's face was frightfully discouraging. The gimlet-eyes seemed to bore into Bunter.

"If—if—if I mum-mum-may have my letter, sir," stammered Bunter. "I—I ain't thinking of the postal order in it, sir, only—only——"

"I quite understand," said Mr. Quelch, grimly.

"Oh ! Thank you, sir ! Mum-mum-may I have my letter ? "

"You may not, Bunter."

"Oh, sir ! I——"

"You may leave my study, Bunter, at once."

Billy Bunter did not leave Mr. Quelch's study at once.

His eyes, and his spectacles, had fallen on the letter under
the paper-weight. Like Fisher T. Fish half an hour ago,
he recognised the letter, although it was partly concealed.
Unlike Fisher T. Fish, he discerned a postal order for £1,
lying across the letter, also pinned down by the paper-
weight.

His eyes popped behind his spectacles.

Perhaps there had been a faint lingering doubt at the
back of Billy Bunter's mind, as to whether there was, really
and actually, a postal order for £1 in that letter. He
hoped there was, he believed there was, he was practically
certain there was : yet he was only too well aware that
there always seemed a lurking element of doubt in the
matter of his postal orders.

But this was proof positive !

For there was the postal order ! Seeing was believing !

Quelch must have taken it out of the envelope. Bunter
had not supposed that Quelch would look at a fellow's
letter, even if it was ready opened. Certainly, he would
have done so himself : but he had believed better things
of Quelch.

But he could not doubt it now—now that he saw the
postal order outside the envelope !

Bunter's eyes and spectacles almost devoured that postal
order. He really did not mind Quelch looking into the
letter, if Quelch, like Bunter, had a taste for nosing into
the concerns of others. He was quite prepared to overlook that, if Quelch let him have the postal order. But
apparently the beast wouldn't ! Still, it was something to
have actually seen it, and to be absolutely assured, beyond
the shadow of a doubt, that it had come !

" I have told you to leave my study, Bunter ! " Quelch
seemed to have borrowed the voice of the Great Huge Bear !

" Oh ! Yes, sir ! " Bunter had fairly to drag his eyes
and spectacles away from that enticing vision on the table.
" Yes, sir ! But——"

" Go ! " rapped Mr. Quelch.

It seemed impossible for Bunter to go : leaving that postal order behind ! The gimlet-eyes glinted at him.

" Unless you leave my study this instant, Bunter, I shall cane you," said Mr. Quelch. He reached out for his cane.

" Oh ! "

Bunter decided to leave the study that instant !

The door closed on the Owl of the Remove : and Mr. Quelch, breathing rather hard, resumed the Latin paper. Not for several minutes did the charms of the tongue of Cicero and Horace chase away the frown from his brow.

CHAPTER VIII

BUNTER'S LATEST

" I SAY, you fellows ! "

" Oh, blow away, Bunter," growled Bob Cherry.

" Oh, really, Cherry——"

" Hook it, fathead," said Harry Wharton. " Nobody's going to raid Quelch's study for your silly letter. Wait till after class."

" Oh, really, Wharton——"

" The hookfulness is the proper caper, my esteemed fat-headed Bunter," said Hurree Jamset Ram Singh. " The jawfulness is terrific."

" Oh, really, Inky——"

" Speech is silvery, but silence is the bird in the bush that goes longest to the well, as the English proverb remarks. Pack it upfully."

" If you fellows would let a fellow get in a word edge-wise——" hooted Bunter. " You're like a sheep's head—all jaw ! I say, you fellows, do listen to a chap ! I've thought of a dodge, and I want to know what you fellows think, see ? "

The Famous Five, when they came out of the House after dinner, did not seem to be yearning for the fascinating society of William George Bunter : least of all Bob Cherry, who was generally very tolerant of the fat and fatuous Owl. They were not deeply interested in Bunter, or in his letter, or in the possible postal order contained in the letter : or indeed in anything that was his ! Moreover, they were discussing a matter of interest to themselves—a football match due with Highcliffe. Bunter was quite superfluous.

To Bunter, of course, a soccer match was a very incon-siderable trifle, in comparison with a postal order. He really had no patience to waste on such frivolity.

" I think it's a pretty good dodge," went on Bunter.
" But before I try it on Quelch, you fellows tell me what
you think."

" Oh, we'll do that," grunted Johnny Bull. " I think
you're a fat, frabjous, footling, foozling, frowsy owl."

" Oh, really, Bull—— "

" I think you're a blinking, blithering, blethering bandersnatch," said Bob.

" The thinkfulness is preposterous ! " grinned Hurree
Jamset Ram Singh.

Billy Bunter gave them an exasperated blink.

" Will you listen to a fellow ? " he howled. " This is
important ! I say, you fellows, Mrs. Mimble has got a
fresh lot of cream puffs in—— "

" You must want a lot of cream-puffs, ten minutes after
dinner ! " remarked Frank Nugent, sarcastically.

" Well, look what measly dinners we get," said Bunter.
" I only had four helpings of the steak-and-kidney pie, and
only three of the pudding. I can tell you I could do with
a snack before class, if Quelch would let me have my postal
order. I've got to get it somehow, and I've thought of a
dodge. It ought to work, if Quelch has any feelings. Do
you fellows think he has ? "

" Are you going to tell him you're perishing of hunger,
after only four helpings of steak-and-kidney pie and three
of pudding ? "

" Ha, ha, ha ! "

" I wish you'd listen to a chap instead of cackling. I
say, suppose my uncle at Folkestone was ill—— "

" Is he ? "

" Oh, no ! But that ain't the point. Suppose he was,"
said Bunter. " Then I should be very anxious to read his
letter and find out whether he was worse or not, see ?
Think that would do for Quelch ? "

" Oh, my hat ! "

" If he's got any feelings, he would be a bit sympathetic,
seeing a chap very anxious about an ill uncle, and all that,

what ? And even a schoolmaster must have some feelings ! "
argued Bunter. " I mean, they're human, in a way."

" Better not try pulling Quelch's leg, you fat ass ! It's
about as safe to pull as a tiger's tail."

" Well, if he hasn't read the letter, he wouldn't know,"
said Bunter. " You see, I got the envelope open before
the beast collared it, so he may have read it. If he has, it's
no good saying Uncle Carter's ill when he ain't ! Do you
fellows think he's read the letter, as it was open ? "

The Famous Five gazed at Bunter.

" You piffling, pernicious porker," said Harry Wharton.
" Do you imagine that Quelch would nose into a letter like
you ? Of course he hasn't, you bloated image."

" Well, if he hasn't, all right," said Bunter. " But he
must have taken the letter out when he took the postal
order out, you know."

" He hasn't taken the postal order out, fathead, if there
was one in it."

" That's all you know," retorted Bunter. " I happen to
know that he jolly well has, because I saw the postal order
lying across the letter on his table, when I went to his
study before dinner."

" Rot ! " said Bob Cherry.

" I tell you I saw it ! " hooted Bunter. " A postal order
for a pound, on the letter, under a paper-weight."

" Rubbish ! " said Harry Wharton. " Why should Quelch
take it out of the letter ? "

" Well, if he read the letter——"

" He didn't, you benighted chump."

" Well, if he didn't, O.K. But he must have taken the
letter out of the envelope, when he took out the postal
order," said Bunter, anxiously. " A fellow wants to be
sure. No good telling him that that letter's about my
uncle being ill, if he's read it, and knows it's only about
sending me a tip. See ? "

Bunter was quite worried.

Not for a moment had it occurred to his fat mind that

the postal order he had seen on Quelch's table was quite a different postal order, purchased by Quelch at Friardale Post Office.

Having overheard a fragment of Prout's talk to Quelch, he was aware that Prout had asked Quelch to call at the post office while he was out : but that was all he knew : and he had, in fact, already forgotten it. That Prout had asked Quelch to get a £1 postal order for him was quite unknown to Bunter.

That postal order on Quelch's table was Bunter's postal order : of that, to Bunter's fat mind, there was no possible doubt, no possible probable shadow of doubt, no possible doubt whatever !

And if that postal order had been taken from Bunter's letter, obviously the letter itself must have been taken out of the envelope : in which case, hadn't Quelch looked at it ? It seemed frightfully probable to Bunter. Like most of us, he was disposed to judge others by himself !

" You see how important it is," went on Bunter, his fat brow corrugated by a worried frown. " If Quelch thinks that letter's about my uncle being ill, he's bound to let me have it, if he's got any feelings at all. But if he's read it, saying ' Dear William, I enclose the pound I promised to send you ', or something like that, he would make out that I was telling untruths——"

" Make out ! " gasped Harry Wharton.

" Well, you know what Quelch is," said Bunter. " Suspicious, you know. He's doubted my word before this. That's the sort of thing you get from schoolmasters—not gentlemanly, you know. I don't want Quelch to make me out a liar. Besides, he would whop me ! Think he's read that letter, after taking it out of the envelope ? "

" He never took it out, you howling ass ! If the postal order's outside, it may have dropped out, as the envelope was open."

" Oh ! " That was a new idea to Bunter. " Think that's possible ? I should think Uncle Carter would fold up the postal order inside the letter. Still, he mayn't have. If it fell out, Quelch would pick it up, and stick it there with the letter, I suppose. If that's what's happened, all right. If he hasn't read the letter——"

"You pernicious owl, his name isn't Bunter, and he hasn't."

"If a fellow could feel quite sure he hadn't——" sighed Bunter. "It's a bit risky! I say, Harry, old chap, suppose you go to Quelch—you can speak to him as Head Boy of the Remove—and tell him I'm anxious about my uncle being ill at Folkestone——"

"What ? "

"Then, from what he says, you'll know whether he's read the letter or not, and you can put me wise, before I try it on, see ? "

"But your uncle isn't ill at Folkestone!" shrieked Wharton.

"I wish you'd keep to the point, old chap ! " said Bunter, peevishly. "That's the worst of you fellows—you keep on wandering from the point. The point is that I want my postal order, see ? "

"Gentlemen, chaps, and fellows," said Bob Cherry, "it's no use talking to Bunter. Boot him ! "

"Hear, hear ! "

"Good egg," said Johnny Bull. "Let's dribble him round the quad. That will keep him too busy for telling lies to Quelch."

"The goodfulness of the egg is terrific."

"Ready, Bunter ? "

"Beasts ! " roared Bunter. And he departed on his highest gear. Dribbling round the quad was not what Bunter wanted, though no doubt what he deserved.

But at all events, he departed, and Harry Wharton and Co. were able to resume their own topic of the Highcliffe match, getting a much-needed rest from Billy Bunter and his postal order.

CHAPTER IX

TOO LATE

Mr. Quelch stared.

He was standing at the open window of Masters' Common-room, looking out into the quadrangle.

In the distance, a number of Remove fellows were punting a footer. Quite a benevolent expression came over Quelch's severe face, as he watched his boys engaged in that cheery and healthy exercise.

And when Coker of the Fifth happened along, and the footer, perhaps by accident, collided with Horace Coker's hat, and knocked it off, Mr. Quelch even smiled. Boys will be boys : and little accidents like that would happen. And when Hobson and his pals in the Shell made a sudden rush for the Remove ball, captured it, and rushed it off, with a horde of Removites whooping in fierce pursuit, Quelch continued to smile benevolently. Quelch had been a boy once, though few fellows in the Remove could quite have realised it.

But Quelch ceased to smile, and frowned slightly, as a fat member of his form came along the path by Common-room window. William George Bunter was not in his good books or his good graces.

Bunter had been very irritating that day. Staring at the clock all through second school : handing out the worst con ever perpetrated in the form-room : getting another fellow to throw a letter in to him while in detention, actually trying to open that letter while Quelch's back was momentarily turned : and then coming to Quelch's study to bother him about that letter after being told quite plainly that he must wait for it till after class—really, Bunter, always a troublesome pupil, had been unusually and superfluously irritating. Hence the frown that replaced the benevolent smile on Quelch's crusty countenance.

But as Bunter came nearer the big bay window in which Quelch stood looking out, the frown followed the smile, vanishing in its turn. And Mr. Quelch, as already stated, stared !

Bunter did not look quite as usual. His fat face had a dismal, dolorous, woebegone expression. And as Quelch's eyes fixed on him, he took a handkerchief, much in need of washing, from his pocket, pushed up his spectacles, and rubbed his eyes. At which Quelch's stare intensified.

Bunter had asked the Famous Five whether they thought Quelch had any feelings. As a matter of fact, he had. And they were moved by the dolorous woe in the fat countenance of William George Bunter. If even that lazy, inattentive, exasperating member of his form had some cause of trouble or grief, Quelch could be sympathetic.

He leaned from the window, and called :

" Bunter ! "

Quelch was well known in the Remove to be a downy bird. He was very wary. It was considered next door to impossible to pull Quelch's leg. Yet that, in point of fact, was exactly what the astute Owl was doing at that very moment.

Wary as he was, it did not occur to Quelch that Bunter knew that he was there in the big bay window of Common-room : still less did it occur to him that the grief and woe in the fat face were specially worked up for his especial behoof. But that, sad to relate, was how the matter stood.

Bunter was resolved, at long last, to ' try it on '. It was getting near time for class and he simply had to have that postal order—if he could ! If Quelch really had any feelings, Bunter was going to stir them. He was not quite certain that Quelch hadn't read that letter. But if he hadn't, all was safe ! Bunter hoped for the best.

As Quelch called him from the window, the fat Owl blinked round. Then he rolled towards the window.

" Yes, sir ! "

" Is anything the matter, Bunter ? " asked Mr. Quelch, quite kindly.

" Oh ! Yes, sir ! My pip-pip-pip——"

" Your what ? "

" My pip-pip-pip-poor uncle, sir," stammered Bunter.

" Your uncle ! " repeated Mr. Quelch. " Is your uncle ill, Bunter ? ".

" Oh, yes, sir ! I—I—I hoped he was getting better, but—but—I—I don't know till I read his letter, sir."

" Oh ! " exclaimed Mr. Quelch.

Bunter felt a spasm of terror. If Quelch had read that letter, he would know that there was nothing in it about Uncle Carter being ill. Harry Wharton and Co. had assured Bunter that Quelch hadn't : and he fervently hoped that they were right !

Anyhow, he had taken the plunge now ! He waited in an anguish of anxiety for his form-master to speak.

" Oh ! " repeated Mr. Quelch. " Do you mean to tell me, Bunter, that the letter you received this morning was from a sick relative ? "

Bunter felt a wave of relief. That question showed that Quelch couldn't have read the letter. Harry Wharton and Co. had been right !

" Oh ! Yes, sir," stammered Bunter. " My pip-pip-pip-poor Uncle Carter, sir——"

" You thoughtless and absurd boy," exclaimed Mr. Quelch. " If that is the case, why did you not tell me so at once, in the form-room this morning ? "

" Oh ! " gasped Bunter, " I—I hadn't——"   He broke off just in time. It was not judicious to say that he hadn't thought of it then ! " I—I—I mean, I—I——"

" You should have told me at once, Bunter ! I should certainly have allowed you to read the letter without delay, in such circumstances."

" Oh ! W-w-would you, sir ? " stuttered Bunter. He wished sincerely that he had thought of this masterly dodge a little earlier !

"Certainly I should." Mr. Quelch glanced up at the clock-tower. "It will be time for class in a few minutes now, Bunter. But there is ample time for you to read your letter. You may go to my study and take it from the table there."

"Oh!" gasped Bunter. "Thank you, sir."

"Go at once," said Mr. Quelch.

"Oh, yes, sir."

Bunter went at once: in fact, he shot away like an arrow from a bow. Grief and woe disappeared from his fat face as he shot.

It had worked!

Quelch clearly hadn't read the letter, and he had feelings! Both circumstances were very fortunate for Billy Bunter. The clouds had rolled by: all he had to do was to speed to Quelch's study, grab up that letter, and all would be calm and bright!

So far from registering grief and woe, Bunter's fat face was irradiated by a wide grin, as he bolted into the House.

He hurtled into Masters' Passage. He hurled open the door of Quelch's study. He bounded into that apartment.

There lay the letter, with the postal order on it, under the paper-weight, just as Bunter had seen them before dinner. To remove the paper-weight, clutch up letter and postal order together in a fat paw, was the work of a second —a split one!

The letter Bunter jammed into his pocket. There was ample time to read that later. It was the postal order upon which the fat Owl concentrated. That was crumpled in a fat grubby paw as he rolled out of the study. He rolled: but he felt as if he were walking on air!

At last, at long, long last, Billy Bunter and Billy Bunter's postal order had established contact! Of the fact that it wasn't his postal order at all, Bunter was still in a state of blissful ignorance. There were some millions of postal orders in existence: but that one among those millions happened to be in Quelch's study that day, did not occur to Bunter. His fat thoughts were wholly concentrated on a pound postal order from his Uncle Carter, and this was it : he did not dream of dreaming otherwise. Postal order crumpled and clutched in grubby hand, Bunter rolled happily out of Mr. Quelch's study, and out of the House.

"Hallo, hallo, hallo ! " Bob Cherry met him as he rolled out into the quad. "You're looking bucked, old fat man ! Got that postal order yet ? "

Bunter chuckled.

" Look ! " he said.

He held it up. Bob Cherry looked at it ! Undoubtedly, indubitably, indisputably, it was a postal order for a pound.

" Gratters ! " grinned Bob.

" I say, old chap, cut across with me, and I'll stand you a jam-tart and a ginger," chirruped Bunter. "Come on."

" Too late, old fat bean : it's just on class ! Tuck-shop's closing."

" Oh, crikey ! "

Bunter bolted across the quad.

The school shop was closed during class. If it was closed now, Bunter had to wait—with the postal order burning a hole in his pocket !

The Owl of the Remove was not accustomed to putting on speed. But this time he fairly stamped on the gas. He flew ! He almost whizzed ! He ran into Tubb of the Third, and sent that youth spinning, with a howl of in-dignant protest. He almost ran into Wingate of the Sixth : but the Greyfriars captain side-stepped in time, and stood staring after the fat junior as he flew on.

But alas for Bunter !

The door of the school shop was closed. Mrs. Mimble had temporarily retired from business, to a back parlour and a cup of tea.

Billy Bunter stared at the closed door. It was a stunning blow. He had 'tried it on' with Quelch, after long hesitation, and he had tried it on successfully—but too late ! It is well said that he who hesitates is lost ! With

a postal order for a pound clutched in a fat paw, Bunter
stared, and blinked, at a shut door, like a fat Peri excluded
from the delights of Paradise.

"Oh, lor'!" groaned Bunter.

The bell was ringing. Bunter did not heed it. He
stared at the door, as if the concentrated stare of a little
pair of round eyes, and a big pair of round spectacles, could
stare it open.

"Bunter!" It was Wingate's voice.

The fat Owl blinked dismally round.

"Eh! Oh! Yes, Wingate."

"What do you mean by bolting across the quad like a
mad rhinoceros?" demanded the Greyfriars captain. "Off
your chump, you young ass?"

"Oh! Yes! No! I——"

"Can't you hear the bell ringing? Deaf as well as
silly?" asked Wingate. "Cut off to your form-room at
once."

"Oh, dear!"

Bunter rolled dolorously away. He slipped the postal
order into his pocket. It was useless till after class. Really,
he might just as well have waited till after class for his
letter! Two endless hours stretched before Bunter, before
he could expend that postal order in refreshment fluid and
solid. His luck was out—and, as he was still blissfully
unaware that that postal order did not belong to him, he
remained unaware also that, in the circumstances, his luck
was in!

CHAPTER X

BUNTER KNOWS HOW

BILLY BUNTER'S plump brow was corrugated with deep thought, as he sat in his place in the Remove form-room.

The lesson was geography : but if Mr. Quelch noted the wrinkles of thought in the fat brow of his fattest pupil, and supposed that Bunter was unusually keen on acquiring knowledge of that important subject, he was in error.

Bunter couldn't have cared less.

Bunter was in the unusual, almost unprecedented, happy state, of having received a postal order after long, long expectation. That was more than sufficient to banish from his fat mind any interest he might otherwise have felt in mountains, rivers, seas, and capital cities.

From the point of view of the Owl of the Remove, there was only one matter of primary importance going on at the moment. In his pocket was a postal order for a pound. In his fat inside was an aching void that almost cried aloud to be filled with sticky things. To translate the postal order into cakes, buns, tarts, doughnuts, was a perfectly simple matter, had it only been a half-holiday that afternoon. But it wasn't ! With an aching void and a postal order, Bunter had to sit in class.

But had he ?

Billy Bunter's brain was not, as a rule, a quick worker. But it could accelerate under pressure : and now it was under the combined pressure of a postal order and an aching void.

If he could get out of class—— ?

And could he not ?

Quelch, it was evident now, had feelings. He did not look as if he had, but he had, or he wouldn't have fallen so easily to Bunter's latest dodge. He had indeed been quite kind about it. That chicken had fought and won, as it were. Might it not fight again ?

It was established now—so far as Quelch was concerned—that Uncle Carter at Folkestone was ill, and that Bunter was anxious about him. He wasn't, and Bunter wasn't : but as Quelch didn't know all that, it did not matter in the least—from Bunter's peculiar point of view. Having been a stranger to truth for so long, Bunter was not likely to think of striking up an acquaintance in the present urgent circumstances.

Bunter resolved to try it on. If Quelch fell for it, he would get out of the form-room ; if Quelch didn't, he would be no worse off. But he was hopeful, owing to the discovery that Quelch, after all, had feelings !

" If you please, sir——"

Quelch, with a big map on the blackboard, and a pointer in his hand, was expounding geography to a more or less interested Remove. He glanced at Bunter as the fat junior squeaked, perhaps expecting some question which would indicate that Bunter, for once, was giving attention to the lesson.

" If—if—if you please, sir—— ! "

" Well, Bunter ? "

" I—I—I'd like to—to answer my uncle's letter, sir, and catch the post, if—if—if I may, sir," stammered Bunter. " The collection goes before we're out of class, sir, and—and my uncle being ill——"

Mr. Quelch gave him a sharp look for a moment. He knew his Bunter ! But his expression melted into benevolence. Bunter, obviously, was very eager, and very anxious. That could be read in his fat face. Quelch would hardly have expected Bunter to be deeply concerned about a sick relative. He was pleased to see it.

" I hope your uncle is not very ill, Bunter," said Mr. Quelch, quite kindly.

" He—he's rather bad, sir, and—and I'd like——"

" Very well, Bunter ! You will be excused this lesson,"
said Mr. Quelch. "You may leave the form-room, Bunter."

" Oh ! Thank you, sir ! " gasped Bunter.

He almost bounded from his seat.

Some of the Remove fellows exchanged glances, and
Vernon-Smith winked at Tom Redwing. If Mr. Quelch
believed that Bunter was moved by anxiety for a sick
uncle, he was the only individual in the Remove form-room
who did !

" You fat spoofer," whispered Peter Todd, as Bunter
passed him.

" Fancy Quelch falling for that ! " murmured Skinner.

Bunter did not heed. The Remove were welcome to
think what they liked, so long as Quelch was satisfied. And
Quelch was.

The old oak door closed behind Billy Bunter. The
Remove were left to the delights of geography, minus that
fat ornament of the form.

Bunter did not grin till the door had closed after him.
Then he grinned so wide and expansive a grin that it almost
met round his fat head.

" He, he, he ! " chuckled Bunter.

He rolled gleefully down the passage.

He had leave from class for a whole ' school '. Ten
minutes of it had elapsed before Bunter's fat brain had
evolved that new dodge. That left him fifty minutes :
more than ample time to write a letter to Uncle Carter
and place the same in the post in good time for collection.
But Billy Bunter was not thinking of writing letters to
avuncular relatives. He had not read his uncle's letter yet,
and certainly was not thinking of answering it. His plump
mind was wholly concentrated on the postal order and what
it would produce in the way of tuck.

He was out of class—that was the first essential. Had
the school shop been open during class, the thing would
have been as easy as falling off a form. But it was closed,
and would not be open again till class was over. Bunter,

seeking like a lion for what he might devour, had to go further afield.

Uncle Clegg's shop in Friardale was the nearest source of supply. But he could scarcely walk a mile there, and a mile back, in the time. Courtfield was the next nearest. That was a good distance off, across Courtfield Common : still further by the road. But with a whole pound in his pocket, the question of transport was easily answered. Bunter could afford a taxi now !

His eyes glistened behind his spectacles at the thought of a happy and glorious spread at the bun-shop in Courtfield—while the other fellows were mugging up geography in the form-room with Quelch.

He had lots of time !

It was easy to borrow Quelch's telephone to ring up a taxi, while Quelch was in the form-room. Easy to drop out over the Cloister wall, and meet the taxi on its way to the school—thus saving time and eluding observation. In a matter of minutes he would be at the bun-shop, enjoying life. The taxi fare was only three shillings—that would leave him seventeen—out of which he would reserve twopence for the 'bus back as far as the corner of Oak Lane, leaving him only a short walk. It was all happily mapped out in Bunter's fat mind. Quelch, believing him up in his study writing that letter, wouldn't know a thing. He would be back in ample time for the next lesson.

Grinning, the fat Owl rolled away to Mr. Quelch's study to borrow the telephone.

But he approached that study rather cautiously.

Quelch was with his form : but other beaks might be about, or a maid with a Hoover or a duster. A fellow had to be careful, when he was supposed to be up in his study, writing an anxious and affectionate letter to a sick relative.

But the coast was clear.

Nobody was to be seen about Masters' studies. Bunter crept cautiously along to Quelch's door.

He gave a little start, and listened, as a sound came from one of the studies—Prout's. Apparently the Fifth-form master was there—it was a sound of scraping chair-legs, as if somebody had just risen.

Bunter whipped open the door of Quelch's study, and popped in. He closed that door quickly behind him. Now he was safe out of sight, in case Prout happened to come out.

He crossed to the telephone.

He was about to lift the receiver, and dial the taxi-rank at Courtfield, when he suddenly paused.

There was a heavy tread in the passage. Prout had come out of his study. He was not going to Common-room—that was up the passage. The heavy tread came down the passage, towards Quelch's door.

" Beast ! " breathed Bunter.

Prout couldn't be coming to Quelch's study : he must know that the Remove master was with his form. He was going out, most likely. But—if he did look in, for any reason—— !

' Safety first ' was Bunter's motto. He backed away from the telephone, and ducked down behind Quelch's writing-table. By the time the heavy tread reached the door, Bunter was under that ample table, keeping company with the waste-paper basket, and a variety of waste-paper which had missed the basket. Crumpled under the table, the fat Owl waited for that elephantine tread to pass the door, when all would be safe.

The next moment, he was glad that he had consulted ' safety first ' : for the elephantine tread did not pass the door.

It stopped there.

The door-handle rattled as it was turned. Prout was coming in ! Had Bunter been at the telephone, he would have been full in Prout's view as he came. But the fat Owl had hunted cover in time : and he was invisible : and deeply thankful for the same. The door opened :

and Bunter had a view of a pair of trouser-ends under a master's gown, as Mr. Prout came into the study : and the alarmed fat Owl could only wonder, with deep feelings, why on earth the unspeakable, unutterable, indescribable beast came to Quelch's study at all when Quelch wasn't there !

CHAPTER XI

RICHES TAKE UNTO THEMSELVES WINGS

" Really ! " said Mr. Prout, aloud. " Really ! "

He seemed puzzled and a little irritated.

Prout had come directly towards the writing-table, leaving the door of the study open. That looked as if he did not intend to remain long, which was a relief to the fat Owl under the table, though he could not imagine why Prout was there at all.

Trouser-ends, and the hem of a master's gown, were quite near Bunter, as Prout stood at the table—looking over it in search of something, so far as Bunter could make out.

" Really—— ! " repeated Mr. Prout, a little more puzzled and a little more irritated, judging by his tone. " Quelch said distinctly, on the table, beside the blotter. Yet it is not there ! It does not appear to be on the table at all ! Really—really—— ! "

Bunter wondered what Prout was looking for. Possibly some paper or book that Quelch was lending him. Certainly it did not occur to his fat mind that Prout was looking for a postal order.

But that, precisely, was what Mr. Prout was doing. Quelch had brought in that postal order for him before dinner. Prout had not contacted him again till after dinner, when Quelch had duly apprised him that the required postal order had been purchased, and lay under a paper-weight on his study table, ready to be called for as it were.

Quelch had then gone to the Remove form-room : and Prout, who had no class at the time, his form being at maths with Mr. Lascelles, had gone to his study to write a letter to his nephew. The letter written, Prout walked along to Quelch's study to pick up the postal order from the table there, to enclose in the letter he had written. It was all quite simple, if Bunter had only known.

Prout was surprised, and a little annoyed, by his failure to discover the postal order on Quelch's table.

Quelch was a careful and methodical man. It was very unusual for him to be careless or forgetful. Yet he had stated that the postal order was there—and the postal order was not there !

Mr. Prout looked all over the table. He saw the paper-weight : but there was nothing whatever under that paper-weight. There were books and various papers on the table : but among them there was nothing that remotely resembled a postal order.

It was not there !

" Really—— ! " said Mr. Prout once more.

The postal order was not on the table. It was not likely to occur to Prout that it was under the table, in the possession of a fat alarmed Owl who was crumpled there.

" Really—— ! " said Mr. Prout, yet again.

He gave a snort.

Quelch, no doubt, had intended to leave the postal order there, under the paper-weight on the table. But he must have forgotten to do so : and the postal order, no doubt, was still in his pocket. It was surprising, in Quelch : and it was annoying, to Prout.

He did not feel that he could interrupt a form-master in his form-room, inquiring after that postal order. Neither was the matter so urgent as all that. Having written his letter, Prout naturally wanted to drop it into the post: still, there was no particular hurry, and the matter could stand over till after class.

So, having expressed his annoyance with an emphatic snort, Prout rolled door-ward again, left the study, and closed the door after him.

Bunter, under the table, gasped with relief.

Whatever the beast had wanted there, he was gone !

A fat and breathless Owl was able to uncrumple himself and crawl out from under the table. He waited till the elephantine tread died away up the passage, and then he emerged.

"Beast!" murmured Bunter.

And he rolled across to the telephone once more.

All was safe now.

The fat Owl proceeded to dial the taxi-rank at Courtfield. In less than a minute a taxi-driver had instructions to drive to the school, and pick up a passenger who would be walking to meet the taxi on its way to Greyfriars.

That done, Bunter replaced the receiver, and rolled across to the door. He opened it a few inches and peered out, wary of Prout.

But Prout had gone back to his study, and closed the door, and the coast was quite clear. Billy Bunter quitted Quelch's study, and rolled away down the passage, and out into the quad.

The quad was deserted, during class. But Bunter did not linger. He cut away to the old Cloisters, where there was a well-known easy spot for climbing the wall, and dropping into the lane outside. Easy, that is to say, for any fellow but Bunter. Bunter negotiated it successfully : but he was gasping for breath when, at last, he dropped into the lane.

Prout had wasted valuable time for him : but he still had plenty of time. He rolled down the lane to the high-road, and blinked along it in the direction of Courtfield.

The taxi was not yet in sight. But it would not be many minutes, and Bunter rolled along the road to meet it.

He had covered about thirty yards, at the pace of a very old and very fatigued snail, when the taxi came in sight on the road across the common.

Bunter waved a fat hand.

The taxi whizzed up and stopped.

"Courtfield Post Office," said Bunter, as he clambered in.

"Yessir."

"COURTFIELD POST OFFICE," SAID BUNTER,
AS HE CLAMBERED IN

The taxi whirled round in the road, and whizzed back
to Courtfield. Billy Bunter leaned back in his seat, in a
state of happy satisfaction.

In five minutes he would be at the post office in Courtfield
High Street, and the postal order cashed. To pay off the
taxi-driver, and roll across to the bun-shop, would be a
matter of moments. And then——!

Bunter's fat thoughts dwelt on a gorgeous feed, on a pile
of enticing, attractive, sticky things, to the exact value of
sixteen shillings and tenpence. Three ' bob ' for the taxi-
man, who, if he expected a tip, would learn that he had
another guess coming : twopence reserved for the motor-
bus fare back : sixteen and ten for tarts, buns, cakes, ginger-
pop, eclairs, doughnuts, cream puffs—it was quite dazzling.
Seldom did Bunter possess such a sum to expend on the
inner Bunter. It was an added pleasure to enjoy that
dazzling spread in lesson-time, while less lucky fellows were
grinding in the form-room. Everything, in fact, was going
Bunter's way : and just at the moment, life seemed to him
one grand sweet song !

The taxi buzzed to a halt outside the post office in the
High Street. Bunter rolled out.

" Wait here a minute," he said.

" Yessir."

Bunter mounted the steps into the post office. He
rolled across to the counter, slipping a fat hand into his
pocket for the postal order.

Then, suddenly, he stopped, an extraordinary expression
coming over his fat face. He gave a gasp.

" Oh, crikey ! "

Frantically, he groped in that pocket. Nothing in the
nature of crumpling paper met his fat fingers. He had
put the postal order into that pocket : he knew that, when
he had turned empty away from the school shop. It was
there—it must be there : it had to be there. But—it
wasn't !

In utter horror, Bunter groped and groped.

But there was no postal order to be found.   All he dis-covered in that pocket was a hole in the lining !

The postal order was gone !

CHAPTER XII

WHERE ?

MR. QUELCH knitted his brow, as the door of the Remove form-room opened, and a fat figure rolled in.

His eyes fixed grimly on Billy Bunter.

Quelch had given Bunter leave from a whole lesson. That was ample time, more than ample time, for what Bunter had to do—or rather, for what Quelch supposed that he had to do. After such a rare concession from his form-master, Bunter should at least have been prompt on time for the next lesson.

So far from being prompt on time, Bunter was not on time at all. He was very late.

The lesson was history : the last for the day. It was half-through when the fat Owl, at length, presented himself in the form-room.

All the Remove looked at him as he came in.

Not a fellow there doubted that Bunter had pulled Quelch's leg, to get out of form. He had got away with it : but it behoved even an ass like Bunter not to overdo it. But he had overdone it to the tune of an extra half-hour. The Remove expected the thunder to roll, when the fat Owl did at last show up : and Quelch certainly looked like it.

" Bunter ! " said Mr. Quelch, in a deep, deep voice.

" Yes, sir," mumbled Bunter, wearily.

Quelch instead of going on, paused. His gimlet-eyes scanned the Owl's fat face. The thunder faded from his brow.

Quelch, as had already transpired, had feelings ! But even a hard-hearted form-master might have been moved by the deep woe in Billy Bunter's dismal fat countenance.

He did not look merely dismal. He did not look merely

dolorous. He looked the picture of woe. He looked like a fellow plunged in the deepest depths of pessimism. A person who sat upon the ground to tell sad stories of the death of kings, would have looked quite cheerful beside him. Never, in all his fat career, had William George Bunter looked such an utterly woebegone object.

Long, very long, had Billy Bunter expected a postal order. At long, long last, it had materialised. And it was gone with the wind! It had vanished like the baseless fabric of a vision, leaving not a wrack behind! It was gone from his gaze like a beautiful dream.

Quelch, luckily for Bunter, was quite unaware of that catastrophe. That awful blow had fairly doubled Bunter up. But Quelch knew nothing of that awful blow. He could only suppose that it was his deep concern for a sick relative that made the fat Owl look as if life had lost its savour.

He was silent for a moment or two, gazing at Bunter. Then he spoke, very mildly.

" You are late, Bunter! But—you may go to your place."

" Yes, sir," moaned Bunter.

He hardly cared, at that moment, whether Quelch whopped him or not. He rolled sadly and sorrowfully to his place.

Fellows looked at him on all sides. Something was the matter with Bunter, that was clear : but they could not guess what.

" What's up, old fat man ? " whispered Bob Cherry.

" I've lost it ! " moaned Bunter.

" Eh ? What ? "

" My postal order ! "

" Oh ! " gasped Bob.

History proceeded in the Remove form-room. Billy Bunter could have taken no interest just then, in the annals of his native land, had he tried ever so hard. But Quelch, touched by the dismal woe in the fat face, passed him over.

Bunter had only to sit through the remainder of the lesson. Kings and queens came and went unheeded by Bunter.

Where was that postal order ?

It had dropped somewhere—but where ?   It might have dropped anywhere—in the quad, or in the passages, in the form-room, in Quelch's study—in the Cloisters, or in the lane, or on the high-road—just anywhere !

It had been awful for Bunter !

There was not only the catastrophe itself—overwhelming as that was.   On emerging from the post office, he had had to deal with a doubtful and rather sardonic taxi-driver : who had made quite a lot of very unpleasant remarks before he finally agreed to wait till the morrow for his fare.   Then there had been the walk back to Greyfriars.   The motor-bus would have borne Bunter most of the way, had the necessary twopence been available.   But the necessary two-pence had not been available.   Bunter had had to walk !

Where was that postal order ?

It seemed most likely to Bunter that it had dropped while he was scrambling over the Cloister wall.   It was a tired Bunter who arrived back at that spot, but he searched for the postal order there, dragging at the old ivy, blinking into dusty and musty recesses.   He searched in vain : nothing like a postal order met his eyes or his spectacles. Quite likely it was there all the time : equally likely, it was somewhere else : and the unhappy fat Owl had given it up at last, and returned to the form-room.

Where was that postal order ?

That question hummed in his fat brain like a refrain. Had he dropped it in the school at all, or somewhere out on the road ?   He hadn't dropped it in the taxi : he had looked all over the taxi.   But he had dropped it in some spot—and there were hundreds, or rather thousands, of spots where it might have dropped.   Searching for that postal order looked like a task akin to that of searching for a needle in a haystack.

Bunter could almost have wept.

Where was that postal order ?

So deeply was Bunter engrossed in that problem, that he did not even know that the lesson was ended, and the Remove dismissed, till the stirring of the other fellows apprised him of the fact.

He rolled out with the Remove.

" I say, you fellows," squeaked Bunter, as soon as the Remove were out, " I say, I've lost my postal order ! Who's going to help me look for it ? "

" Sure it came ? " asked Skinner, with a grin.

" Oh, really, Skinner——"

" It came all right," said Bob Cherry. " Bunter showed it to me before class. Tough luck to lose it, old fat man."

" The toughfulness is terrific."

" Silly ass ! " commented Johnny Bull.

" Oh, really, Bull ! I didn't know there was a hole in the pocket—I mean, I had forgotten it ! I say, you fellows, be pals, and help a fellow look for it," urged Bunter.

" Well, we're going down to footer practice," said Harry Wharton.

" Oh, really, Wharton ! What does that matter ? " yapped Bunter. " Talk about Pontius Pilate fiddling while Carthage was burning ! "

" Ha, ha, ha ! "

" Blessed if I see anything to cackle at ! I say, you fellows, that postal order's about somewhere—do help a fellow look for it."

" Oh, all right ! All hands on deck," said the captain of the Remove. " Where do you think you may have dropped it, you fathead ? "

" Well, anywhere, really," said Bunter. " It might have been in the quad, or in the passages, or in the Cloisters, or in the lane outside, or on the road, or——"

" You've been out of the school ! " exclaimed Harry.

" Eh ? Oh ! Yes ! You see, I never missed it till I was going to cash it at Courtfield Post Office——"

" Oh, my hat ! Then that postal order's strewn about somewhere between Greyfriars and Courtfield Post Office ! " ejaculated Bob Cherry.

" Looks hopeful ! " remarked Frank Nugent.

" The hopefulness is terrific," grinned Hurree Jamset Ram Singh.

" Well, it must be somewhere," argued Bunter. " Might be spotted any minute, if a lot of fellows look for it."

" Well, we'll give the jolly old show the once-over," said Bob Cherry. " If you lost it outside the school, it's a goner : but it may be spotted about here somewhere. Join up, you men."

The Famous Five were all willing to help. Vernon-Smith and Redwing joined them, and Tom Brown, and Squiff, and Peter Todd, and Ogilvy, and six or seven other good-natured fellows. Even Fisher T. Fish joined up— perhaps in the hope of extracting that historic ' bob ' from Bunter if the postal order materialised. Even Lord Mauleverer exerted himself to the extent of wandering round the quad with his hands in his pockets.

They looked almost everywhere for that postal order. They looked up and down passages—they scanned the quad —they glanced behind trees and round buttresses : they hunted in the Cloisters, they examined the spot where Bunter had clambered out—they shook dust, but nothing more valuable, out of old ivy. Really and truly, they took a lot of trouble. But that elusive postal order was not discovered.

No doubt it was, as Bunter asserted, somewhere ! But, as Hurree Jamset Ram Singh sagely remarked, the whereful-ness was terrific.

CHAPTER XIII

MISSING

Buzzzzzzzzzzz !

" Upon my word ! " breathed Mr. Quelch.

It was scarcely possible to avoid feeling irritated.

After class, while a crowd of Remove fellows were helping Billy Bunter in the vain search for a disappeared postal order, Mr. Quelch was going to his study. The Remove were happily done with Quelch for the day : and Quelch, equally happily, was done with the Remove. Now an hour of agreeable leisure stretched before him, before he joined the other beaks at tea in Common-room : and Mr. Quelch was going to put in that happy hour at his ' History of Greyfriars ' : the great work which had been the occupation of his leisure for twenty years or so. In the scholastic quiet of his study, he was going to revel in black-letter manuscripts, which would have made any Remove man's head ache just to look at them. There was a smile of happy anticipation on Quelch's crusty face, as he wended his way to his study. And then——

Buzzzzzzzzzzzzz !

The hum of the Hoover, like the voice of the turtle, was heard in the land.

Quelch had forgotten the Hoover. Had he remembered it, he might have supposed that Mary would return to finish hoovering his study while he was in the form-room, when the Hoover might have hummed like a hive of bees, or roared like the Bull of Bashan, without bothering him. Being a mere man, Quelch did not grasp the fact that women's work has to be mapped out just like men's work. It was, Quelch seemed to think, something that could be done at any old time, the chief consideration being that it shouldn't interrupt Henry Samuel Quelch.

He looked in at the open doorway of his study.

There was Mary—there was the Hoover. It was plugged in, buzzing merrily, and Mary was steering it to and fro, with trailing flex. At the moment, it was engulfing fragments of waste paper under Quelch's writing-table that had missed the waste-paper basket.

Mary, free from other duties, had resumed activities in Quelch's study : very likely quite unaware of the hour at which the Remove were dismissed : perhaps not having given a single thought to Quelch or his form-room ! Mrs. Kebble had ordained that the masters' studies were to be hoovered that day, and that was sufficient for Mary. There she was—hoovering.

" Upon my word ! " repeated Mr. Quelch.

Buzzzzzz !

" Mary ! Please cease that dreadful noise at once," rapped Mr. Quelch.

Mary looked round.

There was blessed silence as she shut off the current.

" Did you speak, sir ? " asked Mary.

Quelch breathed hard, as he stepped into the study.

" I did ! " he answered. " Please take that—that implement out of my study, Mary. I have work to do."

" Only another five minutes, sir," said Mary, encouragingly. " Your carpet is very dusty, sir."

" I have not observed it," said Mr. Quelch, tartly, " and my time is of value, Mary."

" Oh, yes, sir ! " agreed Mary. " Just another few minutes, sir."

Mary turned on the current again, without waiting for a reply. Perhaps she thought that Mr. Quelch assented. Perhaps she did not want to give him time to dissent. Buzzzzzzzzzzzz !

Quelch breathed harder. But he tried to be patient. He could, after all, wait a few minutes, even with that appalling buzz in his ears. Perhaps he realised that if he argued the point with Mary, the few minutes would elapse

just the same, before he could get to work. It was obvious
that Mary and her Hoover were not going to vanish at a
word from Quelch, like a ghost at cock-crow. Quelch stood
in the study and waited, while Mary steered the ' implement '
to and fro, dust vanishing into its maw like magic.

There was a tread in the passage—a heavy tread. A
portly figure loomed in the study doorway.

" Ah ! You are here, Quelch," said Mr. Prout.

Quelch glanced at him. He did not hear the words, in
the buzz of the Hoover. Prout rolled into the doorway.

" My dear Quelch, I came here for that postal order
this afternoon, but did not find it on your table," said Mr.
Prout.

" Eh ? "

" That postal order, Quelch." Prout raised his voice,
in competition with the Hoover. He had to shout. " The
postal order you kindly brought in for me this morning,
Quelch——"

" Oh ! Yes ! It is on my table, Prout," shouted Quelch.

" I came in for it this afternoon, Quelch——"

" Eh ? "

" I came in for it this afternoon ! " roared Mr. Prout.
" But I did not find it on your table, Quelch."

" Indeed ! I certainly left it there——"

" Eh ? "

" It was there, under the paper-weight," roared Quelch.

" I could not find it there, Quelch."

" Eh ? "

" I could not find it there ! " bawled Prout.

" Indeed ! That is very singular——"

" Eh ? "

" Upon my word, this noise is intolerable," exclaimed
Mr. Quelch. " It must cease ! Mary ! "

Buzzzzzzzzz !

" Mary ! " raved Mr. Quelch.

Mary shut off, as she realised that Mr. Quelch was
addressing her.

" Did you speak, sir ? " she asked.

" Take that dreadful thing away ! "

" Another minute or two, sir——"

" Not another minute ! Not another second ! I cannot hear myself speak ! Take it away immediately."

" I have not quite finished the carpet, sir——"

" Take it away ! This instant ! "

" Oh, very well, sir," said Mary, with a slight toss of the head. " If Mrs. Kebble thinks the carpet is still dusty, sir, you will explain to her."

" Eh ? Oh ! Yes ! No ! Go away at once, and take that implement with you."

" Very well, sir."

Mary unplugged the Hoover, and wheeled it out of the study. Quelch breathed more freely when she was gone with it, glad to see the last of Mary and her Hoover. Mary, probably, was also glad to see the last of a testy old gentleman. Anyhow, off she went, Hoover and all : and Quelch, at last, was able to hear his own voice and Prout's.

" You were saying, Prout—— ? " said Mr. Quelch.

" I came in for the postal order, sir, but it was not on the table under the paper-weight," explained Mr. Prout. " No doubt you forgot to place it there, Quelch."

" Nothing of the kind, Mr. Prout. I certainly did place it there. I am not in the habit of forgetting," said Mr. Quelch, tartly.

" It is a matter of no moment, sir," said Mr. Prout, soothingly. " I had no occasion to catch an early post. But if the postal order is still in your pocket——"

" It could scarcely be still in my pocket, Mr. Prout, when I placed it under the paper-weight on my table," said Mr. Quelch.

" It was not there when I looked for it, Mr. Quelch."

" That is very extraordinary, Mr. Prout."

" If you are quite sure—— ! " murmured Prout.

Quelch made no rejoinder to that. Of course he was

sure! He was always sure. Nothing in the history of mankind was more certain than that Quelch had placed that postal order under the paper-weight on his table. Quelch turned to the table, and scanned it.

There was the paper-weight. But there was nothing under it—excepting, of course, the table. Quelch had left the postal order there. It was not there now. Quelch had to acknowledge the fact.

" Extraordinary ! " said Mr. Quelch.

He wrinkled his brows, as he gazed at the paper-weight.

" That stupid boy Bunter—— ! " he said.

" Bunter ? " repeated Mr. Prout.

" As it happens," explained Mr. Quelch, " there was something else under the paper-weight—a letter for Bunter, of my form. The postal order was placed on the letter, both under the paper-weight. Just before dinner I gave Bunter leave to fetch his letter from this study, and he must have done so, as it is gone. To take it he must have lifted the paper-weight. He should, of course, have re-placed it on the postal order, after taking his letter. Apparently he did not do so."

" But the postal order, in that case, should still be there, Quelch, whether under the paper-weight or not."

" Certainly it should," assented Mr. Quelch.

" I do not see it," said Mr. Prout.

Quelch scanned the table. Obviously, the postal order should have been still there, lying on the table, even if Bunter had carelessly omitted to replace the paper-weight on it. Quelch expected to spot it, among the various papers that lay on the table. He did not succeed in spotting it. It was not there !

" You do not see it, Quelch ? "

" I do not, Prout."

" It is very singular."

" Very ! "

Quelch was silent for a moment or two, puzzled and annoyed. Prout waited. Having handed Quelch a pound,

F

plus the poundage, for the purchase of that postal order,
Prout, naturally, wanted it.

" I will send for Bunter," said Mr. Quelch, at last.   " No
doubt the foolish boy can tell me where it is, as he must
have moved it.   I will bring the postal order to your study,
Mr. Prout."

" Thank you, Mr. Quelch."

Prout revolved his axis, and elephantined out of the
study.   Quelch touched the bell for Trotter, and des-
patched him to call Bunter—waiting for Bunter's arrival
with a deepening frown on his brow.

CHAPTER XIV

A STARTLING DISCOVERY

" No go ! " said Bob Cherry.

" Oh, really, Cherry——"

"Nothing doing, Bunter," said Frank Nugent.

" Oh, really, Nugent——"

" We've looked jolly nearly everywhere," said Harry Wharton.

" Oh, really, Wharton——"

" The lookfulness has been terrific, my esteemed fat Bunter," said Hurree Jamset Ram Singh, " but the spotfulness of the idiotic postal order is a boot on the other leg."

" Oh, really, Inky——"

" Chuck it," said Johnny Bull.

" Oh, really, Bull——"

The Famous Five and Bunter were in the old Cloisters. That seemed to them the most likely spot, as Bunter had clambered over a wall there. It would be very like Bunter to drop things about when he was clambering, even without the aid of a hole in his pocket. But they searched in vain : and indeed, with so very many possible spots to choose from, the search seemed rather hopeless. The chums of the Remove had done their best—sacrificing games practice to the search for that elusive postal order. Now they thought it time to ' chuck ' it. Bunter, on the other hand, did not.

" I say, you fellows, stick to it," he urged. " Don't be slackers, you know. The postal order must be somewhere."

" O where and O where can it be ? " sang Bob Cherry.

" The wherefulness is terrific."

" Look here," said Johnny Bull. " We can't find it ! But you can get a lost postal order replaced, if you can prove it's lost, and give the number."

" Oh ! " said Bunter.

It was a gleam of hope !

True, it was no present help in time of need : Bunter wanted the postal order at once, to translate into terms of tuck. But a pound to come, at a later date, was better than a pound irretrievably lost—much better. If the postal authorities, on being satisfied that the postal order was lost, shelled out the pound, there was at least a prospect of tuck to come.

" Did you notice the number ? " asked Harry.

" Oh ! No."

" Most likely your uncle took the number, before posting it," said Johnny Bull. " Did he mention it in his letter ? "

" I don't know."

" You don't know ? " repeated Johnny Bull, staring at him. " How don't you know, you fat ass, after reading the letter ? "

" I haven't read it yet," explained Bunter.

" Oh, my hat ! " said Bob.

Bunter, evidently, was interested only in the remittance, and not in any avuncular remarks that might have accompanied it. He had, indeed, quite forgotten the letter, in his anxiety about the postal order.

Harry Wharton laughed.

" Well, you'd better read it now, and see if Mr. Carter said anything about the number," he said.

" Unless you've lost the letter as well as the postal order," grunted Johnny.

" It was in a different pocket," said Bunter. " I expect I've got it all right." He groped. " Oh ! Here it is."

From a pocket which did not happen to have a hole in it, Bunter drew Mr. Carter's letter.

He took out the folded missive from the envelope, and unfolded it. He blinked at it through his big spectacles.

Then an extraordinary change came over Bunter's fat face.

It was quite startling.

Harry Wharton and Co., watching him, could only wonder what there was in that letter to cause Billy Bunter's jaw to drop, and his little round eyes to pop behind his big round spectacles.

Whatever it was, evidently it had given the fat Owl a shock.

Bunter read that letter through. Then he read it through again, as if doubting his eyes or his spectacles. Then he ejaculated :

" Oh, crikey ! "

" What on earth's up ? " asked Nugent, blankly.

" Oh, crumbs ! "

" Does your uncle mention the number ? " asked Johnny Bull.

" Eh ? Oh ! No ! Oh, jiminy ! "

" Bad news ? " asked Harry.

" Oh, lor ' ! "

" Look here, you ass——"

" I—I—I say, you fellows, I—I—I—oh, crikey ! I—I don't understand this ! I—I—I—oh, lor ' ! I—I—I say, mum-mum-mum-my uncle never sent me a postal order at all ! "

" WHAT ! "

" I can't make it out ! Look at the letter ! " gasped Bunter. " I—I—I thought that postal order had been taken out of it—of course I did ! But—but—but—but it couldn't have been ! Look ! "

Blankly, the Famous Five looked at the letter from Uncle Carter. It was really rather unfortunate that Bunter had not looked at it a little earlier ! It ran :

> Dear William,
>
> I have received your letter, in which you mention that you have not yet received the £1 I promised you. I have not forgotten it, and I shall post it to you, in the form of a postal order, next week.
>
> Your affectionate Uncle,
> Humphrey Carter.

The Famous Five gazed at that letter. Then they gazed at one another. Then they gazed at Bunter.

Bunter blinked at them anxiously.

" I—I say, you fellows, doesn't that sound as if my uncle never put a postal order in the letter at all ? " he stuttered.

" It does, you unbelievable ass ! " said Harry Wharton. " Mr. Carter's sending you a postal order next week. He hasn't sent you one in this letter."

" Oh, crikey ! "

" But the blithering idiot had a postal order," said Bob. " He showed it to me—it was a postal order for one pound, all right."

" It wasn't Bunter's," said Johnny Bull.

" Oh, scissors ! "

" Holy smoke ! " said Harry Wharton. " Quelch must have had a postal order for something or other, on his table, and that fat chump—— "

" Oh, jiminy ! "

" And he's lost it—— ! " said Nugent.

" Oh, lor ' ! I—I say, you fellows, I—I thought it was my pip-pip-postal order," moaned Bunter. " Uncle Carter promised it, and of course I thought it was in his letter, and then I saw it on the letter in Quelch's study—and the envelope was open, you know—you fellows remember I asked you whether you thought Quelch had read the letter as it was open and he'd taken the postal order out—— "

" You blithering owl ! "

" Oh, suffering cats and crocodiles ! " said Bob Cherry. " That unlimited idiot has bagged a postal order that belongs to Quelch—and lost it—— "

" Quelch will miss it—— ! " said Nugent.

" There'll be a row—— "

" Bunter, you priceless chump—— "

" Bunter, you potty porpoise—— "

" I—I say, you fellows, that beastly postal order's got to be found," gasped Bunter. " If we find it, I can take it back to Quelch's study before he misses it. I—I suppose it can't be mine, from what Uncle Carter says——".

" Of course it can't, you blithering bloater."

" Well, 'tain't my fault, is it ? " yapped Bunter. " What the thump did Quelch have a postal order on his table for ? Of course I thought he'd taken it out of the letter. What was a fellow to think ? "

" Oh, you chump ! "

" It—it's all right, if we find it——"

" It can't be found, fathead ! Very likely it's blowing about Courtfield Common this very minute," said Bob.

" But I—I—I say, Quelch might think it was pinched ! " gasped Bunter. " He might make out that I'd taken it, if—if he knew I had, you know."

" You did take it, you howling fathead ! You'd better go to Quelch at once and tell him——" said Harry Wharton.

Yell, from Bunter.

" You silly ass ! He mightn't believe that I thought it was my postal order at all ! Watch me telling him ! "

" Well, it wants some believing," said Johnny Bull, with a very sharp look at Bunter. " Look here, you unspeakable ass, if——"

" Easy does it, Johnny," said Bob Cherry. " Bunter wouldn't——"

Another yell from Bunter.

" Beast ! Think I'd pinch a postal order ! Of course I thought it was out of my letter ! I—I say, you fellows, you jolly well know——"

" We know that you're fathead enough for that, or any-thing else," said Harry. " You'd better go to Quelch at once and tell him the whole thing——"

" I'll watch it ! " gasped Bunter. " Look here, I—I never had anything to do with it. Don't you fellows get saying that I had a postal order, or—or anything. If—if it can't be found, keep it dark, see ? I'm not going to have Quelch making out that I snooped a postal order from his study."

" For goodness sake, have a little sense, Bunter," exclaimed the captain of the Remove. " If you begin telling Quelch lies about it, he will think you pilfered the rotten thing. Tell him the truth, and——"

" Oh, really, Wharton——"

" The truth, the whole truth, and nothing but the truth, old fat man," said Bob Cherry. " That's your best guess."

" Oh, really, Cherry——"

" If you begin lying to Quelch, you're done for," said Johnny Bull.

" I hope I'm not the fellow for lying," said Bunter. " I'm a bit more particular than some fellows I could name. Look here, Bull——"

" Hallo, hallo, hallo ! Here comes Trotter ! " exclaimed Bob Cherry. " Looks as if he's looking for somebody."

The House page came into the Cloisters. Evidently he was looking for somebody : and the Famous Five could guess for whom. Quelch must have gone to his study after class, and they could guess that he had missed the postal order. Trotter looked round, and came across to the group of juniors.

" I've been looking for you everywhere, Master Bunter," he said. " Mr. Quelch wants you in his study."

" Oh, lor ' ! "

Trotter, with a rather curious look at the fat Owl's dismayed face, departed. Bunter blinked dolorously at the Famous Five.

" I—I say, you fellows, think Quelch wants to see me about my lines ? " he asked, hopefully.

The Co. made no reply to that. They had no doubt that Quelch wanted to see Bunter about a more serious matter than lines.

" I—I say, think it's about that beastly postal order ? " groaned Bunter.

" It must be," said Harry. " For goodness sake, Bunter, tell Quelch the truth for once——"

" Beast ! "

Billy Bunter rolled dismally away : but whether with the intention of telling Quelch the truth, was very doubtful. Such a sudden change in Bunter's manners and customs was considerably improbable.

CHAPTER XV

CALLED TO ACCOUNT

MR. QUELCH's face was grim, as he eyed the fat figure at his doorway.

"Come in, Bunter!" he rapped.

Bunter rolled reluctantly in.

Quelch had been quite kind that day : since he had learned about Bunter's anxiety for a sick relative ! But Bunter could see that he did not look very kind now.

Mr. Quelch was, in point of fact, deeply disturbed.

A postal order for £1 was missing from his study. Bunter, it was certain, must have moved that postal order, in getting his letter. He was careless enough to leave it lying anywhere on the table, without replacing it under the paper-weight. But Quelch had gone through all the papers on the table, and made assurance doubly sure that the postal order was not among them. He was driven to believe that it was no longer in the study at all. But if it was no longer in the study, what was Mr. Quelch to think ?

He was very anxious to see Bunter, and clear up this extremely disturbing and disagreeable matter. But he had had to wait : it had taken Trotter some time to track the fat Owl to the Cloisters. However, here was Bunter at last—dragging himself reluctantly into the study, as if his fat little legs almost refused to carry him in.

"I have sent for you, Bunter—— !" began Mr. Quelch.

"Yes, sir ! I—I haven't had time to do them yet, sir——"

"What ? What ? To what do you allude, Bunter ? "

"Mum-mum-my lines, sir——"

"I have not sent for you about your lines, Bunter."

" Oh ! Haven't you, sir ? Thank you, sir. M-m-may
I go now, sir ? " gasped Bunter.

" Listen to me, Bunter," said Mr. Quelch, quietly.
" Just before class this afternoon, I gave you leave to take
your letter from this study."

" Oh ! Yes, sir."

" You took the letter ? "

" Yes, sir."

" On that letter, under the same paper-weight, was
a postal order for £1," said Mr. Quelch. " You must
have noticed it, Bunter, when you took your letter. That
postal order is missing. What can you tell me about it ? "

Mr. Quelch's eyes were fixed on Billy Bunter's fat face.
Never had those gimlet-eyes seemed so penetrating.

Bunter quaked inwardly.

It was coming now !

Quelch was putting it gently, mildly. That Bunter must
know what had become of the missing postal order was
clear to his mind. But the bare thought of possible pilfering was so repugnant to him, that he would not entertain
it, if he could help it. He hoped that, improbable as it
seemed, there might be some other explanation.

Harry Wharton and Co. had earnestly advised Bunter to
tell the truth, and though in this peculiar case, the truth
might have sounded stranger than fiction, it was undoubtedly
Bunter's best guess. Unfortunately, the truth was a re-
source of which Billy Bunter thought last, if he thought of
it at all.

Bunter wasn't going to have Quelch making out that he
had snooped that postal order ! That was fixed in Bunter's
fat and fatuous mind. Now that he knew that that postal
order wasn't his, he knew what it looked like—what it must
look like. If he could have produced the postal order, it
would have been different. But he couldn't, as he had
lost it. Prevarication was always Billy Bunter's first line
of defence. He was not thinking of adopting new methods
now.

" Well ? " rapped Mr. Quelch.

" Did—did—did you say a pip-pip-pip—— ? " stammered Bunter.

" What ? "

" A pip-pip-postal order, sir ? "

" I did," said Mr. Quelch. " I must know what has become of that postal order, Bunter. You must have moved it when you took your letter. What did you do with it ? "

" I—I didn't, sir," gasped Bunter.

" Be careful what you say, Bunter. This is a very serious matter."

" Is—is—is it, sir ? "

" It could hardly be more serious, Bunter. The postal order is missing. It has been taken from my study."

" Has—has—has it, sir ? "

" It has, Bunter. I purchased that postal order, this morning for Mr. Prout, at Friardale Post Office. I placed it under that paper-weight, with your letter. When Mr. Prout came here for it this afternoon, it was gone."

" Oh ! " gasped Bunter. He knew now why Prout had come to the study, and driven him to take cover under the table.

" It cannot be found, Bund, r."

" Kik-kik-kik-can't it, si it, si "

" It cannot, Bunter. just before class, you came here and took your lett rom under the same paper-weight——"

" Oh ! No, sir ! " gasped ter. " I—I—I didn't——"

" What ? A few minutes go you told me that you did ! "

" Oh ! I—I mean—— "

" Well, what do you mean, Bunter ? " inquired Mr. Quelch, his eyes boring like gimlets into the fat Owl's alarmed face.

" I—I—I mean, I—I di. my letter, sir—— "

" Be careful how you answer me, Bunter," said Mr.

Quelch. " I warn you, if only for your own sake, to tell me the truth."

" Oh, yes, sir. I—I always do, sir——"

" You removed the paper-weight, and took your letter," resumed Mr. Quelch. " You must, therefore, have moved the postal order, which lay on the letter. What did you do with it ? "

" I—I—I didn't, sir——" gasped Bunter.

" What ? "

" It—it wasn't there, sir ! I—I should have noticed it, if—if it had been—I—I'm certain I should have noticed it, sir."

" Upon my word ! "

" Pip-pip-perhaps it blew out of the window, sir," suggested Bunter, hopefully.

" Do not be absurd, Bunter."

" Oh, yes, sir ! I mean, no, sir. It wasn't me, sir," groaned Bunter. " I never touched it, sir. I—I wouldn't ! It wasn't there at all, sir, and—and I left it there quite safe under the paper-weight when I went away, sir——"

" What ? " gasped Mr. Quelch.

" C-c-can I go now, sir ? "

" Bunter ! I warn you to tell me the truth ! " exclaimed Mr. Quelch. " A postal order for £1 has been taken from my study. I am reluctant to believe any boy in my form capable of pilfering—"

" Oh, crikey ! "

" Tell me at once what you did with that postal order, Bunter," rapped Mr. Quelch.

" N-n-nothing, sir ! I—I never knew you'd got a postal order for Mr. Prout, sir. I—I don't know anything about it," groaned Bunter. " I never touched it at all, and I wouldn't have, only I thought it was mine. Not that I did, sir. I never even saw it——"

" You thought it was yours ! " ejaculated Mr. Quelch. " What do you mean, you utterly stupid boy, if your words have any meaning at all ? "

"I—I mean I—I was expecting a postal order, sir," stammered Bunter, "and my letter being open, I—I thought you'd taken it out——"

"Bless my soul!" said Mr. Quelch.

"I wouldn't have touched it, sir, only I thought it was mine——"

"Then you did take it, Bunter?"

"Oh!" gasped Bunter. "No! I—I never saw it, sir! It wasn't there!"

"Grant me patience!" breathed Mr. Quelch. "Bunter, it is scarcely possible for me to believe that you can have been so obtuse, so stupid, so utterly stupid as to have acted in the way your words would imply. But if you took the postal order under such an extraordinary error, return it to me at once."

"I—I can't, sir!"

"And why?" thundered Mr. Quelch. "Have you changed that postal order, Bunter, and expended the proceeds?"

"Oh, crumbs! No, sir," howled Bunter, in alarm.

"Then why cannot you return it?"

"I—I—I never had it, sir."

"What?"

"I—I never touched it, sir. It wasn't there when I came to the study for my letter. Besides, I—I never came."

Mr. Quelch gazed at that member of his form. He did not speak. It really seemed that William George Bunter had taken his breath away.

"M-m-m-may I go now, sir?" ventured Bunter.

"Bunter! I command you to return the postal order you took from my table. If you do not return it, it is obvious that you have cashed it: in which case you will be taken to your headmaster——"

"Ow!"

"And charged with pilfering——"

"Oh, crikey!"

" And expelled from Greyfriars——"

" Ooooooh ! "

" Produce it ! " thundered Mr. Quelch.

" Oh, lor' ! "

" For the last time, Bunter—— ! "

" Oh, dear ! I—I I kik-kik-kik-can't ! I—I—I—I've lost it ! " wailed Bunter.

CHAPTER XVI

DOUBTING THOMASES

" I SAY, you fellows."

" Blow away, Bunter."

" But I say—— ! "

" Give us a rest ! "

Harry Wharton and Co. were at tea in No. 1 Study. Over tea they were talking Soccer.

Soccer was a more interesting subject than Bunter. And they really did feel that they needed a rest from Bunter. Fascinating fellow as Bunter had no doubt that he was, it was possible to have too much of him. The Famous Five felt that they had had enough for one day, at least, and perhaps a little over. So with one accord they bade him blow away as he presented himself in the doorway of the study.

Bunter, however, did not blow away.

Instead of blowing away down the passage, he blew into the study.

" I say, you fellows, you might be a bit sympathetic," he said, reproachfully.

" Awfully cut up about your uncle, who isn't ill ? " asked Johnny Bull, sarcastically.

" Oh, really, Bull—— "

" The too-muchfullness of the esteemed Bunter is terrific," remarked Hurree Jamset Ram Singh.

" I'm in an awful jam, you fellows," said Bunter, pathetically.

" Same jam you had in the form-room this morning ? " asked Bob Cherry.

" Ha, ha, ha ! "

" It's jolly serious ! I say, I've been to Quelch," moaned Bunter. " I say, he makes out that I had that postal order."

" Well, you had it, you fat villain," said Harry Wharton.

" It turns out that it was Prout's," said Bunter. " The old ass asked the other old ass to bring it in for him this morning. That's how it came to be on Quelch's table. Of course, I thought——"

" You thought ? " asked Johnny Bull, still sarcastic. " What did you do that with ? "

" I thought it was mine, or I shouldn't have taken it along with the letter," groaned Bunter. " It would be all right if I hadn't lost it. Quelch only wants me to hand it back. I think he would believe that I took it by mistake, if I handed it back. He doesn't seem to believe it now. He fancies that I've snooped it and spent the money ! Me, you know."

" Haven't you ? " asked Johnny Bull.

" Beast ! " roared Bunter.

" Even Bunter wouldn't—— ! " said Bob.

" Quelch knows that he snoops tuck," said Johnny. " He's whopped him for it more than once. Now there's a postal order gone, and Bunter tells him a cock-and-bull story of taking it by mistake and losing it. What does it look like ? "

" It does look pretty bad," said Harry Wharton, slowly. " But——"

" Well, Quelch can't be expected to get it down, even if it's true," said Johnny. " And is it ? "

" I've told you I lost it," howled Bunter, indignantly.

" You've told us lots of things," answered Johnny. " Generally crammers."

" Beast ! No wonder Quelch won't take my word, if my own pals won't ! " said Bunter. " Actually, he wouldn't believe what I said, when I told him that I never saw the postal order in the study at all."

" You told him that ? " gasped Harry Wharton.

" Yes, and he as good as called me a liar," said Bunter, sorrowfully. " That's the sort of thing a fellow has to put up with at school. A schoolmaster ought to take a fellow's word. Then it would be all right."

G

The Famous Five gazed at Bunter.

"As the matter stands," continued the fat Owl, "Quelch thinks that I bagged that postal order from his study——"

"You mean he knows you did," hooted Nugent.

"And he doesn't believe I've lost it," went on Bunter. "I say, if I don't take it back, I'm going up to the Head."

"You haven't cashed it ?" asked Johnny Bull.

"I've told you I haven't," yelled Bunter.

"I know that ! But have you ?"

"Beast !"

"Bunter's idiot enough to do exactly what he says he did," said Bob Cherry, slowly. "But losing the postal order on top of it—that sounds jolly thick ! Quelch can't be expected to swallow that."

Snort, from Johnny Bull.

"A fellow takes a postal order that doesn't belong to him," he said, "and when he's asked for it, says that he's lost it ! If Quelch swallowed that, he would swallow anything."

"But it's true !" wailed Bunter.

Johnny shrugged his shoulders. The other members of the Co. looked at Bunter dubiously.

They hardly knew what to believe.

Bunter's reputation as an Ananias had come home to roost, as it were. He was too well known to have no use for facts. No doubt he told the truth sometimes. But if trouble threatened, Bunter was rather like Mr. Jaggers' celebrated witness, who was prepared to swear ' in a general way, anythink '. After telling Mr. Quelch that he had not even seen the postal order he had taken from the study, he really could hardly expect Quelch to believe his further statement that he had lost it. And the Famous Five could not help having doubts.

"Look here, you fat spoofer," said Harry Wharton, at last. "We know you pulled Quelch's leg to get out of class, and hiked off to Courtfield to cash that postal order and gorge at the bun-shop. If you did it——"

" I didn't ! " howled Bunter. " I tell you it was gone, when I felt in my pocket for it."

" If you did it, and then spun us a yarn about losing it——"

" If you can't take a fellow's word, Harry Wharton——"

" Fathead ! "

" Beast ! "

" Blessed if I know what to think," said Frank Nugent. " But if you've really lost that postal order, Bunter, you'd better find it again, before you go up to Dr. Locke."

" But I can't find it," wailed Bunter. " I say, you fellows, Quelch has given me a quarter of an hour to take that postal order to his study——"

" Lots of time, if you haven't cashed it," said Johnny Bull.

" I tell you it's lost ! " shrieked Bunter.

" Um ! " said Johnny.

" If I don't take it to him, he's going to take me to the Head ! I can't take it to him when it's lost. I say, you fellows, do you think the Head will believe that I never took it from the study at all ? The Head's a gentleman, which Quelch ain't, and he might take a fellow's word."

" Oh, my hat ! "

" But Quelch will be there, and he's against me," said Bunter. " Think the Head will take Quelch's word against mine ? "

" Help ! "

" Quelch is always against me," said Bunter, sadly. " I never get justice. He's down on me. Some schoolmasters know when a fellow's a credit to his school. Does Quelch ? Why, he wouldn't care if the Head bunked me."

Herbert Vernon-Smith looked into the study from the passage.

" Bunter here ? " he asked. " Oh, here you are, Bunter ! You're wanted."

" Oh, crikey ! "

" Wingate's looking for you," said Smithy.

" I—I—I say, what does Wingate want me for ? " asked Bunter. " Think he wants to—to ask me to tea in his study, Smithy ? "

The Bounder chuckled.

" Not quite," he answered. " He wants you for Quelch, fathead. You'd better go down."

Smithy walked on up the passage. Billy Bunter turned his spectacles on the Famous Five with a dolorous blink.

" I—I—I say, you fellows, that means that Quelch wants me, to take to the Head," he gasped. " I—I ain't going to the Head."

" No choice about that, ass," said Bob. " If you don't go down, Wingate will come up here after you."

" I tell you I ain't going to the Head, when Quelch is going to make out that I snooped old Prout's postal order," howled Bunter. " I—I say, hide me somewhere, and—and tell Wingate I ain't here——"

" You howling ass—— ! "

" Beast ! "

Billy Bunter blinked into the passage. A glimpse of a stalwart figure on the landing was enough for him. He bolted back into the study like a scared rabbit.

" I say, you fellows, he's coming ! " gasped Bunter. " I say, I—I ain't going to the Head ! Don't you tell Wingate I'm here."

The fat Owl backed out of sight behind the open door.

There, he was full in view of five fellows in the study : but invisible to anyone looking in from the passage—unless that one looked round the door.

" You benighted ass—— ! " gasped Bob Cherry.

" Shut up, you beast ! Keep it dark."

Wingate's tread was heard in the passage. Harry Wharton and Co. stared at Bunter, behind the door, and then at one another. Then they hurriedly resumed tea, as the stalwart form of the captain of Greyfriars appeared in the doorway.

" Is that young ass Bunter up here ? " asked Wingate.

Bunter, behind the door, hardly breathed.

" Bunter ? " repeated Bob Cherry. " Bunter's study is No. 7, Wingate."

Wingate nodded, and went on up the passage. Bob's answer was perfectly veracious, though perhaps it savoured a little more of the wisdom of the serpent than of the innocence of the dove. Bunter's study, certainly, was No. 7—and the Greyfriars captain went on to No. 7 to look for him.

" You'd better get out, Bunter," said Harry Wharton.

" Beast ! "

" How long do you think you can keep this game up ? " asked Johnny Bull.

" Beast ! "

" Look here, you ass—— ! " said Nugent.

" Beast ! "

Bunter, evidently, was not to be reasoned with. It was extremely doubtful how long he could keep this game up : but apparently he was going to keep it up as long as he could !

CHAPTER XVII

BOLTED

WINGATE of the Sixth looked into No. 7 Study in the Remove. Peter Todd and Tom Dutton, who were at tea there, jumped up with due respect, at the sight of the captain of the school.

Wingate glanced round the study.

" This is Bunter's study, isn't it ? " he asked. " He doesn't seem to be here. Know where he is, Todd ? "

" I think he went to Quelch——" answered Peter.

" I know he did ! Quelch wants him again," grunted Wingate. " The young sweep has been up to something, I suppose. Know where Bunter is, Dutton ? "

" Eh ? " asked Tom Dutton.

Wingate had forgotten, for the moment, that Tom Dutton was deaf. He raised his voice as he repeated the question.

" Know where Bunter is ? " he asked, in a voice that could be heard as far as No. 1 Study, and that reached the fat ears of a terrified Owl behind a door. But it did not seem quite loud enough for Dutton.

Dutton looked astonished.

" Eh ? Of course I do," he answered.

" Well, where is he, then ? "

" A hunter is a fellow who hunts," said Dutton, staring. " What about it ? "

Wingate stared, and Peter Todd grinned.

" You young ass ! " gasped Wingate. " I'm not talking about a hunter. Have you seen Bunter ? "

" Well, I don't know that I've seen a hunter. I've seen a huntsman," answered Dutton.

" Not Hunter—Bunter ! " roared Wingate. " I said Bunter, not hunter."

" I know Bunter's not a hunter. What about it ? "

"Do you know where Bunter is ?" howled Wingate. "I've got to take him to Quelch."

"Bunter isn't Welsh, that I know of——"

"What ?"

"If he was Welsh, he would know one tune from another, and he doesn't," said Dutton, shaking his head. "He's never told me that he's Welsh."

"I said Quelch !" shrieked Wingate.

"Is Quelch Welsh ?" asked Dutton. "First I've heard of it."

"Ha, ha, ha !" yelled Peter Todd.

"What are you laughing at, Toddy ?" asked Dutton. "I've never heard that Quelch is Welsh, and it's not a joke, if he is. Look here, Wingate, I don't know whether Quelch is Welsh or not : if you want to know, you'd better ask him."

"Have you seen Bunter ?" bawled Wingate.

"Yes, I saw him in the quad, after class—I think he was looking for something. You needn't yell at a fellow—I'm not deaf."

"Haven't you seen him since ?"

"Do you mean Hurree Singh ?"

"What ?"

"He's the only prince I've ever seen—they say he is a prince in India. No other princes at Greyfriars, that I know of."

Wingate gave it up at that. It seemed rather less exertion to look for Bunter, than to inquire after him in his study. He tramped out of No. 7, leaving Peter Todd grinning, and Dutton looking puzzled.

He decided to 'draw' the studies one after another for Bunter, beginning with No. 2, as he had already looked into No. 1. But as he stopped at the door of No. 2, he gave a little jump, at the sound of a fat squeak from No. 1.

"I say, you fellows, look out and see if that beast's still in the passage. If he's gone into a study I'll cut."

"Oh !" ejaculated Wingate.

He strode into the doorway of No. 1 Study.   Five fellows looked as innocent as they could under a grim glare.

" You young sweeps ! " exclaimed Wingate.   " Bunter was here all the time.   I've just heard him speak.   Where is he ? "

" Oh, crikey ! "

That startled ejaculation from behind the door apprised the Greyfriars captain of Bunter's whereabouts.   He circumnavigated the door, and stared at the fat Owl.

" You young rascal—you're here ! " he snapped.

" Oh ! No ! I—I ain't here, Wingate," gasped Bunter. " I—I mean—oh, crikey ! "

A muscular hand on a collar hooked Bunter out from behind the door, like a fat winkle from a shell.

" Ow ! Leggo ! " roared Bunter, as he was twirled into the doorway.   " Ow ! Beast ! I ain't going to the Head ! Yaroooh ! "

" It's not the Head, you young ass ! It's your form-master wants you.   Get a move on."

" Yow-ow ! He's going to take me to the Head ! " howled Bunter.   " I never had that postal order, Wingate ! It's all a mistake."

" What ? " exclaimed Wingate.

" I never had it ! It wasn't on Quelch's table when I went to his study," yelled Bunter, " and I told Quelch it was still there when I went away, and—and I never went to the study at all——"

" Good gad ! " said Wingate, staring at him.   " Is that what's up ? Come along, you young rascal—you're going to Quelch, anyway."

" Poor old Bunter ! " murmured Bob Cherry, as the squeaking fat Owl was hooked out of the study.   " He's for it now."

" Still time for him to cough up Prout's postal order," said Johnny Bull.

" But if he's lost it—— "

" Then he'd better look in his pocket and find it," said Johnny, sarcastically.   " Those who hide can find."

" I say, Wingate, leggo my collar ! " came a howl from the passage. " I'm coming, ain't I ? "

" Well, come on," grunted Wingate.

Billy Bunter was extremely reluctant to come. But he came. A dozen fellows stared at him, as he went down the stairs with the Greyfriars captain. His little round eyes blinked right and left behind his big round spectacles, as he went. Bunter was going—but he was watching for a chance to dodge. There was room in Billy Bunter's fat head for only one idea at a time : and the idea now fixed in it, was that he wasn't going to be taken to the Head to be ' bunked ' from Greyfriars. Somehow or other, he was going to elude that painful interview with his headmaster— if he could !

Buzzzzzz !

The sound of the Hoover greeted Bunter's fat ears, as Wingate marched him into Masters' passage. Mary was busy again, hoovering the long strip of carpet that ran the length of Masters' passage, to the door of Common-room.

However, Mary and the Hoover were some distance up the passage, beyond Quelch's door. Wingate walked Bunter as far as that door, and knocked.

He opened the door, and pushed the fat Owl in.

" Here is Bunter, sir," he said.

" Thank you, Wingate."

The Greyfriars captain walked away down the passage, glad to be done with Bunter. The hapless fat Owl stood just within the doorway, eyeing Mr. Quelch through his big spectacles, as a fat rabbit might have eyed a particularly ferocious fox. Mr. Quelch's eyes fixed sternly on the fat Owl.

" Bunter ! Have you brought the postal order to me ? "

" Oh, crikey ! "

" Answer me at once, Bunter."

" Nunno."

" Very well ! " Mr. Quelch compressed his lips hard. " I shall now take you to Dr. Locke, Bunter, and your head-

master will deal with you.   I shall—Stop !   Bunter !   How
dare you ?   STOP ! " shrieked Mr. Quelch.

Bunter did not stop.   He bolted !

Wingate was gone !   It was a chance at last !   Bunter
made one bound through the open doorway into the
passage.

" STOP ! "

Quelch rushed after him.

Bunter flew.

Down the passage, Wingate was yet in sight, going.
Behind was Quelch, and a clutching hand.   Up the passage
was Mary, steering the buzzing Hoover along the carpet-
strip, with the flex trailing.   With Wingate or Quelch,
Bunter could not hope to deal : but Mary was not
dangerous : and Bunter bolted up the passage.   Quelch's
clutching hand, sweeping out of the doorway, missed him
by a foot.

" STOP ! " thundered Quelch.

Wingate looked round, and came hurrying back.

" Oh, gad !   Stop, Bunter, you young ass ! " he shouted.

Bunter heeded neither of them.   He flew.

Mary, notwithstanding the buzz of the motor in the
vacuum-cleaner, heard those shouts, and looked round, the
Hoover still buzzing.

" Law-a-mercy ! " ejaculated Mary, in astonishment, as
she beheld a fat junior, his eyes popping with terror behind
his spectacles, charging up the passage like a runaway bull :
with a form-master and a Sixth-form prefect in pursuit.

Bunter charged on.

He swerved to avoid Mary and the Hoover.   But he did
not see the trailing flex.   He was not aware of it till his
feet caught in it, and he went headlong.

" Yaroooh ! " roared Bunter, as he crashed.

It was a terrific crash.   Billy Bunter, yelling frantically,
rolled over on the floor, wildly mixed up with the Hoover.
The Hoover suddenly ceased to buzz.   Mary did not need
to switch it off : the motor went off song as Billy Bunter's

" YAROOOH ! " ROARED BUNTER, AS HE CRASHED

uncommon weight crashed on the machine. No doubt it
was damaged. Few machines could have escaped damage,
under the tremendous impact of Billy Bunter's avoirdupois.
But if the Hoover was silent, Bunter was not. Yell on yell,
and roar on roar, resounded from Bunter, waking every echo
of Masters' studies.

CHAPTER XVIII

THE LAST CHANCE

" Bunter—— ! "

" Yaroooh ! "

" Be silent——"

" Yoo-whooooop ! "

" Cease that ridiculous noise instantly, Bunter——"

" Yow-ow-ow-ow-woooop ! "

Study doors were opening in the passage. Mr. Hacker looked out of one, Mr. Prout out of another, Mr. Capper out of a third, Mr. Wiggins out of a fourth, Monsieur Charpentier out of a fifth.

Bunter was getting an audience.

Mr. Quelch, almost crimson with anger and vexation, stooped, grasped the fat Owl by a podgy shoulder, and heaved him to his feet. Wingate, grasping the other podgy shoulder, lent aid. Between the two of them, Bunter resumed the perpendicular, still yelling.

" Upon my word ! What is this disturbance ? " boomed Mr. Prout, from his doorway. " Quelch ! What is all this ? "

" What has happened ? " piped Mr. Capper.

" One of Quelch's boys," said Mr. Hacker, sardonically, and he went back into his study, and closed the door with a bang.

" Mais qu'est-que-c'est ? " ejaculated Monsieur Charpentier. " C'est affreux, cela ! Mon bon Quelch——"

" Bunter, be silent ! "

" Yow-ow-ow ! Whooop ! "

" Will you be silent, Bunter ? Otherwise, I shall cane you before taking you to the Head ! " thundered Mr. Quelch.

" Ow ! I'm hurt ! I believe my leg's broken ! I—I

believe I've broken the spinal column in my elbow—wow ! "

" What is the matter, Quelch ? " boomed Prout.

" Nothing ! " snapped the Remove master. " This foolish boy has collided with the vacuum cleaner, that is all, running up the passage——"

" Are Remove boys permitted to race about Master's passage, Mr. Quelch ? Such a disturbance——"

" Extraordinary ! " said Mr. Capper.

" Really—really——" said Mr. Twigg, looking out of his study, and adding himself to the audience. " Really—really——"

" Unprecedented," said Prout.   " Indeed, unparalleled ! Really, Quelch——"

Mr. Quelch breathed very hard and very deep. With a grip of iron on Bunter's fat shoulder, he jerked him away.

" Come with me, Bunter, and be silent," he breathed. " Another sound, and I will take you back to my study and cane you with the greatest severity."

Bunter spluttered. But he ceased to roar. Quelch evidently was in no mood to be trifled with.

" Mary." Quelch, with an effort, forced himself to speak courteously. " I am sorry that this stupid boy of my form has interrupted you. I am taking him away—you may resume your work with that—that implement."

Mary tossed her head.

" It's gone off," she said.

" Then you may switch it on——"

" I mean it's gone off," said Mary, lucidly. " I think the motor's busted. Anyhow it won't switch on. I shan't be able to finish the carpet."

" Bunter, you stupid boy, you have damaged the vacuum-cleaner," said Mr. Quelch, severely.

Grunt, from Bunter. He was not worrying about having damaged the Hoover. The Hoover had damaged him : and that was worry enough for Bunter.

" You are sure it is out of action, Mary ? "

" Look at it ! " said Mary.   " It's switched on all right !
Is it buzzing ? "

" Thank goodness it is not—I—I mean, apparently not,"
said Mr. Quelch, hastily.   " I regret—ahem——"   Really,
Mr. Quelch could not regret very sincerely that the vacuum-
cleaner was out of action.   He had had more than he
wanted of its musical effects.

" I shall have to tell Mrs. Kebble, and she will have to
get the young man from Courtfield," said Mary, " and it
may be days ! "

" Dear me ! " said Mr. Quelch.   " Come, Bunter."

He walked Bunter away, with a hand on his shoulder.
The fat Owl was not to be given another chance to bolt.

Mary, with a perceptible sniff, wheeled the disabled
Hoover away.   Prout and the other masters exchanged expressive looks, from door to door, and returned into their
studies.   Wingate, with a rather compassionate glance at
the hapless Bunter, went down the passage again : while
Bunter, with fingers of steel compressing his fat shoulder,
was led to the headmaster's study.

He went with dragging feet, quaking.

Few fellows liked visiting that dread apartment.   Kindly
old gentleman as Dr. Locke was, Greyfriars fellows were
content to respect him at a distance : and did not enjoy
being summoned into the Presence.   Least of all did Billy
Bunter desire to interview his headmaster.   But for the
grip on his fat shoulder, Bunter certainly would have bolted
again.   He was going to the Head to be ' bunked ' : and
the prospect was too awful.

But Quelch gave him no chance to bolt on the way.
They arrived at the door of Dr. Locke's study.

There, however, Quelch paused.   He still gripped
Bunter's fat shoulder, but he did not, for the moment,
raise his other hand to tap at the door.   He fixed his
gimlet-eyes on the fat scared face.

" Bunter ! " he said, quietly.

" Oh, dear !   Yes, sir," moaned Bunter.

"I shall give you a last opportunity, Bunter, before taking you in to Dr. Locke. Knowing your almost incredible stupidity——"

"Oh, really, sir——"

"Knowing your incredible, amazing, extraordinary stupidity," said Mr. Quelch, "I can believe that you really did take the postal order from my study by mistake, as you have stated—if you return it at once, Bunter. If you do not return it, Bunter, you will be expelled from the school for pilfering. I am bound to make every possible allowance for so utterly obtuse a boy. I will give you one more opportunity to make restitution."

"I—I—I kik-kik-kik-can't, sir—— !" stuttered Bunter.

"For the last time, Bunter ! It will be too late, in the presence of your headmaster."

"I—I—I——"

"Is it in your pocket, Bunter ?"

"N-n-n-no ! "

"Is it in your study ?"

"N-n-n-no."

"Where is it, then, Bunter ?"

"I—I—I don't know, sir."

"Very well." Quelch set his lips. "You leave me no recourse but to place the facts before Dr. Locke. Come !"

Quelch raised his free hand to tap at the door.

Then Bunter had a brain-wave : the sort of brain-wave that Bunter would have ! Bunter's object was to get Quelch's grip off his fat shoulder, before he was hooked into the Head's study. And it flashed into Bunter's powerful brain that he knew how.

"Oh, sir ! Please——" he gasped.

Quelch paused, with upraised hand.

"Well ?" he rapped.

"Kik-kik-kik-can I—I go and fetch it from my study, sir ?" gasped Bunter.

"Upon my word !" said Mr. Quelch. "Then you admit —upon my word ! Bunter, you utterly unscrupulous boy,

I hardly know how to deal with you ! Go and fetch it from your study at once."

" Yes, sir ! " gasped Bunter.

That iron grasp on his fat shoulder relaxed. Bunter was free ! The moment he was free, he shot down the corridor, and turned the nearest corner. If Mr. Quelch waited for him to return with the postal order, he waited in vain. Quelch was not destined to see that hopeful member of his form again in the near future.

H

CHAPTER XIX

WHERE IS BUNTER ?

" HENRY looks shirty ! " whispered Bob Cherry.

Henry did !

It was very fortunate for Bob Cherry that Henry Samuel Quelch, looking in at the doorway of the Rag, did not hear that whisper.   He did not look in a mood for jesting.

Really, Bob's whisper was an understatement.   Henry did not look merely ' shirty '.   He had a look of concentrated anger : quiet and calm, but all the more deadly in its quietness and calmness.   Something, evidently, had stirred Quelch's deepest ire.   The juniors, looking at him, realised that whoever had brought that expression to Quelch's face, was booked for the time of his life.

There had been a cheery buzz of voices in the Rag.   Now there was a hush.   The crowd of juniors waited, as it were, for the thunderbolt to crash.

Somebody was ' for it '.   That was plain.   Fellows who had sins on their consciences felt an inward quake.   Skinner and Snoop exchanged a stealthy glance of uneasiness, thinking of cigarettes in the study.   Fisher T. Fish felt a spasm of dread lest Quelch might have learned of money-lending activities among the fags.   The Bounder, with all his nerve, felt a slight tremor, as he wondered whether a Greyfriars cap had been seen over the fence of the Cross Keys !

It was only a moment or two before Quelch spoke.   But that moment or two seemed very long to the juniors in the Rag.   But it came at last :

" Is Bunter here ? "

There was almost a gasp of relief.   It was only Bunter ! Nobody in the Rag was ' for it ' : Bunter not being there. It was the Owl of the Remove who was the cause of the

deep, deep wrath discernible in Quelch's speaking countenance.

Harry Wharton, as Head Boy of the Remove, answered :
" No, sir."

" Do you know where he is, Wharton ? "

" No, sir."

" Where did you see him last ? "

" In my study, sir, some time ago, when Wingate came
to fetch him."

" Has any boy here seen him since ? "

There was a sort of suppressed sensation in the Rag, at
that question. Bunter, it seemed, was not to be found.
Quelch wanted him, but could not find him. That was
very extraordinary : but Quelch's question could mean
nothing else.

" Oh, gum," breathed Bob Cherry. " What has that
potty rhinoceros been up to now ? "

" The upfulness must have been terrific," murmured
Hurree Jamset Ram Singh.

Quelch's keen eyes scanned the staring crowd of juniors.
He waited for a reply to his question.

" I saw him coming downstairs with Wingate, sir," said
Hazeldene.

Quelch gave a faint grunt. He wanted later information
than that.

" Kindly attend to me," he snapped. " Half an hour
ago, Bunter left me at the door of the headmaster's study.
I desire to know whether he has been seen since. Has any
boy here seen Bunter during the last half-hour ? "

There was no reply to that. Apparently none of the
fellows in the Rag had seen Billy Bunter during the last
half-hour.

" Todd ! " Quelch broke the silence with a rap.

" Oh ! Yes, sir," answered Peter.

" Bunter shares your study. Do you know anything of
his movements ? "

" Not since Wingate came up for him, sir."

" He told you nothing of his intentions ? "

" No, sir."

" Dutton ! " rapped Quelch.

Tom Dutton, like the other fellows, was staring at Quelch. He continued to stare at him, without answering, not having heard the rap.

Peter Todd gave him a nudge. Dutton transferred his stare from Quelch to Peter.

" What—— ? " he began. Peter made a sign towards Mr. Quelch : and the deaf junior transferred his stare back again to the Remove master.

" Did you speak to me, sir ? " he asked.

" I did, Dutton. Have you seen Bunter since Wingate came up to the study ? "

" I didn't notice whether Wingate was muddy or not, sir. I don't think he was."

" I did not say muddy, Dutton," gasped Mr. Quelch.

" I thought you said Wingate, sir ! I don't know anything about muddy mutton," said Tom, looking quite bewildered.

There was a gurgle in the Rag. It was immediately suppressed, as a gimlet-eye glinted round. It was no time for gurgling.

" Haven't you seen Bunter, Dutton ? "

" I didn't know he had any, sir."

" What ? Any what ? "

" Mutton, sir ! Did you say mutton ? "

" Bless my soul ! I did not say mutton, Dutton."

" Oh ! Button ! " said Tom. " I thought you said mutton, sir ! No, I don't know anything about Bunter's buttons, sir."

" I did not say button," shrieked Mr. Quelch. " Do you know where Bunter is ? "

" Oh, no, sir ! I know he bursts a button sometimes, but I haven't noticed any about."

Peter came to the rescue. He bawled into Dutton's ear :

" Have you seen Bunter since Wingate came up ? "

" No, I haven't, and you needn't yell at a fellow as if he were stone deaf, either. You're interrupting Mr. Quelch. I'm sorry, sir, but I haven't seen anything of Bunter's buttons, if he's dropped any. I remember I picked up one of his waistcoat buttons yesterday, but I gave it to him."

" That will do, Dutton," said Mr. Quelch, hastily.

" Did you speak, sir ? "

" I said that will do."

" Two what, sir ? "

Mr. Quelch did not answer that question.

" Wharton ! " he rapped.

" Yes, sir."

" Bunter cannot be found. There can be no doubt that he is deliberately keeping out of sight, in order to avoid being taken to his headmaster. I desire him to be found at once. Please search for him, and the others may help you."

" Oh, certainly, sir," answered Harry. " May I ask, sir, if it is about the postal order that was lost ? "

" It is about the postal order taken from my study by Bunter, Wharton : but it was not lost."

" Bunter has told us about it, sir. He took the postal order by a silly mistake, and lost it——"

" He did not lose it, Wharton ! He has admitted to me that the postal order is still in his possession."

" Oh ! " gasped Harry, quite taken aback. The captain of the Remove had felt impelled to put in a word for the hapless fat Owl, if he could. He had believed, or at least tried hard to believe, that Bunter had lost that postal order, as he had stated. Quelch's answer took all the wind out of his sails. " He—he—he has admitted it, sir ? "

" He has, Wharton ! He left me at the headmaster's door to fetch it from his study."

" Oh ! " gasped Harry, again.

" But he did not return ! " said Mr. Quelch, in a grinding

voice. "He is deliberately keeping out of sight, to elude the consequences of his unscrupulous action. He must be found at once. I shall be obliged, Wharton, if you will find him, with the help of the other boys of my form."

"Oh, certainly, sir."

Mr. Quelch rustled away, leaving the Rag in an excited buzz. Johnny Bull gave an emphatic snort.

"Still think that Bunter lost that postal order, you fellows?" he inquired, sarcastically.

"Not if he's admitted to Quelch that he's still got it, of course, fathead," said Bob Cherry. "By gum! Was the fat villain just pulling our leg, when he made us hunt all over the shop for it?"

"Camouflage!" grunted Johnny. "He wanted to make out that it was lost, when Quelch got after it."

"But—but he really took it by mistake," said Harry.

"Did he?" grunted Johnny.

"I—I'm sure he did! I—I'm sure that that much was genuine, at any rate. We all know he's ass enough." But the captain of the Remove spoke rather haltingly.

"If he took it by mistake, why doesn't he hand it back now that he's found out his mistake?" asked Johnny. "He told us it was lost! Now he's owned up to Quelch that he had it in his study."

There was no answer to be made to that.

"Well, we'd better look for the fat ass, as Quelch wants him," said Bob Cherry. "Come on, you men."

The Famous Five left the Rag, to look for Bunter. A dozen other Remove men joined in the search.

But the search for Bunter proved as futile as the earlier search for Bunter's postal order. Bunter was not to be found. Bunter, like the postal order, was no doubt somewhere: but where he was, was a mystery. Nothing had been seen of the fat Owl when the bell went for prep.

Billy Bunter had disappeared: and for the present, at least, he was staying disappeared.

CHAPTER XX

PREP IN COKER'S STUDY

HORACE COKER, of the Fifth Form, gave an irritated grunt.

" For goodness sake," he said. " Give a fellow a bit of room. Ain't this table big enough for three fellows ? "

Potter and Greene looked up from prep.

Coker often found something to grouse about. But what he was grousing about at the moment was quite unknown to his study-mates.

The table in Coker's study was a large one. Coker's study had been furnished for him by his affectionate Aunt Judy, regardless of expense. It was quite a handsome table, with ample room for three fellows to sit round it at prep, and pack their legs underneath : even though Horace Coker's legs were an out-size in legs, and his feet designed on the same generous scale.

" What's the trouble ? " inquired Potter.

" Can't you give a fellow room for his legs ? " demanded Coker.

" They want some room," agreed Potter. " But I'm not in your way, Coker."

" Well, you, Greene——"

" Not guilty, my lord ! " said Greene.

Coker frowned.

" Don't be a funny ass ! " he snapped. " Rotten enough to have to chew on this tripe, without a fellow bumping against a fellow's legs all the time. Keep over your own side."

" I'm keeping over my own side."

" Oh, don't argue," said Coker.

" So am I," said Potter.

" Don't jaw, Potter."

" Well, look here——"

"Oh, dry up, the two of you," said Coker, crossly. "We've got to mug up this tripe for Prout. Think I can mug it up with two silly asses jawing all the time? Give us a rest."

"But you said——"

"I said don't jaw."

Potter and Greene gave the great Horace rather expressive looks, and resumed prep. Neither of them was conscious of having bumped Coker's extensive legs under the table: but Coker, it seemed, fancied that his legs had been bumped, and was not open to argument on the subject.

Prep went on: Coker's rugged brow corrugated over it. Latin did not come easily to Horace Coker: and he rather resented the fact that he had to give it any attention at all.

But the silence established in Coker's study did not last. Coker broke it.

"This tripe!" he said. "Piffle!"

Neither Potter nor Greene answered. The historical works of Titus Livius might be, in Coker's valuable opinion, tripe and piffle: but that did not alter the fact that there was 'con' in the morning in the Fifth-form room, and that Mr. Prout would expect them to have some knowledge of the section of Liber XXI assigned for preparation.

"We mug up this stuff," said Coker, glaring across the table at Potter and Greene, as if it were their fault. "Well, what's the good? Suppose we mugged up Latin till we could talk it like parrots. Who are we going to talk it to?"

Potter and Greene grinned at that question, perhaps thinking that Coker needed to mug up English as well as Latin.

"Do you mean whom?" asked Potter.

"No, I don't."

"Oh, all right."

"What's the good?" went on Coker, frowning. "You

can't mug it up without swotting your head off. And when you've done it, you've got no use for it, unless you become a schoolmaster, and pass it on to somebody else. Fat lot of good that is! I'm not going to be a schoolmaster!"

"Oh, crumbs!" ejaculated Potter and Greene together. They seemed a little overcome, at the bare idea of Horace James Coker in the role of schoolmaster!

"Just tripe," said Coker. "Virgil, Livy, and the whole crowd of them! Tripe! I've a jolly good mind to tell Prout so."

"Prout might like to know what you think of the classics, old chap," said Potter, blandly.

"There's one jolly good thing about this blighter," went on Coker, thus alluding to Titus Livius. "Some of his books were lost, and have never been found. Pity it didn't happen to the lot! Remember Prout telling us once of a rumour that Livy's lost books had been found? He thought we'd like to hear it! That's Prout!"

Coker gave a snort.

Coker had been quite relieved to hear that that rumour, which had excited and delighted Prout, was unfounded. Coker would have been more interested in losing the known books of Livy, than in discovering the lost ones.

"Bellum maxime omnium memorabile," snorted Coker. "Biggest war ever—fat lot Livy knew about it! And who cares, anyhow? Yah!"

Coker, at least, couldn't have cared less for that tremendous war 'quod Hannibale duce Carthaginienses cum populo Romano gessere'.

"But we've got to swot at it!" added Coker.

"We have," agreed Greene. "Better push on with it."

Snort, from Coker.

However, he decided to push on with it. Gladly, had it been possible, he would have knocked Livy's and Hannibal's heads together. But it was a good many centuries too late

for that : and he settled down once more to mugging up
what Livy had written about Hannibal. He stretched his
long legs under the table for greater ease, and gave an
irritated yelp.

" Can't you keep your hoofs over your own side, Potter ? "

" If you mean my feet, I've got them tucked under my
chair," answered Potter.

" Well, yours, Greene——"

" Do you want the whole study to park your feet in,
Coker ? " inquired Greene.

" I want a bit of room, Greene, and if you bump me again
under the table, I'll jolly well give you a hack."

" I haven't bumped you——"

" Think I dreamed it ? " demanded Coker.

" I tell you——"

" Oh, don't jaw ! Just keep your hoofs on your own
side, and for goodness sake, don't jaw."

Greene breathed rather hard. However, he refrained
from ' jaw ', and went on with his prep. But a minute or
two later he looked up sharply.

" Who's bumping a fellow's legs under the table now ? "
he demanded.

" Eh ! Is anybody ? " asked Coker.

" It wasn't you, was it, Potter ? "

" No ! Mine are under my chair."

" Then it was you, Coker——"

" Don't be a silly ass, Greene. I haven't moved."

" You bumped against my legs without moving ? " asked
Greene, sarcastically.

" I never bumped against your silly legs ! Blow your
silly legs ! Keep your silly legs to yourself, and shut
up."

" Somebody bumped on my legs," hooted Greene.

" Oh, don't talk rot ! Give a fellow a rest ! Why, you
howling ass, what are you bumping on my knees for ? "
roared Coker.

" Who's bumping on your silly knees ? "

" You are ! Or else Potter ! Look here, if you fellows think this sort of thing is funny, while a fellow's mugging up this tripe——"

" I never moved," howled Greene.

" Well, look here, Potter——"

" I never moved either."

" Oh, didn't you ? " said Coker, with withering sarcasm. " You never moved, and Greene never moved, but my knees got bumped just the same. Well, I'll tell you what—next time I get a jolt, I'm going to land out. If you're not tired of this silly game, I am, and I can jolly well tell you so. You bump me under the table again, either of you, and you get it—hard ! I mean that ! "

" I never——"

" And I never——"

" Oh, cheese it ! Take my tip, that's all," said Coker. " I'm not going to tuck my legs under my chair, when there's plenty of room under the table. I'm going to stretch them out just as far as I jolly well like, and if anybody gives me another jolt, I'll jolly well—My hat ! Take that ! " roared Coker, as he felt something bump against his stretching legs under the table : and drawing one of them back, he delivered a hack. " Now, then——"

" Yaroooooh ! "

It was a fearful yell, as Coker's hack landed. But it did not proceed from Potter or Greene. That hack had not landed on either of them. But it had landed on somebody, as that fearful yell testified.

Coker jumped.

" Why—what—— ! " he stuttered.

" Great pip—— ! "

" Holy smoke ! "

" Yow ! Oooooogh ! Yarooooooooop ! " came a roar. " Wow ! wow ! wow ! "

" There's somebody under the table ! " gasped Coker. He bounded to his feet, pushing back his chair. He grasped the table, and dragged it aside. Three pairs of eyes fixed,

in amazement and wrath, upon a figure that was revealed—
a fat figure, with a fat face adorned by a big pair of spectacles,
with a fat hand clutching a fat shin where Coker's hack had
landed—and still yelling.

"Yow-ow-ow-ow-ow!"

CHAPTER XXI

STOP HIM

" BUNTER ! " stuttered Coker.

" Bunter ! " repeated Potter and Greene.

" Yow-ow-ow ! " roared Bunter. " Ow ! Oh, my shin ! Wow ! Beast ! Wow-ow ! "

Billy Bunter was squatted on Coker's carpet, in the centre of the spot hitherto covered by the table. The mystery of those bumps and jolts under the table was now revealed. It was not Fifth-form legs and knees and feet that had administered those bumps and jolts—it was Billy Bunter !

There was a good deal of space under the table. There was really room for him to squat untouched by feet, if the Fifth-form men had arranged their legs and feet to suit. But, of course, they hadn't. And Bunter had had some dodging and squirming to do—keeping out of the way of some legs, and inevitably colliding with others in doing so. It had been irritating to Coker and Co. : but it had been a very trying time indeed to Bunter.

They gazed at him.

News that a Remove junior was missing from the list had not reached the Fifth. All the Remove were greatly excited about it, and the Shell and the Fourth had heard something of it : but senior men of the Fifth Form were as yet blissfully ignorant of any unusual happening in the Lower Fourth. That Bunter was in flight, and in hiding, was quite unknown to Coker and Co., and they could not begin to guess why he was squatted under the table in their study. But there he was !

" Bunter ! " repeated Coker. " That fat Remove tick ! Hiding under our table ! It was him all the time," went on Coker, with his usual independent disregard of grammar. " It was him——! "

"What is the fat freak doing here ?" ejaculated Potter. "The Remove are at prep now."

"Yow-ow-ow ! I say, you fellows—wow ! That beast kicked me ! Wow !" howled Bunter. "I—I say——"

"What are you up to in our study ?" roared Coker. "What do you mean by sneaking under the table, and bumping a fellow's legs ? If that's your idea of a lark——"

"Oh ! No ! I—I say——"

"Have you been after my tuck ?" That was a natural suspicion to arise in Coker's mind. It was not uncommon for Bunter and missing tuck to happen simultaneously.

"No ! Oh ! No !" gasped Bunter. "I—I never even looked into the cupboard ! I—I never saw the pie there, Coker, and I never ate any——"

"By gum !" said Coker. "Open that door, Greeney. I'll kick him right out into the passage ! I'll give him snooping my tuck !"

Billy Bunter bounded to his feet. He had already sampled the weight of Coker's foot. He did not want another sample.

As Greene threw the door open, Bunter rushed for it.

Thud !

Bunter's rush was rapid. But it was not rapid enough to escape Horace Coker's lunging foot. That heavy foot thudded on his tight trousers : and Bunter, thus accelerated, fairly flew through the doorway.

There was a bump in the passage, and a roar. Five or six study doors opened, and Fifth-form men looked out, startled by the sudden uproar. Hilton, Price, Tomlinson, Blundell, Bland, all stared blankly at a sprawling fat Owl, rolling and roaring.

"Yow-ow-ow-ow-ow-wooooh !"

Coker emerged from his doorway after Bunter.

"I'll jolly well kick him as far as the landing," he exclaimed. "I'll give him snooping tuck in a Fifth-form man's study."

"Yaroooh !"

Bunter bounded up again. He flew down the passage towards the landing. After him rushed Coker. Hitherto, Bunter's chief desire had been to keep doggo. That was why he had parked himself in a senior study. But with Coker, and Coker's lunging foot, behind him, Bunter forgot all about keeping doggo. He forgot everything but Coker and Coker's foot.

He charged down the Fifth-form passage, yelling.

Thud ! thud ! thud !

Bunter flew—but Coker's long legs easily kept pace. He dribbled Bunter as far as the landing, every jolt behind eliciting a fresh frantic roar from the hapless fat Owl.

" Oh ! Ow ! wow ! Beast ! Stoppit ! Wow ! "

Bunter flew across the landing. He was heading for the stairs, as the nearest way of escape. But as he reached the top of the staircase, his eyes fell on Wingate of the Sixth, coming up.

" Bunter ! " exclaimed Wingate.

He put on speed, coming up two at a time.

" Oh, crikey ! " gasped Bunter.

He whirled round, and flew for the Remove passage. Coker had halted, a little breathless. Bunter dashed up the steps to the Remove landing, and bolted into the passage. Coker turned back to go to his study.

" Bunter ! " exclaimed a startled voice.

It was Loder of the Sixth, in the Remove passage.

" Oh, scissors ! " gasped Bunter. He pounded to a halt, as Loder came along the passage with a hand outstretched.

Evidently, the Sixth-form prefects were looking for him. Probably they would not have thought of looking for him in a Fifth-form study. Bunter would have been safe under Coker's table, but for Coker's legs. But now that he had been rooted out of that unsuspected refuge, it looked as if Bunter's number was up.

" Stop ! " shouted Loder. He broke into a run, as Bunter whirled round, and dashed back to the landing.

Bunter did not heed. He charged back across the

landing. Wingate's head was just rising into view from
the stairs. But Coker was gone : and Bunter, doubling
like a hunted hare, rushed back into the Fifth-form passage.

" Stop ! " roared Wingate.

" Stop ! " yelled Loder.

Both the Sixth-form men rushed after Bunter.

Bunter did not stop. He raced. He went up that
passage as fast as he had come down it a minute ago.

Coker had reached his study door. He looked back at
the commotion behind him, and stared blankly at Bunter,
coming back.

" Oh, my hat ! " ejaculated Coker. " If that fat freak
wants some more——"

" Stop him, Coker ! " shouted Wingate and Loder together.

" I'll stop him all right," called back Coker.

Coker stepped into the middle of the passage, facing
Bunter as he came. He was not quite prepared for what
followed. He expected to stop Bunter with perfect ease.
But the wildly excited Owl, with two prefects in pursuit
behind him, was desperate now. He did not stop. He
lowered his fat head, and charged Coker.

Crash !

Almost before Coker knew what was happening, a bullet
head crashed into his waistcoat. Coker staggered. His
hands, extended to grasp Bunter, sagged. He tottered.
He gurgled. He guggled. Every ounce of wind inside
Coker was driven out by that sudden impact on his waistcoat. Utterly heedless of Bunter, Coker staggered against
the passage wall, clasped both hands to his waistcoat, and
moaned and gurgled horribly.

Bunter reeled, for a moment, from the shock. But only
for a moment. Then he flew on, and disappeared by the
back staircase at the end of the Fifth-form passage.

Wingate and Loder came speeding on.

" You ass ! " snapped Wingate, as he passed Horace
Coker.

" You dummy ! " snapped Loder, as he passed a second later.

They tore on, after Bunter, without waiting for a reply. Not that Coker could have made any reply, except in the shape of a gurgle or a guggle. Coker was winded, and he could only lean on the passage wall and make queer sounds of woe and distress.

Bunter vanished, and after him vanished the two prefects, unheeded by Coker. He caressed his waistcoat and moaned. Whether Bunter escaped, whether Wingate and Loder got him, whether they all three tumbled down the back staircase and landed in a heap at the bottom, Coker did not know, and did not care. His internal convulsions were sufficient to occupy Coker's whole attention.

" Ooooh ! wooooh ! moooooooooh ! " moaned Coker.

Potter and Greene came out of the study.

" What's up ? " asked Potter.

" Mooooooooooh ! "

" Anything happened ? " asked Greene.

" Mooooooooooh ! "

They gazed at him. They had not seen the collision, and why Coker was mooing like a distressed cow they did not know. They went back into the study, leaving him to his farmyard imitations.

It was some minutes before Coker was able to follow them in. Potter and Greene were at prep again. But it was long before Horace Coker could turn his attention to prep. Long he sat in his arm-chair, caressing his waistcoat, mumbling, moaning, and mooing, indifferent to Livy, to the Carthaginian War, and to Prout in the morning.

CHAPTER XXII

NO BUNTER

CLANG ! clang !

The rising-bell rang in the dewy morn.

Greyfriars School turned out to a new day. And, in the Remove dormitory, all eyes turned on one particular bed—Bunter's.

That bed was vacant.

It had not been slept in.

" Bunter never came back to roost, then," said Bob Cherry. " He's not been here. Where on earth can he be ? "

" There wherefulness is terrific," remarked Hurree Jamset Ram Singh. " The esteemed and idiotic Bunter is asking for preposterous trouble."

" The fat ass ! " said Harry Wharton. " He can't keep this game up."

" They can't have found him," said Frank Nugent. " He's hiding somewhere—goodness knows where."

" What a game ! " remarked the Bounder, with a chuckle. " Puzzle—find Bunter ! "

" The dear boy doesn't want to be bunked for pinching Prout's postal order," grinned Skinner. " But is even Bunter idiot enough to think that this game will do him any good ? "

" Isn't he idiot enough for anything ? " grunted Johnny Bull.

" Bunter didn't pinch Prout's postal order, Skinner," said Lord Mauleverer, mildly. " He fancied it was his when he lifted it."

Skinner laughed.

" Does he still fancy it's his ? " he asked. " He's owned up that he's got it—Quelch said so."

Mauly made no reply to that.

" Blessed if I make the fat duffer out," said Harry Wharton. " Now he knows that the postal order isn't his, why the dickens doesn't he hand it over, and get off with a licking ? It can't be lost, as he admitted to Quelch that he had it. He will be sacked if this goes on."

It was a puzzle to all the Remove. Bunter, evidently, was eluding a painful interview with his headmaster, but the extraordinary expedient of disappearing and hunting cover. But what use he thought it would be, was a mystery. It was possible, of course, that he was not thinking at all : thinking not being his long suit.

All the Remove were anxious for news of Bunter, when they came down from the dormitory. But there was no news of Bunter.

It was known that he had been rooted out of Coker's study in the Fifth, and that Wingate and Loder had chased him down a back staircase, and lost him there. Bunter, apparently, had dodged into some remote corner, and was staying there. Fisher T. Fish remarked that the pesky piecan must have got into a hole and pulled it in after him : and really it began to look like it.

Before breakfast, Sixth-form prefects could be discerned, in all sorts of odd corners, looking about them. Evidently, the search for Bunter was still going on.

The news had spread to all forms now, and almost every fellow at Greyfriars was asking the question, where was Bunter ? But echo answered, where ?

" They'll have him soon," Skinner told the Famous Five, when the school came out after prayers.

" It doesn't look like it," answered Harry Wharton.

" Wait till the breakfast-bell rings," said Skinner. " Think Bunter could resist that ? He will hear it, wherever he is."

" By gum, though, Bunter must be getting hungry," remarked Bob Cherry. " He had to cut supper last night. A fellow can't carry on without food——"

" Not Bunter, at any rate," said Nugent.

" The grubfulness is the sine qua non with the esteemed Bunter," said Hurree Jamset Ram Singh, with a nod. " He will show up when he gets terrifically hungry."

But when the breakfast-bell rang, there was still no sign of Billy Bunter.

Undoubtedly the fat Owl, wherever he was, must have heard the bell. All Greyfriars could hear it. That bell must have apprised him that it was a meal-time : and for Bunter to miss a meal was an unprecedented occurrence. But Skinner's prediction was not fulfilled : the breakfast-bell did not draw Bunter from his lair.

There was a vacant place at the Remove table. At the head of that table sat Quelch, with a face reminiscent of a gargoyle.

Hurree Jamset Ram Singh whispered to his comrades that the esteemed Quelch was terrifically infuriated. There was, at least, no doubt that Quelch was deeply incensed.

After breakfast, he was seen speaking to Sammy Bunter, of the Second Form. Perhaps he thought that Bunter minor might know something about the mysterious movements of Bunter major. But Sammy, it appeared, had no information to impart : at all events, nothing was heard of Billy Bunter : and he was still in a disappeared state when the Remove went to their form-room.

The Remove were on their very best behaviour that morning. Quelch was only too clearly not in a mood for trifling.

True, Quelch was a just man, and would never have dreamed of visiting Bunter's sins on innocent heads. The Remove had only to be good ! But nobody doubted that if they failed to be good, the vials of wrath would be poured out in unusual abundance.

It was necessary to be circumspect. That morning the Remove were very circumspect indeed. A visitor to the school, looking into the form-room, might have supposed —quite erroneously—that the Lower Fourth were a model form, with no desire in life but to hang respectfully and attentively on the words of their form-master !

Such unusual goodness was rather a strain on the Remove, and all were glad when the bell rang for break.

In break, there was a rumour of a spot of trouble below stairs. It was said that the House-dame was making a fuss about a pie missing from the pantry. From which Harry Wharton and Co. deduced that the Owl of the Remove was not quite so hungry as they had supposed : and it became more comprehensible how Bunter had been able to resist the lure of the breakfast-bell.

But where was Bunter ?

Out of class, Wingate, Loder, Gwynne, Sykes, Carne, Walker, and other prefects, were still looking for him. Perhaps their search was growing a little desultory. Loder remarked to Walker that Sixth-form men had something better to do with their leisure than expend it in hunting for a silly fag, and Walker fully agreed. Still, the search went on.

But Greyfriars School was a very extensive and rather rambling ancient place. There were disused attics, and passages that seemed to lead nowhere in particular : all sorts of holes and corners and remote recesses. A fellow who was determined to keep out of sight had at least a sporting chance : and Bunter, so far, seemed to be getting away with it.

Billy Bunter, and Billy Bunter's amazing antics, were the reigning topic at Greyfriars that morning. But there was another matter that interested a good many of the Remove, even to the exclusion of the Bunter topic : the circumstance that it was a half-holiday that afternoon, and that the Remove eleven were booked to play football at Highcliffe. Apart from Soccer, most fellows were glad that it was Wednesday and a half-holiday : in view of the extreme circumspection that was required in the form-room in present circumstances. It was going to be a real pleasure to get a good distance from a gimlet-eye.

There was no news of Bunter during break. But just before class, Harry Wharton ran up to his study for a book needed in third school. He found the book on the table in No. 1 Study : and something else that made him jump.

" Oh, my hat ! " ejaculated the captain of the Remove, as he stared at it.

It was a half-sheet of impot paper. On it was scrawled a message in a well-known hand. Wharton would have known that it was from Bunter, even without reading it : it looked as if a spider had dipped himself into an inkpot and crawled over the paper. There was no mistaking Bunter's hand !

It ran :

> Deer Wharton,
>
>   Pleeze do be a pall, and kepe on looking for that beestly poastal order I lost. If it is fownd it will be all rite. Quelch will kno it wasn't pilphered if it is fownd. If it isn't fownd I shall be sakked. Never mind about Sokker this afternoon. Kepe on looking for that beestly poastal order.
>
> Yores,
W. G. Bunter.

" Oh, holy smoke ! " said Harry Wharton.

Bunter, apparently, was still keeping it up that the postal order was lost—after having admitted to Quelch that he had it !   Wharton put the note in his pocket, and went down to show it to his comrades. It was very perplexing : but the Famous Five were at least able to get a laugh out of Bunter's happy suggestion that they should cut a Soccer match in order to spend the afternoon looking for that postal order !

CHAPTER XXIII

MUSIC HATH CHARMS

" Lucky bargee ! " said Hobson, of the Shell.

Claude Hoskins, of that form, nodded.

He was, in his own opinion and that of his chum, indeed a lucky bargee.

Third school, that morning, in the Shell, was maths with Mr. Lascelles. There were fellows in the Shell, like Stewart, who were good at maths, and indeed almost revelled in them. But they were few in number. Most of the Shell would have preferred even Latin with their own beak, Hacker : though, otherwise considered, that was the limit. The mere word ' maths ' gave James Hobson a feeling that he had a headache coming on. And that lucky bargee, Hoskins, was able to cut that school : being up to Mr. Flatt for music instead of up to Lascelles for maths.

" Well, it's not all lavender, you know," said Hoskins. " I'm not really satisfied with that man Flatt."

" I daresay you know as much about it as he does," said Hobson. Hobby had a tremendous admiration for his musical chum. Hoskins could compose music—or, at least, believed that he could, and Hobson shared his belief. Hoskins, indeed, believed that he was a musical genius : and Hobson shared that belief also. It was true that Hobby preferred to admire old Claude's compositions from a safe distance. It was only with difficulty that old Claude could ever persuade him to listen to them.

" More ! " said Hoskins. " Flatt's out of date ! Flatt doesn't care for Russian music, for instance. He can't see anything in Buzzumoff, or Bangski, or even in Snatchis-wiskersoff. He's a back number ! You'd hardly believe that he's down on my consecutive fifths."

"Is he ?" said Hobson. Hobby had only the vaguest idea of what consecutive fifths might possibly be. But Hobby was a loyal pal. "Must be an ass!"

"Absolute idiot!" said Hoskins. "When he looked over my capriccio in G minor, he actually thought I put them in by mistake."

"D-d-did he ?"

"He did," said Hoskins. "He just stared when I explained to him that I produce my particular effects by a free use of consecutive fifths. Just stared like a calf at a train."

"Oh!" said Hobson.

Claude Hoskins glanced up at the clock-tower.

"Five minutes to class," he said. "Flatt won't be in the music-room yet. Come along with me now, old man, and I'll play over my capriccio to you."

"Oh! I—I was just going to ask young Wharton whether there was any news of that chap Bunter who's dodging about somewhere——"

"Eh! Who's Bunter ?"

"Fat chap in the Remove! They say his beak's in a fearful bait because he's dodging about out of sight——"

"Eh ? Is he ?" Claude Hoskins, evidently, was not interested in a fat chap in the Remove, or in his beak. "Never mind him! Come on."

"There's Stewart calling me——"

"I didn't hear him. Come on, Hobby. I shan't have time to play the whole thing through, but I can show you how it goes."

"Oh! I—I think I'll wait till another time, old chap, when—when you have time to play it right through——"

"No time like the present," said Hoskins. "Come on."

"I say, there's Hacker at his study window. I—I think he's—he's beckoning to me——"

"He isn't, old chap! He's looking the other way. Come on."

Claude Hoskins took his chum by the arm, and led him

away, as it were to execution. Hobson suppressed a groan and submitted to his fate. Not for worlds would he have hurt old Claude's feelings. He admired old Claude, and was proud of him. And after all, he had listened-in to Claude's music before, and lived to tell the tale. It was only one more sacrifice on the altar of friendship. But he was glad to remember that it was only five minutes to class —even maths !

The music-room was at some distance from the form-rooms. Claude, as they went down a long corridor, explained happily his theory of consecutive fifths, of which Hobson loyally tried to understand a few words, without success.

But as they reached the door of the music-room, Claude broke off suddenly, at a sound from that apartment. It was a sound as of somebody moving.

" Oh, scissors ! Has Flatt come early ? " he ejaculated. " What rotten luck ! "

Hobson breathed more freely.

If the music-master was already on the spot, Hoskins wouldn't be able to play over that capriccio after all. Hobby could only hope that Mr. Flatt had been unusually punctual. Generally he was unpunctual.

Claude Hoskins opened the door, with a grunt. Hobson paused.

" Well, if Flatt's here, I'd better not come in," he remarked, casually.

" Hold on ! He isn't ! " said Hoskins, staring about the room. " I thought I heard somebody—didn't you ? "

" I—I thought so. Isn't he here ? " asked Hobson, sadly. " Well, look ! "

Hobson looked. There was nobody to be seen in the music-room. Unless Mr. Flatt had ducked down behind the well-worn old grand piano, or parked himself in the wall-cupboard where music was kept, Mr. Flatt had not arrived.

" Bit of luck, what ? " said Hoskins, cheerily. " False

alarm, after all! Come in, Hobby, old chap! You'll remember afterwards that you were one of the first to hear my capriccio in G minor—I mean, in later years, old chap, when audiences at the Albert Hall are going wild about it. When that time comes, you'll remember me playing it to you in the old music-room at Greyfriars, what ? "

" Oh ! Ah ! Yes ! I say, I mustn't be late for class——"

" Where's my music ? I left it on the piano ! Has some idiot moved it—has some blithering cuckoo shifted my music ?—has some dangerous maniac been handling my cappricio in G minor—— ? " Hoskins was getting excited. " By gum ! If anything's happened to my music ? "

" Is this it, old chap ? "

" Eh ! Can't you see that that's a piano concerto in D ? "

" Oh ! Is it ? Perhaps this is it ? "

" How could that be it, you ass, when that's a prelude for strings ? "

" Oh ! Perhaps it's in the cupboard——"

" I left it on the piano ! Nobody ought to have touched it ! Goths ! Vandals ! Huns ! Cannibals ! Where's my capriccio ? "

" Is—is that eleven striking from the clock-tower ? "

" No ! Look among all that music——"

" Is this it ? "

" Great pip ! Don't you know the difference between Mendelssohn's ' Lieder ohne Worte ' and a capriccio in G minor ? Oh! Here it is ! Some blithering idiot—some born ass—some hopeless blockhead—shoved it out of sight under that Beethoven. O.K., old chap. Now listen."

Claude arranged his music on the piano desk, planted himself on the music-stool, pushed back his cuffs as if he were going to box, and started.

Hobson listened to the crash that followed. He had to. He dared not put his fingers to his ears, lest old Claude should spot him out of the corner of his eye. Hobson of the Shell stood up to it like a Trojan, while Hoskins, who had rather a fancy for the loud pedal, dragged out of that old piano every discordant sound that it was capable of producing.

If eleven o'clock struck, Hobson did not hear it. He would hardly have heard an atom bomb, while Claude Hoskins was playing his capriccio in G minor. Old Claude, at the piano, believed in putting his beef into it. But for the evidence of his suffering ears, Hobby could never have believed that a single piano could possibly have produced such a thundering row.

Hobson was feeling somewhat like Mr. Quelch when Mary was busy with the Hoover in his study. But more so! Ever so much more so! The hum of the Hoover was a mere whispering zephyr compared with this. Indeed, shunting railway-trains would have had little chance against Hoskins playing his capriccio in G minor. Trumpeting wild elephants might have passed in a herd, unnoticed.

Hobson, as a musician's chum, had had to learn to suffer and be strong. He stuck it out. He knew that he was getting late for class—but it was futile to speak to Hoskins while he was thumping the piano—Claude would not have heard, neither would he have heeded had he heard. And he couldn't very well back out of the music-room and leave old Claude wasting his sweetness on the desert air—old Claude would have been offended. Hobby had to risk being late with Lascelles—luckily, Lascelles wasn't an Acid Drop like Hacker. But with his whole being did Hobby long for the priceless boon of silence.

It came at last. With a final crash, as if old Claude was determined to knock the stuffing out of the piano in the last round, that composition in G minor ceased from troubling, and the weary were at rest.

Hobson stood dazed. Hoskins swung round on the music-stool, and fixed him with a triumphant eye. He waited for his meed of praise. And Hobby—as soon as he recovered—would have ladled out the praise. But that moment of happy and glorious silence was broken by another voice—a very unexpected voice, ejaculating:

" Oh, crikey ! "

And James Hobson and Claude Hoskins stared round blankly, quite astonished to hear the fat voice of Billy Bunter of the Remove, proceeding from the music-cupboard in the corner of the music-room.

CHAPTER XXIV

BUNTER ON THE RUN

" Bunter ! " gasped Hobson.

He dragged open the cupboard door.

A fat figure, a fat face, and a pair of glimmering spectacles, were revealed. There was Bunter ! It was the missing Owl !

Hobson stared at him. Hoskins stared at him. Billy Bunter blinked at both of them.

The music-room, it appeared, was the fat Owl's mysterious refuge. Hobby and Hoskins remembered the sound they had heard in the room as they came along. Evidently Bunter had dodged into the cupboard at the sound of footsteps.

He had remained there, unseen and unsuspected by Hobby and Hoskins, till the effect of the capriccio in G minor had caused him, unintentionally, to reveal his presence.

Probably Bunter had uttered more than one ejaculation during that performance. But they had been, of course, unheard. No doubt, with Hoskins at the piano, Bunter had regretted his choice of a hiding-place. Now, however, he was revealed : and his hide-out was a hide-out no longer.

It was a large cupboard, walled with shelves, laden with music. There was plenty of room for Bunter, if he had been a little careful. But he hadn't been. Quite a quantity of music had been knocked off the shelves, and was strewn around Bunter. He stood in a sea of Beethoven, Handel, Mendelssohn, Bach, Arne, and Purcell.

" I—I—I say, you fellows, keep it dark ! " exclaimed Bunter, anxiously. " Don't you tell Quelch I'm here."

" You fat ass—— ! "

" Oh, really, Hobson—— "

" I've heard that you pinched a postal order from your beak's study——"

" I—I didn't ! I—I never took it at all. Besides, I lost it afterwards. I say, don't you fellows give a chap away."

The quarter chimed from the clock-tower, and Hobby gave a jump.

" Oh, crumbs ! I'm fifteen minutes late for Lascelles ! I shall have to cut, Claude——"

" Hold on, Jimmy. Look here, chance it with Lascelles," said Hoskins. " I'll play you my march in F major, as Flatt hasn't come yet——"

Hobson repressed a shudder.

" I'd like it no end, old chap, but Lascelles would be shirty. I've simply got to cut ! "

And Hobby, whether because Lascelles would be shirty, or because he had reached the limit of human endurance, dashed out of the music-room, and fled. Hoskins, taking no further heed of Bunter, went back to the music-stool.

Bunter blinked at him.

" I—I say, was it you kicking up that awful row, Hoskins ? " he asked. Bunter had not seen the performance. But he had heard it. Emphatically he had heard it.

Claude Hoskins looked round at him again.

" That what ? " he asked.

" I mean, is there something wrong with the piano ? " asked Bunter. " Have the wires got loose, or something ? It was awful, wasn't it ? "

Claude Hoskins stood looking at him fixedly. Hobson would never have dreamed of telling him that his capriccio in G minor was an awful row. Hobby had tact. Bunter had absolutely none.

" I—I say, you ain't going on, are you ? " asked Bunter, anxiously. " I mean to say, it's a bit thick, ain't it ? More than a fellow can stand, you know. I mean, if you want to play the piano, why not play a tune or something ? Not much sense in just sitting there hitting the keys anyhow."

Still Claude Hoskins did not answer. But he breathed very hard, and he breathed very deep. That, apparently, was Billy Bunter's impression of the capriccio in G minor, which was to make audiences at the Albert Hall go wild —some day in the happy future. Bunter had supposed that Hoskins was just sitting at the piano hitting the keys anyhow !

"Don't tell anybody I'm here," went on Bunter. "If the music-master's coming, keep him away from this cupboard, won't you, old chap ? But I say, you might give a fellow a rest—you've made my head ache, thumping the thing like that, all the keys at once. It was jolly thick, you know."

Still in silence, Claude Hoskins turned to the piano. From the piano-top he picked up a volume of Beethoven sonatas. It was a large and somewhat weighty volume. Taking it in both hands, Hoskins came towards Bunter.

Bunter blinked at him, as he came, supposing that Hoskins was going to put that volume away in the cupboard shelves. But that was not Claude's intention.

Whop !

"Yaroooh !" roared Bunter, in surprise and anguish, as the hefty volume suddenly established contact with the fattest head at Greyfriars School.

Whop !

"I say, keep off !" Bunter dodged frantically. "I say, gone mad ? Yarooooh !"

Whop !

Bunter bounded out of the cupboard. He flew across the music-room. After him flew Hoskins, still speechless, but with an absolutely deadly expression on his face.

Whop !

"Yooo-hoooop !" roared Bunter.

Why Claude Hoskins had cut up rusty, in this unexpected and extraordinary manner, Bunter did not know. But it was clear that Hoskins had, and that he seemed to derive a ferocious satisfaction from whopping Bunter with that volume of sonatas. Bunter roared, and yelled, and dodged.

He dodged round the piano, with Hoskins in fierce pursuit. Another whop caught him as he circumnavigated the piano, and yet another as he streaked across to the door, Hoskins close behind. With Claude Hoskins in this savage mood, the music-room was no refuge for the fugitive Owl. Bunter was not thinking now of hiding from Quelch—he was thinking only of escaping from Hoskins. Another whop caught him as he tore the door open.

" Oh, crikey ! wow ! "

Bunter bounded through the doorway. A terrific swipe just missed him as he bounded, and Hoskins, over-balancing with the force of the swipe, stumbled over, and landed on the floor. Bunter had a split second : and he made the most of it. He went down the corridor at about 60 m.p.h. By the time Hoskins scrambled up, still grasping Beethoven with a vengeful intent, Billy Bunter had vanished round a corner.

Hoskins gave it up, at that, and went back to the piano, to wake the echoes with his capriccio in G minor until the unpunctual Mr. Flatt arrived. But the guilty flee when no man pursueth : and Bunter, still in terror of swiping sonatas, charged on wildly, and hurtled out into the quad in a breathless state.

Everybody but Hoskins was in third school, and the quad was deserted. But though neither beaks nor boys were to be seen, a gnarled countenance stared at Billy Bunter from the direction of the porter's lodge.

" My eye ! " said Gosling. " It's that there Bunter ! My eye ! "

Billy Bunter came to a panting halt, pumping in breath. He had lost his refuge in the music-room : and he had to find another before eyes fell on him. Then he became aware that eyes were already on him, as William Gosling, the ancient porter of Greyfriars, bore down on him, and a clutching hand grasped a fat shoulder.

" Oh ! " gasped Bunter. " Leggo ! "

HE DODGED ROUND THE PIANO, WITH HOSKINS
IN FIERCE PURSUIT

K

" Gotcher ! " said Gosling.   " Wot I says is there 'ere
—I gotcher ! "

" Look here, you beast——"

" Looking for you all over the school, they is," said
Gosling.   " Keep your heyes open for 'im, Gosling, Mr.
Quelch says to me, he says.   Now I gotcher."

" Beast ! "

" You come along o' me," said Gosling.   " I'm taking
you to Mr. Quelch, now I gotcher."

The horny hand on his shoulder led Bunter back towards
the House.   But the fat Owl was desperate.   He was not
going to be taken to Quelch, thence to the Head, and sacked
—not if he could help it !

A sudden fat fist jammed into William Gosling's ancient
ribs.

" Ooooh ! " gasped Gosling, taken by surprise.

His grasp relaxed for a moment.   That moment was
enough for Billy Bunter.   He tore his fat shoulder away,
and flew.

" My eye !   'Ere, you, stop ! " roared Gosling.   " You
'ear me, young Bunter ?   Stop ! "

Bunter flew on.   After him rushed Gosling.   Bunter
gave one blink over a fat shoulder, and put on speed,
dashing into the old Cloisters.

But fast on his track came Gosling.   Bunter gave another
blink behind, and scrambled frantically up the wall, at the
spot where he had clambered the previous day.   On that
occasion he had clambered slowly and laboriously.   But
fear lends wings.   Bunter went over that old wall almost
like a bird.

" 'Ere !   You stop ! " spluttered Gosling, as he came
charging up.   He grabbed at disappearing fat legs.

His grasp closed on one leg.

" Leggo ! " yelled Bunter.

" Gotcher ! " gasped Gosling.

But he had not quite got Bunter.   He had captured one
leg—but Bunter kicked out frantically with the other.   The

roar that came from Gosling, as a heel banged on his ancient nose, would have done credit to the Bull of Bashan, famed of old time for his roaring.

Gosling let go Bunter and clasped his nose. Bunter vanished over the wall. A sound of running feet was heard in the lane, dying away in the direction of the high road. But Gosling gave it no heed. He tottered away clasping his nose, which felt as if it had been driven into his head like a nail. Not for quite some time did Gosling feel equal to reporting to Mr. Quelch, in the Remove form-room, that the missing member of his form had turned up : and was now outside the school, hitting the open spaces.

CHAPTER XXV

BUNTER AT LARGE

" HALLO, hallo, hallo ! "

"Look ! "

"That ass ! "

"Bunter ! "

"The esteemed idiotic Bunter ! "

The Remove footballers were rolling over to Highcliffe in their brake. The junior eleven, and seven or eight other fellows, were packed in : and there was a cheery buzz of talk, on the subject of Soccer, and the prospects of beating Courtenay's team at Highcliffe : and not a word on the latest topic at Greyfriars. Sad to relate, Harry Wharton and Co. had forgotten all about Bill Bunter and his antics and his tribulations.

They had heard Gosling report to Mr. Quelch, in third school, the latest development in the Bunter Odyssey. They were aware that the fat Owl, like the much-enduring Ulysses, was still on his travels. But at the moment, Soccer filled their minds, and Bunter was forgotten.

Now they were suddenly reminded of him. The brake was rolling along the Courtfield road, across the common, when Bob Cherry spotted a fat figure at the roadside, waving a fat paw.

All eyes at once turned on Bunter. There he was : a good mile from Greyfriars. The juniors had heard that Wingate, Gwynne, Loder, and other prefects, had gone out on their bicycles to look for him. Evidently they had not found him yet—for there he was.

"I say, you fellows, stop, will you ? " yelled Bunter, as the brake drew abreast. " I say, I want a lift."

Harry Wharton signed to the driver to stop. Billy

Bunter rolled out into the road, and blinked up at staring faces.

"You howling ass," said the captain of the Remove. "What are you doing here?"

"Eh! I've been waiting for you," answered Bunter. "Did you find my note in your study, Harry, old chap?"

"Yes, you benighted chump."

"I asked you to chuck Soccer and look for that postal order, Wharton. You might have found it by this time. I jolly well knew you wouldn't, though," added Bunter, shaking his head. "Selfishness all round, as usual."

"Is that the lot?" asked Harry. "Then we'll push on."

"Oh, really, Wharton——"

"Good-bye, Bunter! Look out for the pre's—there's a bunch of them out on bikes scouting for you," called out Squiff, the Remove goal-keeper.

"Hold on! I want a lift in that brake," howled Bunter. "Wait till I get on. I can't walk all the way to Highcliffe."

"You can't come to Highcliffe, fathead, with the pre's after you," said Vernon-Smith.

"I jolly well can," hooted Bunter. "I can't go back to Greyfriars till after dark, or they'll cop me."

"The copfulness is the proper caper, my esteemed fat Bunter."

"Beast!"

"Why not go back and hand that postal order over to Quelch?" asked Johnny Bull. "You'd get off with a licking, then."

"It's lost, you beast."

"Gammon!"

"Look here, you fellows, give a fellow a lift," howled Bunter. "Nice sort of pals you are, turning a fellow down when he's in a jam."

"Oh, let him hop on," said Bob Cherry. "He can stand round and cheer our goals at Highcliffe. The pre's won't think of looking for him there."

"The sooner they get him, the better," grunted Johnny
Bull.

"Beast!" roared Bunter.

The fat Owl was allowed to hop on, and the brake rolled
on its way. The fat Owl wedged himself into a seat, and
blinked round at grinning faces. The present circumstances appeared, to Bunter, tragic: but to the other
fellows they seemed rather comic.

"I say, you fellows, got any toffee?" asked Bunter.

"No!"

"Got any chocs?"

"No!"

"Got anything to eat?"

"No!"

"Oh, lor'!"

"Bunter's cut tiffin," remarked Bob. "Poor old Bunter!
He must be feeling like any other fellow after three weeks
in an open boat at sea. Look here, Bunter, if you go back,
Quelch will let you have some dinner before the Head bunks
you."

"Beast!"

"What are you keeping up this idiotic game for?"
demanded Johnny Bull. "Do you think you can keep that
postal order, or what?"

"Think I want to keep a postal order that doesn't belong
to me, you beast?" hooted Bunter.

"Then why haven't you handed it over?"

"I haven't got it!" yelled Bunter. "Don't I keep on
telling you it was lost, through that jacket in my lining—I
mean that lining in the hole—that is, the hole in the
lining——"

"But you owned up to Quelch that you had it!" roared
Johnny. "He told us so."

"I didn't say I had it! I said I'd fetch it from my
study!" roared back Bunter.

"Well, that's the same thing, isn't it?" asked Frank
Nugent, staring at the fat Owl.

" The samefulness is terrific."

" 'Tain't ! " hooted Bunter. " Quelch was taking me to the Head, and he had hold of my shoulder. He wouldn't let go. I said that to make him let go, see ? "

" Oh, holy smoke ! "

" You benighted chump ! "

" That was strategy," explained Bunter. " I had to make the beast let go, or he'd have hiked me in to Dr. Locke. He let go all right when he thought I was going to fetch the postal order from my study. See ? "

The Remove fellows gazed at Bunter.

" You—you—you owned up that you'd got the postal order, when you hadn't, just to get away from Quelch ? " articulated Harry Wharton.

" I'd have said anything to get away from Quelch," explained Bunter. " That was important, you know."

" Oh, scissors ! "

" Besides, I never said I had it—I asked Quelch if I could fetch it from my study," said Bunter. " I had to make him let go. Of course I couldn't fetch it from my study when it wasn't there. It's lost."

" Oh, crumbs ! " said Bob Cherry. " I wonder whether that postal order really is lost, after all ! "

" I've told you it is ! " roared Bunter.

" That's pretty good evidence that it isn't," remarked the Bounder.

" Oh, really, Smithy——"

" But—but—but—you unlimited chump," gasped Harry Wharton. " Can't you see that now you've owned up to having it, Quelch and the Head can't have any doubt about it, and you'll be bunked if you don't hand it over ? "

" How can I hand it over when I haven't got it ? Talk sense, old chap."

" You've made Quelch and the Head think you've got it ! " roared Wharton. " What else are they to think ? "

" Well, you never know what a schoolmaster may think—

silly lot ! " said Bunter. " But it will be all right when the postal order's found."

"When ! " snorted Johnny Bull.

"The whenfulness will probably be terrific."

"Well, it's got to be found," said Bunter. "Otherwise they will make out that I had it, especially after what I said to Quelch. I think you fellows might chuck football, just for once, and put in the afternoon hunting for it."

"Ha, ha, ha ! "

"Oh, don't cackle ! I'm not joking," howled Bunter.

"You are ! " said Bob Cherry. "One of your best, old man."

"Ha, ha, ha ! "

"Well, after all I've done for you fellows, I think you might stand by a fellow in a jam," said Bunter, reproachfully. "I've got to keep doggo till that postal order's found. If the Head gets hold of me, I shall be bunked. How would you fellows like that ? " added Bunter. "How would you like never seeing me at Greyfriars again ? "

"Fine ! " said the Bounder.

"Ripping ! " said Peter Todd.

"Splendid ! " said Johnny Bull.

"Glorious ! " said Ogilvy.

"One of those happy dreams that never come true ! " said Bob Cherry, with a sad shake of the head.

"Why, you—you beasts ! " exclaimed Bunter. "After all I've done for you ! Talk about gratitude being sharper than a serpent's tooth ! "

"Ha, ha, ha ! "

"Hallo, hallo, hallo ! There's Loder ! " exclaimed Bob Cherry. A cyclist had come in sight on one of the paths over the common, heading for the high-road and the Greyfriars brake.

There was a howl of terror from Bunter. He cast one startled blink round, dived, and disappeared among innumerable legs and feet.

"I—I—I say, you fellows, don't you tell Loder I'm here,"

he gasped. " I—I say, if he asks you, tell him you haven't seen me, and—and that you saw me taking the train at Courtfield——"

" Keep quiet, fathead," said the Bounder. " Loder hasn't seen you—but if he hears a pig squeaking, he will guess you're here."

" Ha, ha, ha ! "

" Beast ! "

Loder came out on the road, waving his hand to the brake to stop. The vehicle stopped, and Loder came alongside. He was not looking in a good temper. Probably he was not enjoying putting in a half-holiday looking for an elusive fat Owl. He rewarded the Removites with a scowl when they obligingly stopped for him.

" Seen Bunter about anywhere ? " snapped Loder.

" Yes, we saw him on this road, about half a mile back," answered the Bounder with cheery coolness. " Two or three minutes on your bike, Loder."

" Oh, good ! "

Loder of the Sixth whirled round his machine, and pedalled back along the road. The Bounder grinned after him, and then glanced round at the other fellows.

" Think Loder fancies that I meant that Bunter was still there, you fellows ? " he asked.

" Sort of ! " chuckled Bob Cherry.

" Well, I never said so ! We did see Bunter on the road half a mile back."

" Ha, ha, ha ! "

Loder disappeared down the road, going all out on his bike. Billy Bunter emerged from a sea of feet, gasping for breath. It was one more narrow escape for the fugitive Owl. But a miss was as good as a mile : and Billy Bunter, still at large, rolled on to Highcliffe with the footballers.

CHAPTER XXVI

PIG IN CLOVER

" Caterpillar, old chap ! "

Rupert de Courcy, of the Highcliffe Fourth, gave a slight start. Then he gazed at Billy Bunter, of the Greyfriars Remove.

De Courcy was ' Caterpillar ' to his friends. In that list was not included the name of William George Bunter. So no doubt it was a slight surprise to him when a fat thumb poked him in the ribs, and he turned, to be addressed by Billy Bunter as ' Caterpillar, old chap '.

But the Caterpillar was always urbane. He was about to enter the changing-room when Billy Bunter happened. He paused, in polite inquiry.

" Glad to see you again, old fellow," said Bunter, with an amicable blink.

" The gladness would be on my side," said the Caterpillar, gravely, " if I happened to know you."

" Oh, really, de Courcy——"

" Have we met before ? " asked the Caterpillar.

" I'm Bunter."

" Really ?   So pleased to meet you, Punter——"

" Bunter——"

" I mean Bunter !   It's a real pleasure to make your acquaintance.   Good-bye."

Rupert de Courcy moved into the doorway. But a fat paw clutched his arm before he could escape into the changing-room.

" I say, hold on," exclaimed Bunter.   " Just listen to a fellow a minute——"

" I'd listen for hours, with real pleasure, Grunter——"

" Bunter——"

" Bunter—only they want me to play football," explained

the Caterpillar. "There's a team here from Greyfriars. Know any of the Greyfriars men ? "

"Oh, really, de Courcy——"

"There's Courtenay callin' me. I shall have to go in and change. Good-bye." The Caterpillar jerked his arm loose.

"But I say——"

De Courcy disappeared into the changing-room.

"Beast ! " hissed Bunter.

Billy Bunter did not quite believe that the Caterpillar had forgotten his fat existence. It was only a few weeks since, on an occasion when Harry Wharton and Co. had come over to tea in No. 3 Study with their Highcliffe friends, the fat Owl had succeeded in wedging into the party.

Bunter had never forgotten that tea in No. 3 Study at Highcliffe. The Caterpillar's teas were lavish. In his present state, having missed dinner, the fat Owl thought of the good things in No. 3 Study, with the longings which the famished Israelites felt for the fleshpots of Egypt.

It was not with the idea of watching Harry Wharton and Co. beating Highcliffe, or being beaten by them, as the case might be, that Bunter had come with the team. Billy Bunter just now was like a lion seeking what he might devour. His interest in Soccer had never been at a lower ebb. His interest in foodstuffs, always deep, had never been stronger.

But evidently there was nothing doing so far as the Caterpillar was concerned. Fascinating fellow as Bunter was, there were quite a lot of people who did not want to know him : and the Caterpillar seemed to be one of them. The beast was playing in the match, anyhow, so he would not be free for more than an hour and a half—even if he did feel disposed to ask Bunter to tea in his study ; and that, Bunter could not help realising, seemed improbable.

"Beast ! " repeated Bunter, disconsolately.

He blinked at the footballers as they came out, and went into the field. Quite a number of Greyfriars juniors had come over, in the brake or on their bicycles, to watch the game. They gathered round the field with a crowd of Highcliffe men. But Billy Bunter did not join them. He did not heed the whistle, and did not care a boiled bean who kicked off, or whether anybody kicked off at all. His thoughts were on more important things.

He rolled away to the doorway of the House.

There, for a few minutes, he hesitated.

There was a shout from the direction of the football-field.

" Goal ! "

Herbert Vernon-Smith had scored, in the first few minutes. Bunter did not even turn his head. He was thinking of No. 3 Study in the Highcliffe Fourth, and debating in his fat mind whether he could make the venture.

At Greyfriars, there would have been no hesitation. No fellow's study cupboard was safe from Bunter, in the Remove passage. How often he had been booted for snooping tuck in the studies, Bunter could not have calculated, without going into very high figures. But even Bunter hesitated to transfer his predatory manners and customs to another school.

Yet, ten to one, there were good things galore in the Caterpillar's study. Fellows might stare, at seeing a Greyfriars man wandering about inside the House. Still, so long as they only stared, it would not really matter.

Bunter, finally, rolled in.

If that supercilious swob, the Caterpillar, had shown the faintest sign of giving him the glad hand, with a prospect of tea after the match, Bunter might have held out till the whistle went. But the swob hadn't. He had passed him by like the idle wind which he regarded not. It was borne in upon Bunter's fat mind that if he wanted to sample the probable good things in No. 3 Study—as assuredly he did—it was no use waiting for the Caterpillar to ask him to tea : and that it might be injudicious to wait till the swob came back to his study !

So, at last, in he rolled.

He almost rolled into Mr. Mobbs, the master of the Highcliffe Fourth. Mr. Mobbs gave him an inquiring look. Under that inquiring look, Bunter realised that he had better explain why he was heading for the stairs.

" Please may I go up to de Courcy's study to fetch his muffler, sir ? " he asked.

" Oh ! Certainly," said Mr. Mobbs.

Bunter heaved his weight up the staircase.

He knew his way, having been there before. In a few minutes he arrived in the Fourth-form quarters, and stopped at the door of No. 3 Study. He rolled into that study, and shut the door.

His fat heart was beating a little fast. This was an unusual experience, even for Bunter. But Bunter was hungry : and when Bunter was hungry, all lesser considerations had to be disregarded.

He gave one blink from the study window. It gave a view of the football field in the distance. The Owl of the Remove, at that distance, could not pick out the players : but he had a dim view of the Highcliffe yellow-and-black mingled with the blue-and-white of Greyfriars. They were going it—and would be going it for well over an hour yet. The Caterpillar and his chum Courtenay were both in the team : and nobody else was likely to come to their study. Really, it was safe as houses.

Having blinked at the distant footballers, Bunter rolled across to the study cupboard : which, as he well remembered, had exuded all sorts of good things, on the occasion when he had wedged into the tea-party. Most likely, almost certainly, it contained good things for tea. Bunter fervently hoped that it did. If he had found an empty cupboard, it would have been a crushing, overwhelming blow.

But all fears were relieved when he opened the cupboard door. The first object that met his eyes, and his spectacles, was a large cake. There were several paper bags, which he soon ascertained to contain eclairs and meringues. There was a box of chocolate creams, and a packet of toffee. There were several pots of jam, one of marmalade, and one of honey. Billy Bunter's little round eyes popped behind his big round spectacles as he gazed.

"Oh, crumbs!" gasped Bunter.

If any hesitation had lingered in Bunter's fat mind, it vanished now. He was hungry—fearfully hungry. The spot where his dinner should have been was an aching void. Even with a dinner inside him, Bunter could hardly have resisted cake, and meringues, and jam. Minus a dinner, it was not to be thought of—by Bunter. Bunter's emotions were those of a pig in clover!

He began, standing at the cupboard. But when half the big cake, and a few meringues, had taken the edge off his appetite, he sat down to it, transferring the provender from the study cupboard to the study table. Generously, he left a few of the paper bags in the cupboard. He was not going to wolf the whole supply.

That, at least, was his first idea. But when the liberal supply on the table had gone on the downward path, his eyes and spectacles turned on the cupboard again.

By that time, Bunter was feeling a little full, and he was very sticky and shiny, and a little short of breath. But he was capable of further exertions. He rolled back to the cupboard.

On the football field, Harry Wharton and Co. were busy, and had quite forgotten Bunter. In the Caterpillar's study, Billy Bunter was equally busy, and had quite forgotten Harry Wharton and Co. The Remove footballers were having a good time. Bunter was having the time of his life.

But he slowed down at last. Even Bunter had his limit, though it was an extensive one. He sat down in the Caterpillar's comfortable arm-chair, with a pot of jam on his fat knees, a tablespoon in his fat hand, and absorbed jam. But he slowed down more and more.

He leaned his fat head back on soft leather. He had to go—it was quite clear to him that he had better go—before Courtenay and the Caterpillar came in. But there was lots of time yet—time for a fellow to take a rest. Bunter had had a hectic time of late : and, with that gargantuan feed to wind up with, he felt that he needed a rest. So he rested.

His eyes closed behind his spectacles. The pot of jam on his knees slipped over, and slowly but surely exuded jam over his trousers—unheeded by Bunter. With his eyes shut, and his mouth open, Billy Bunter slept—and snored.

CHAPTER XXVII

AFTER THE FEAST, THE RECKONING

" GOAL ! "

It was a cheery roar on Little Side at Highcliffe.   It was
followed by the whistle.

It had been a good game, hotly contested on both sides.
Smithy's goal in the first five minutes had been ᵗhe only
score in the first half : but after the interval, the Caterpillar had put the leather in, in spite of Squiff's sturdy
defence between the posts, and Frank Courtenay had
followed it up with another.   After which the Greyfriars
men fought hard to equalize : and succeeded at last with
a lucky shot from Hurree Jamset Ram Singh.   Then it was
ding-dong ding-dong right up to the finish, and looked
like a draw.   Twice, thrice, the yellow-and-black shirts
came down on the Greyfriars goal, like wolves on the
fold : but twice, thrice, Sampson Quincy Iffley Field, of
New South Wales, put paid to all their efforts, saving shots
that looked certain winners.   And then, at length, the
blue-and-white got well away, and yellow-and-black fell
back to pack their goal—in vain.   The ball went in from
Harry Wharton's foot, and the winning goal was scored on
the very stroke of time.

And the Greyfriars men round the field roared ' Goal ! ',
and waved their caps, or tossed them into the air, as the
Remove footballers came off the field winners by three goals
to two.

Which was eminently satisfactory to Harry Wharton
and Co., and they were a cheery crowd in the changing-
room.   But Courtenay and Co. were good losers, and all
was merry and bright.   And not a fellow gave a single
thought to a fat Owl who had rolled over in the brake
with the Greyfriars team.

It was not till the Greyfriars party were going to their brake, that Bob Cherry remembered Billy Bunter, and glanced round for him.

But no rotund figure was in sight : no spectacles glimmered in the sun. Bunter was not to be seen.

"He's gone, I suppose," remarked Bob.

"He ? Who ? " asked Harry Wharton. Not only had the captain of the Remove forgotten Bunter : but he had not yet remembered him.

"Bunter," said Bob.

"Oh ! Bunter ! " Wharton glanced round. "I expect he cleared off pretty early. Blessed if I know what he came for—he wouldn't want to watch Soccer."

"Well, the pre's are hunting him, and this is a safe distance," said Bob. "Queer that he didn't hang on for the brake. 'Tain't like Bunter to walk if he could help it."

"Well, he's not here," said Harry.

And the footballers, dismissing the fat Owl once more from mind, departed. The brake rolled away, a bunch of cyclists following it. Courtenay and the Caterpillar waved a parting hand from the gate.

"Jolly good game," Frank Courtenay remarked, as he walked back to the House with his chum, after the Greyfriars fellows were gone.

"Toppin'," agreed the Caterpillar. "We ought to have had that odd goal, though."

"Better luck next time."

"I was goin' to stand a spread to celebrate the jolly old victory—if any ! " said the Caterpillar, "and as I've asked the fellows, we'd better stand it to celebrate the jolly old defeat, what ? "

Courtenay laughed.

There was no victory to celebrate : but the Highcliffe footballers were ready, indeed eager, to attend the spread in No. 3 Study. Courtenay and the Caterpillar arrived at that study with a crowd of fellows at their heels, all happily anticipative.

L

A strange and unexpected sound from the study greeted their ears as they arrived.

Snore !

" What on earth's that ? " asked Courtenay, in astonishment.

" What the dooce—— ? " said the Caterpillar.

" Oh ! " ejaculated Courtenay, as he opened the study door.

" Oh, gad ! " ejaculated the Caterpillar, in his turn.

They stared into the study. It was quite an unexpected sight that met their astonished eyes.

They stared blankly at a fat figure reclining, not to say sprawling, in the Caterpillar's arm-chair.

Billy Bunter's eyes were closed behind his big spectacles. His mouth was open. The pot of jam on his fat knees had exuded most of its contents over his trousers. A jammy tablespoon had dropped from a sticky hand to the Caterpillar's expensive carpet.

Billy Bunter had fully intended going while the going was good. But Bunter, once asleep, did not wake easily.

He was still sleeping—and snoring !

There he was, sticky, shiny, jammy : and on the table lay the mere wreckage of a spread that had been intended for a dozen fellows. He was fast asleep : and on his fat face, as he slept, was a smile. No doubt he was dreaming of the good things now parked in his capacious interior : though how even Billy Bunter could have made such a clearance of such a supply, was rather a mystery.

But he had ! There was no doubt that he had !

The spread was gone ! Billy Bunter, rather unluckily for himself, wasn't ! But as yet unconscious of peril, the fat Owl of Greyfriars happily slept and snored. There was no doubt that he needed a rest ! Bunter, undoubtedly, had done himself well—very well indeed !

" Oh, gad ! " repeated the Caterpillar.

" Oh, my hat ! " said Courtenay, blankly. " He's bolted everything in the study and gone to sleep——"

They gazed at Bunter. A crowd of juniors in the door-way gazed at him. They had come to a spread in No. 3 Study—one of the Caterpillar's lavish spreads. Evidently, the spread had already taken place. Only the wreckage of that spread remained for the hungry footballers. They gazed at Bunter—their gaze growing more and more expressive.

Undisturbed by the sound of voices, the fat Owl snored happily on.

Snorrrrrrrrre !

" The Sleepin' Beauty ! " remarked the Caterpillar. " I shall have to do the Prince Charmin' act ! "

He stepped behind the arm-chair, grasped the back, and tilted it. There was a wild splutter as Billy Bunter rolled out on the carpet.

" Ooooooooooogh ! "

Bunter sat up, spluttering. He set his spectacles straight on his little fat nose, and blinked round him like a startled owl.

" Oh ! " gasped Bunter.

He realised that he had left it late. He read the danger-signals in the crowd of wrathful faces staring at him. He scrambled to his feet.

" I—I say, you fellows, I—I—I'm just going—— ! " he gasped.

" You are ! " agreed the Caterpillar.

He grasped a fat neck, and slewed Bunter round. Bunter flew from his foot like a fat football.

" Yaroooh ! " roared Bunter, as he flew.

" Pass ! " shouted the Caterpillar.

Courtenay's foot caught Bunter in its turn, and passed him to the doorway. Smithson took the pass, and his foot lifted Bunter into the passage.

" Ow ! wow ! I say, stoppit ! " roared Bunter. " I say, you fellows, I never—I didn't—it wasn't me—I say—Yaroooooooop ! "

Billy Bunter had had the feast. After it came the reckon-

ing.   There was quite a scramble for Bunter in the passage.
Every fellow there seemed eager to get in a kick. Bunter
went down the passage, his voice floating back on its top
note, his fat little legs in their highest gear.   How many
kicks he collected before he escaped down the stairs, Bunter
never knew—it seemed to him like millions.   It was a sore
and suffering Owl that bolted into the quad, careered away
to the gates, and charged out into the road.

CHAPTER XXVIII

AFTER DARK

CLINK !

Harry Wharton and Frank Nugent both looked up startled.

It was prep in the Remove studies. Wharton and Nugent, in No. 1 Study, were sitting at the table with their books, preparing that section of the Æneid which Mr. Quelch would expect them to be ready to construe in the form-room next morning. The sudden clink at their study window was quite unexpected.

" What the dickens——! " exclaimed Harry.

" Sounded like a stone," said Nugent, in wonder.

" Can't be an ass out in the quad after lock-up, buzzing stones at a study window ! "

" Hardly ! But——"

Clink !

" There it is again ! "

The two juniors rose from the study table. Amazing as it was, and quite unaccountable, that clink told of the contact of a pebble on a pane of glass : someone, inexplicably, was out in the quad, after lock-ups, in the dark, ' buzzing ' stones at the window.

And whoever it was seemed to be impatient. For as the two juniors stood staring at the window, there came a third clink—followed by a crack !

Crack !

" Oh, my hat ! There goes the glass ! " exclaimed Nugent.

" The howling ass ! " exclaimed Harry. " Who the deuce—what the deuce—why the deuce——" He cut across to the window.

One pane was cracked. It was rather urgent to put a stop to that fusillade from below, before the glass went.

Wharton threw up the sash. The next moment he gave a howl.

" Ow ! "

A fourth missile was whizzing up. Wharton had thrown up the sash in time to save the glass. But the natural consequence was that the pebble whizzed in at the open window. It caught the captain of the Remove on the tip of his nose. It was quite a hard rap.

" Ow ! " repeated Wharton. " Oh ! My nose ! Oh ! What blithering idiot—— ? "

He leaned out of the window, and stared down with a wrathful face, and shouted. It was dark in the quad, with only a dim glimmer of stars, and he could see nobody : but obviously, somebody was there !

" Stop that ! You howling ass, whoever you are, stop it ! Do you hear me ? "

" Oh, really, Wharton—— " came a fat squeak from the dimness.

" Bunter ! " exclaimed Nugent.

" I say, you fellows—— "

" Bunter ! " Wharton stared down, and caught a glimmer from below—the glimmer of a big pair of spectacles in the starlight. " You burbling bandersnatch, is it you ? What are you buzzing stones at this window for, you footling fathead ? You've cracked a pane—— "

" Well, I had to make you hear—— "

" You got me on the nose," yelled Wharton.

" He, he, he ! "

A fat cachinnation floated up from below. The fact that he had got the captain of the Remove on the nose seemed to amuse Bunter.

" You fat gurgling ass—— ! "

" I say, old chap—— "

" What do you want ? " hooted Wharton.

" I want to get in ! " came the answering squeak. " I

say, I couldn't get back till after dark, or they'd have had me——"

" The sooner the better."

" Beast ! "

" Go and tap at Quelch's window if you want to get in. It will be all right if you hand him that postal order."

" You jolly well know it's lost——"

" I jolly well don't ! Go and eat coke."

" If that's what you call pally, Wharton, when a fellow's in a jam——"

" What do you want ? " hooted Wharton. " You can't get in at this window, you blithering ass ! Think I could let down a string and pull you up ? "

" I've got to get in ! Think I can stay out all night ? " hooted Bunter. " I can't get in anywhere, unless a pal lets me in. Look here, you come down and unlock the door of our lobby, see ? "

" I can't get out in prep."

" You can chance it."

" And run into a prefect ? "

" You can tell him you have to speak to Quelch—as Head Boy, you know—if you run into a prefect——"

" You fat villain ! "

" Beast ! I mean, look here, old chap, I can't stay out all night, can I ? " came the anxious fat squeak from the shadows below. " Besides, I'm hungry. I haven't had anything to eat since I was at Highcliffe this afternoon. And the beasts made an awful fuss because I had a snack in Caterpillar's study. They kicked me——"

" I hope they kicked you hard ! "

" Beast ! " roared Bunter.

" Is that the lot ? " asked Harry Wharton. " Then I'll shut the window, and get back to prep."

" I say, old fellow, hold on. I've simply got to get in," wailed Bunter. " I've got to sleep somewhere, haven't I ? It would be all right by this time, if you'd found that postal order. But you would play football

instead—I say, don't shut that window! Be a pal, old
chap."

Harry Wharton did not close the window. He was not
insensible to the woes of the fugitive fat Owl. There was
Bunter, shut out of the House, like a fat Peri outside the
gates of Paradise. Unless he could get in, his lodging was
going to be on the cold, cold ground! On the other
hand, any fellow discovered helping the fat junior in his
extraordinary game of eluding beaks and prefects, was
certain to be dealt with grimly and efficiently by Mr.
Quelch. Wharton was not exactly yearning for an interview with Mr. Quelch in his grimmest mood!

"Look here, you ass, I can't go down in prep——" he
said at last.

"Beast! I say, Nugent, old chap, will you go down
and open the lobby door? You ain't funky like Wharton,
old fellow."

"Fathead!" was Nugent's reply.

"You blithering, blethering, burbling bloater," said
Harry Wharton. "I'll cut into the lobby after prep, and
unlock the door. That's all I can do. If I try it on now
I shall be spotted, and they'll lock the door again."

"But look here——"

"And if you stand there yelling, somebody will hear
you—the pre's are still looking for you."

"But I'm hungry!" wailed Bunter. "I say, haven't
you got something you could drop out of the window
for me?"

"Yes! Stand steady, and I'll drop a Latin dick on your
silly nut."

"Beast!" roared Bunter.

"Look out," exclaimed Nugent, suddenly, as he caught
sight of a moving figure in the dimness below. "Somebody's coming."

"Oh, crikey!"

There was a patter of feet. Billy Bunter did not wait
for something to be dropped from the window—whether

a Latin dictionary, or something more edible. He bolted.

Wharton and Nugent backed promptly out of sight. But the window remained open, and from the dimness below the sound of footsteps and voices floated up.

" Quelch ! " breathed Nugent.

" I am sure that I heard someone calling, Wingate." It was the Remove master's voice. " You heard——"

" Yes, sir ! I think it was Bunter's voice."

" I have no doubt that that foolish and troublesome boy will return, and he will doubtless attempt to communicate with some other boy, to be let in——"

" Most likely, sir."

Wharton and Nugent exchanged a glance. Quelch, evidently, was wise to the probable proceedings of the fugitive Owl.

" He was probably calling up to a window, Wingate. I have no doubt that he is at hand. Let us look round."

" Certainly, sir."

Footsteps and voices receded. Harry Wharton quietly closed the study window.

" The ass ! " he said.

" The fathead ! " said Nugent.

" How long does the potty porpoise think he can keep this up ? "

" Goodness knows."

" I'll get that door unlocked for him after prep. Six on the bags if I'm spotted at it," growled Wharton. " Bother him ! "

" Blow him ! " agreed Nugent.

And they returned to prep : which was not further interrupted by William George Bunter.

CHAPTER XXIX

SHUT OUT

" Oh, crikey ! " breathed Billy Bunter.

He breathed that ejaculation inaudibly.

He dared not make a sound.

It was very dark in the quad. Lights glimmered only from masters' and sixth-form windows. Other forms were in their dormitories. It was ten o'clock: an hour at which, in normal circumstances, Billy Bunter would have been safe in the embrace of Morpheus, and waking the echoes of the Remove dormitory with his snore. But the circumstances now were not normal : they were exceedingly abnormal : and the Owl of the Remove was not even thinking of slumber.

Mr. Quelch and Wingate had looked round, but they had seen nothing of the fat junior in the dark. They had gone back into the House : but several times since, shadowy figures had moved about the quad, and once, Bunter had had an alarming glimpse of Gosling. It was clear that Quelch knew, or at least felt certain, that the missing member of his form had returned to the school : and it was equally clear that he was very keen to lay hands on that missing member.

Bunter, at the moment, was sitting dismally on a bench under one of the old elms. He was not likely to be seen there by searchers : like the heathen of old, he sat in darkness. By that time the lobby door was unlocked, and there was a way in : but with Quelch on the prowl, Bunter dared not approach the House. He was hungry and he was sleepy : he longed to get within reach of foodstuffs, and to find a corner to curl up in for the night : but ' safety first ' was his motto. He dared not risk Quelch's clutching hand. Dismally, disconsolately, and dolorously, he waited for the lights to go out. Once all was dark, and that unspeakable beast Quelch gone to bed, it would be safe to make the venture.

But a sound of footsteps, and a murmur of voices, from the shadows, apprised him that the beast had by no means gone to bed yet. Bunter had been sprawling on the bench : now he suddenly sat up, with fat ears pricked to listen, like a startled fat rabbit.

" You have seen nothing of him, Gosling ? "

" I think I 'eard 'im once, sir, but I ain't seen him."

" I am assured that he is within the precincts of the school. I have every reason to believe that he was seeking to communicate with some boy in a Remove study. But in this darkness he might be quite near at hand and we should see nothing of him."

Billy Bunter grinned, for a moment.

" 'Ardly see your 'and before your nose, sir," said Gosling. " But the young rip——"

" What ? "

" The young rip——"

" Kindly do not use such expressions, Gosling."

" Oh ! Yessir—no, sir ! I mean, the young idjit——"

" If you are alluding to Bunter, of my form, please express yourself more decorously, Gosling."

" Oh ! Yessir ! What I means to say is, the young— ahem—Master Bunter, sir, will 'ave to get in for the night, and mebbe he'd get another of the young rips—I mean the young gentlemen, sir—to leave a door or a winder un- fastened for 'im——"

" Bless my soul ! " said Mr. Quelch. " That is a very timely suggestion, Gosling. I am almost sure that he was calling up to a Remove study window. Very probably it was with that object in view."

" If you find a winder open, sir——"

" I shall certainly make a very careful investigation, Gosling. Most certainly. If either a door or a window is found unfastened——"

" Then you only got to wait there and cop 'im, sir."

" I shall certainly take every measure——"

The voices passed on. Quelch and Gosling passed within six or seven feet of a scared fat Owl, blissfully ignorant of his proximity. Billy Bunter shook a fat fist after them, as they went.

" Beasts ! " groaned Bunter.

The lobby door would be unlocked : there was no doubt that Wharton would have done that for him. And that indescribable beast, Quelch, was going to make a round of the House, examining doors and windows. He would find that lobby door unlocked—he would know exactly why : and he would wait there for a fat Owl to walk into his hands !

Bunter realised that he had had a narrow escape. But that was not very much comfort to the dolorous fat Owl.

There was an unlocked door : but he dared not approach it, even after all lights were out. Quelch would be on the watch inside ! It looked as if Bunter was booked for a night out ! He had not had a very comfortable time, the previous night, in the music-room. But this was worse —awfully worse ! A mist was creeping up from the sea. It was dark, it was cold, it was clammy. Billy Bunter simply couldn't envisage a night out. But he was not going anywhere near that lobby door !

" Oh, lor ' ! " groaned Bunter.

He had banked on that lobby door. But really, it seemed as if the stars in their courses fought against Bunter, as against Sisera of old. There was only one way in—and that led direct into Quelch's clutches.

Bunter sat on the bench and groaned.

He was hungry, and getting hungrier. Even that gargantuan feed at Highcliffe could not be expected to last all this time. He had thought of another raid on the pantry—of scouting in the studies in the dark—but such resources were barred to a fellow shut out of the House. Almost was Bunter tempted to give himself up, for the sake of a square meal and a warm bed. But if he fell into the hands of authority, before that wretched postal order was found, it was the ' sack '. He just sat and groaned.

One by one the lighted windows in the House went dark. The sixth-form study windows no longer glimmered. Common-room windows no longer showed a gleam. Even Quelch's window disappeared in blackness. Beaks, at last, were gone to bed. Now all would have been safe, if only that unlimited beast, Quelch, wasn't on the watch in the junior lobby. But Bunter knew that the beast was—waiting for him !

But he rose from the bench at last, and rolled away to the House. He was going nowhere near the junior lobby —but some door or window might be negotiable—hope springs eternal in the human breast ! Smithy, as Bunter knew well, sometimes ' broke out ' after lights out : and it might happily have happened this very night, with a window left ajar for his return. Or perhaps some Sixth-form sportsman—there were rumours about Loder of the Sixth, and whispers about Price of the Fifth. Bunter had innumerable windows and doors to choose from : but anything was better than sitting on that bench in the thickening mist, and thinking how awfully hungry he was.

All was dark, and silent, and still, as the fat Owl prowled round the House. Greyfriars slept—and if anyone was awake, there was no sign of it. He was prowling under the Sixth-form windows, on the ground floor, when a sudden sound came to his ears, and he jumped in alarm.

It was not a loud sound. But in the night-silence it came clearly and distinctly. It was the sound of an opening window.

Bunter's fat heart almost missed a beat.

It was a Sixth-form window that opened, not three yards from him. His immediate thought was that a prefect had spotted him from that study. He blotted himself close to the wall in the angle of a buttress, his fat heart thumping.

Deep silence followed the sound of the sash pushing up. Was it Wingate, or Gwynne, or Sykes, or Loder, or some other beastly prefect, looking out? Bunter peered round the buttress. All he could see of the window was a dim glimmer of glass, with a black space below, where it was open. But in that black space, he made out, dimly, like a shadow, a head and shoulders. Somebody was looking out, with bent head, listening.

Bunter's fat head popped back, like that of a tortoise into its shell. If that beast had heard him prowling—— !

Then another sound came fainly to his fat ears from the window. It was a faint rustling, brushing sort of sound. He realised that the Sixth-form man was climbing cautiously and stealthily, out of the window.

" Beast ! " breathed Bunter.

The brute had heard him or seen him, and was getting out the quickest way, to collar him ! That was Bunter's impression. But——

To his amazement, he heard another sound—the sound of a window cautiously and quietly closing. Then faint footsteps. He glimpsed a figure, its back to him, that immediately disappeared in the dark.

" Oh ! " breathed Bunter.

He understood now, and he grinned. It was not a dutiful prefect after Bunter. Prefect or not, it was a fellow getting out of bounds at a late hour, when all was safe. Bunter remembered what he knew, or had heard, about Loder of the Sixth, and his secret manners and customs. Whoever it was, he was evidently not thinking of a fugitive fat Owl, and knew nothing of the fat figure blotted in the the dark in the angle of the buttress. Whoever it was, he was gone.

" Oh ! " breathed Bunter again.

His eyes gleamed behind his spectacles ! This was luck ! He had been prowling to find a way into the House—and here was a way open ! The breaker of bounds must have left the window unfastened for his return. Billy Bunter could get that window open—drop into an unoccupied study—and he would be safe in the House : safe and un-suspected, while Quelch was still keeping up his vigil in the junior lobby !

Bunter grinned from ear to ear. Now that he had a way in, it was rather amusing to think of Quelch sitting in the dark, waiting—for nothing !

For several minutes, the fat Owl waited and listened, till he was assured that the breaker of bounds was quite gone. Then he crept to the window. He reached up to the stone sill with his fat hands. A tall Sixth-former could get in and out without much difficulty. But it was a somewhat different proposition to a fat Removite who was tall only sideways.

Bunter clambered desperately. It was not easy to lift his weight : and he was almost on the sill, when he slipped, lost his hold, and sat down on the quad with a sudden concussion.

Bump !

" Ow ! wow ! Oooogh ! " gasped Bunter.

He sat for a few moments spluttering. But he had to get in at that window, or pass the night under the stars. He scrambled up, grabbed the sill, and tried again. Slowly, laboriously, he heaved himself up, till his fat chest rested on the still. Another tremendous effort, and he was on the sill, where for a long minute he pumped in breath before making further efforts.

But all was plane sailing now. The senior had left the lower sash an inch up, for his return. Bunter inserted fat paws under the sash, and it rose easily. He heaved himself in, felt the floor with his feet, and made a safe landing. After all his trials and tribulations, the fugitive Owl was under a roof again, and assured of a lodging for the night.

CHAPTER XXX

HAPPY LANDING

" Prime ! " murmured Billy Bunter.

He grinned.

Bunter's thoughts, in negotiating that study window, had been concentrated on getting into the House, out of the cold clammy mist in the quad. But once safely inside, they reverted to a fact of scarcely less importance—the aching void in his extensive inside.

Bunter was hungry !

He was fearfully hungry. He was ravenously hungry. He knew now what it was like to drift for days and days in an open boat at sea—for that was exactly what he felt like !

In a senior's study there was certain to be something to eat. Something to eat was now the most urgent matter in the universe, so far as William George Bunter was concerned. If there was anything to eat in that study, Billy Bunter was going to eat it, before he went further afield.

He drew the blind carefully over the window, groped to the switch, and turned on the light.

As soon as the light was on, he knew in whose study he was—Loder's. That—as Loder was absent—was an agreeable discovery : for Gerald Loder was a fellow who ' did himself ' well, very well, in the foodstuffs line.

Bunter opened the study cupboard, blinked into it, and ejaculated ' Prime ! ' with a grin of happy satisfaction.

There was half a cold veal pie. There was half a cake. There was a bag of biscuits. There was a pot of jam. There was a plateful of scones. There was, in fact, enough for a supper for even Bunter. It was nothing like that magnificent spread in the Caterpillar's study at Highcliffe ; but it was a windfall to a hungry Owl.

Bunter lost no time.

How long Loder was likely to be absent, he did not know. The sportsman of the Sixth could hardly be back for some little time; but the experience at Highcliffe had not been lost on Bunter. He was not going to linger.

But the demolition of Loder's provisions was not a matter of long duration. In such matters Bunter was a quick worker.

He helped himself with rapid fat hands. The veal pie disappeared in record time. With the assistance of a table-spoon, the jam followed.

Bunter was about to follow this up with the biscuits. But he reflected in time that a hungry day stretched before him. With unusual foresight, Bunter crammed the biscuits into his pockets, and followed up the jam with the cake instead.

Then one by one, the scones followed the cake, the jam, and the veal pie. There were a dozen scones : and by the time the twelfth had vanished, Bunter was feeling fairly satisfied.

He was also feeling very sleepy.

He cast a blink towards Loder's bed : the Sixth-form rooms being bedrooms as well as studies. The bed looked very comfortable and very inviting. But the fat Owl was not thinking of going to sleep in that bed, as he had in the Caterpillar's arm-chair at Highcliffe. He was only thinking of helping himself to some of the bedclothes.

Even Bunter could learn by experience. It had been chilly in the music-room the previous night. He turned back the bed, jammed Loder's pillow under a fat arm, and extracted two blankets, which he draped over a fat shoulder.

He would have been glad of the quilt also : but he was now loaded with as much as he could conveniently carry. And he had some little distance to go, to the spot he had decided upon in his fat mind as a secure retreat for a sleepy Owl.

M

Laden with blankets and pillow, he opened the study door, and peered out into the Sixth-form passage.

All was silent and still. Behind those closed doors, were slumbering prefects who certainly would have jumped up quickly enough, had they known that the hunted Owl was in the offing. But if Wingate, Sykes, Gwynne, and the rest, were dreaming, they certainly did not dream that Billy Bunter had clambered in at the window of a Sixth-form sportsman who had gone out of bounds. All was safe for Bunter.

He switched off the light in Loder's study, closed the door softly, and rolled away, with a cautious roll.

There was no sound—not a glimmer of light—in all the great pile of Greyfriars. Bunter wondered whether Quelch was still sitting in the dark in the junior lobby, waiting for him. If he was, Bunter wished him joy of it. Stealthily, Bunter made his way to the form-rooms.

He stopped at the door of the Fourth-form room. Quelch, who was a careful and methodical gentleman, always locked his form-room door. Capper, who was neither careful nor methodical, seldom or never did. Bunter, as he expected, found the door of Capper's form-room open to his fat hand.

He rolled in, and closed it after him.

It was about half an hour later that Mr. Quelch, after a long, tiresome, and fruitless vigil in the junior lobby, gave it up and went to bed : carefully locking the door Harry Wharton had unlocked : so that Bunter, if he wanted to get in, would have to knock and deliver himself up. Happily unaware that Bunter was already in, and fast asleep, the Remove master went to bed : and as his way lay nowhere near the form-rooms, he did not hear a deep and rumbling snore that was awakening the echoes in that quarter.

And a little later still, a slinking figure dodged among the shadows of the dark quad, and Loder of the Sixth arrived under his study window. He was surprised, and startled, to find the sash wider open than he had left it.

He stood and stared at it, his heart palpitating.

Somebody had been there !

Discovery of his nocturnal excursions would have meant dire results for the Sixth-form sportsman. 'Pub-crawling' was an amusement that had to be kept very dark by a fellow who did not want to catch a morning train for home. For a long uneasy minute, Loder wished that he had not selected that particular night for seeing his sporting friends at the Cross Keys.

He peered into the study. It was dark and silent. He clambered in at last, his heart beating unpleasantly. He drew the blind carefully over the window, and switched on the light. Then he guessed.

"That fat scoundrel ! " breathed Loder.

His cupboard was wide open—and empty of foodstuffs. Only a sea of crumbs on the floor remained to tell the tale of what had become of them. His bed was dismantled, the blankets and pillow gone. Evidently a fat Owl who had been lurking in the quad had found that unsecured window, and made use of it. It was a relief to know that it was not a 'beak' who had visited the study. But Loder's feelings were deep, as he stared from his denuded cupboard to his dismantled bed, and back from his dismantled bed to to his denuded cupboard.

Gladly would Loder have picked up his ashplant, and gone in search of the Owl of the Remove. But he did not think of doing so. Loder had his secrets to keep, and he had to make the best of it. Loder turned in that night with a couple of overcoats on his bed in lieu of blankets, and a cushion in lieu of a pillow. And in Mr. Capper's form-room, a fat Owl, rolled in Loder's blankets, with his fat head on Loder's pillow, slept and snored, till the rising-bell rang in the dewy morn.

CHAPTER XXXI

NO TAKERS

" I say, you fellows ! "

Harry Wharton and Co. jumped, as that unexpected voice fell on their ears.

They were, as a matter of fact, thinking of Billy Bunter : though certainly not expecting to hear his dulcet tones.

After prayers that morning, the Famous Five were taking a trot round the quad till the breakfast-bell rang. The thought of breakfast naturally made them think of Bunter. Whether the fat Owl had got in by the lobby door the previous night, or whether he had had a night out, they did not know, and they wondered what had become of him. And then, as they were passing the form-room windows, that unexpected fat squeak fell upon their ears, and made them jump.

" Bunter ! " ejaculated Bob Cherry.

" Or his ghost ! " said Nugent.

" But where—— ? " Harry Wharton stared round in search of a fat Owl, without seeing one.

" The wherefulness is terrific."

" Where on earth is the fat ass ? " grunted Johnny Bull. " I heard him squeak——"

" I say, you fellows."

This time the Famous Five spotted the direction of the voice. They stared up at the form-room windows.

One window, that of the Fourth-form room, was partly open. At the opening appeared a fat face which looked considerably in need of a wash, and a pair of spectacles glimmering in the morning sunshine.

" Hallo, hallo, hallo ! " ejaculated Bob. " There he is ! As large as life, and twice as natural."

" So you got in last night ? " said Harry Wharton,

staring up at the fat face. " What are you doing in Capper's form-room ? "

" Well, I had to sleep somewhere," answered Bunter. " I say, I've been looking out ever since the bell rang. I'm jolly glad to see you fellows. I say, have you found that postal order yet ? Have you been looking for it ? "

" Better look for it yourself," suggested Johnny Bull.

" How can I look for it, you silly ass, when Quelch will cop me if I show up ? " yapped Bunter.

" Those who hide can find," retorted Johnny.

" Beast ! "

" If that postal order's really lost, it doesn't seem likely to be found, Bunter," said Harry. " But——" He paused. " Look here, you fat chump, if you've got it, all the time——"

" Oh, really, Wharton——"

" He hasn't got it," said Bob, shaking his head. " Even Bunter would have sense enough to cough it up now, if he had it."

" I say, you fellows, it's got to be found," groaned Bunter. " I've got to go on dodging the beaks till it's found, see ? And I jolly well can't keep this up for ever, you know."

" You jolly well can't ! " grinned Nugent.

" I've been having an awful time," said Bunter, pathetically. " I should be simply starving now, if I hadn't found some grub in Loder's study last night."

" Loder's ! Loder will be wild ! " chuckled Bob.

" Oh, blow Loder ! And I say, it would have been awfully cold in here, if I hadn't got hold of Loder's blankets——"

" Oh, my hat ! "

" And I've nothing for brekker excepting Loder's biscuits——"

" Ha, ha, ha ! "

" Well, you can cackle," said Bunter. " But it's pretty tough, I can tell you. I'm jolly well not going to the Head to be bunked. I say, if you fellows hunt for that putrid postal order——"

"Nothing doing," said Harry. "If it's really lost, it can't be found."

"Have you looked in Quelch's study ? "

"Quelch's study ! " ejaculated the captain of the Remove. "Not likely."

"The esteemed Quelch would probably be infuriated, if we rooted in his ridiculous study," chuckled Hurree Jamset Ram Singh.

"Well, it might be there," said Bunter. "I had to huddle under the table when Prout nearly copped me there, the day before yesterday, and it might have dropped there. Of course it might be in the Cloisters, or in the lane, or on the Courtfield road somewhere. I really think you fellows might look for it, when a fellow's in such an awful jam."

"Anybody got a small comb ? " asked Johnny Bull, sarcastically. "If we go along the Courtfield road combing it with a small comb——"

"Ha, ha, ha ! "

"Well, look here, you fellows, if you think it's gone for good——"

"It's gone for good if it's really lost," said Nugent.

"Don't I keep on telling you it's really lost ? " howled Bunter.

"What difference does that make ? " asked Johnny Bull.

"Beast ! "

It was really rather hard on Billy Bunter. He was somewhat in the position of the fellow who cried ' Wolf ' so often when there was no wolf, that he was not believed when the wolf really came. So long and so often had the hapless Owl prevaricated, that now he was, for once, telling the truth, truth had no more effect than his customary fiction. The chums of the Remove would willingly have believed him : but, as Johnny remarked, anything that Bunter said on the subject made no difference at all.

" Well, I've got another idea," said Bunter. " I've been thinking it out, you know. I jolly well know how it can be worked, if you fellows will stand by a pal——"

" 'Ware beaks ! " breathed Bob Cherry, as an angular figure came in sight on the path under the form-room windows.

" Oh, crikey ! "

Bunter vanished from the window.

Mr. Quelch glanced at the group of juniors as he came along. The Remove master was not looking his bonniest that morning. No doubt the strange problem of Bunter was weighing on his mind. What he would have said— and done—had he guessed that the fat Owl was only a few yards away, and that the juniors had been speaking to him a minute ago, would hardly bear thinking of.

" Jolly good goal of Smithy's yesterday," Bob Cherry was saying, as Mr. Quelch came within hearing—for Mr. Quelch's special behoof.

" Topping ! " agreed Harry Wharton. " I hardly thought he'd get through——"

" The Caterpillar nearly had it away from him," chimed in Nugent. " But Smithy got round him——"

" It was touch and go," said Johnny Bull.

" The touch-and-gofulness was terrific," agreed Hurree Jamset Ram Singh. " But the esteemed Smithy got away with it."

" We were lucky to win, really," said Harry. " High-cliffe were in great form yesterday. It was anybody's game right up to the finish."

Mr. Quelch passed on out of hearing : after which the chums of the Remove ceased to discuss the Highcliffe match. A fat face reappeared at the window of Capper's form-room.

" I say, you fellows——"

" All serene, old fat man," said Bob Cherry. Mr. Quelch had turned a corner, and disappeared. " But the bell will be going in a minute or two——"

"Never mind that, old chap! Just listen to a fellow," said Bunter. "I've got an idea, as I was telling you. If that putrid postal order can't be found——"

"It can't be, unless you find it," said Johnny Bull.

"Beast! If it can't be found, I'm done for," hooted Bunter. "I can't go on dodging the beaks for ever—you can see that, I suppose? I may not be able to get hold of any grub——"

"Ha, ha, ha!"

"Oh, don't cackle! Look here, you fellows can raise a pound, or if you can't, you can borrow it off Mauly——"

"That's no good," said Harry Wharton. "If you pinched that postal order, you fat ass, it's pilfering, and paying up the pound wouldn't make any difference. Quelch wants that postal order—not a pound."

"I know! But don't you see?" said Bunter, eagerly. "You go down to Friardale and get a postal order for a pound, Harry, old chap——"

"Eh?"

"And take it to Quelch——"

"What?"

"And tell him you picked it up in the quad——"

"You fat villain!"

"Oh, really, Wharton! Don't you see? That will make it all right! Postal orders are much alike. Quelch won't suspect a thing. He will think it's the same postal order, if you tell him you picked it up in the quad——"

"You pernicious porpoise!" gasped the captain of the Remove. "Is that the idea?"

"Yes, old chap! You tell Quelch you picked it up in the quad—and the other fellows can all tell him they were present when you picked it up—nothing like making sure, you know—all the fellows can swear they saw you pick it up——"

"Well, you're enough to make a fellow swear, if he knew the words!" gasped Bob Cherry. "You piffling, pie-faced, pernicious porker——"

" Oh, really, Cherry——"

" Oh, let's," said Johnny Bull, sarcastically, " let's touch Mauly for a quid, and then go to Quelch and tell him a string of lies, so that Bunter can keep that postal order he's got in his pocket all the time !   Anybody keen on it ? "

" The keenfulness is not terrific," chuckled Hurree Jamset Ram Singh.

Harry Wharton stepped closer to the form-room window. Judging by the expression on his face, he was not greatly taken with the bright idea evolved by Bunter's powerful brain.

" Lean out of the window, will you, Bunter ? " he said.

" Eh !   What for ? "

" So that I can pull your nose."

Bunter did not lean out of the window !

" Beast ! " he roared.

The famous Five trotted on their way.   They seemed to have had enough of Billy Bunter's entertaining conversation and bright ideas.

" I say, you fellows," yelled Bunter.

He blinked after five disappearing backs.

" Beasts ! "

Really, it was quite a bright idea—one of Bunter's brightest !   But evidently there were no takers !

CHAPTER XXXII

A SPOT OF LIVELINESS IN THE FOURTH

"Temple !" said Mr. Capper.

"Yes, sir."

"We shall require the large map," said Mr. Capper. "Kindly get the large map of Europe, Temple."

Cecil Reginald Temple rose in his place in the Fourth Form. He crossed the form-room to the map-cupboard. It was geography in the Fourth in first school that morning.

The blackboard was on its easel. Over the blackboard was to be unrolled the large map of Europe : which at the moment was rolled up and parked in the form-room cupboard. In that cupboard rolled-up maps and other articles were kept till wanted. That it might have, at the moment, additional and unsuspected contents, neither Mr. Capper nor his form could be aware.

In the Remove room, Mr. Quelch was taking his form —one member missing. If Mr. Quelch wondered where that missing member was, certainly he did not suspect that he was in an adjacent form-room : or that he had taken cover in the map-cupboard there when the bell rang for class. Still less did Mr. Capper. Little did Mr. Capper dream, as he spoke to Temple of the Fourth, that his voice reached a pair of fat ears, and caused alarm and despondency in the map-cupboard !

Temple grasped the handle of the door to turn it. To his surprise, it did not turn.

It was quite a large handle on the map-cupboard door, and gave plenty of room for a grip. Cecil Reginald Temple gripped it hard, and strove to turn it.

But it did not stir. It was exactly as if it was held inside ! The oaken door was solid, and that solid oak hid from Temple's eyes a fat and terrified Owl, who was grasp-

186

ing the door-handle with both fat hands, to prevent him from getting the door open.

" Oh, gad ! " murmured Temple. " What's the matter with the dashed thing ? "

It was quite perplexing.

Temple, and other Fourth-form fellows, had often handed articles out of that cupboard when required in a lesson : and had never found any difficulty with the door-handle before. Something, however, seemed the matter with it now.

Mr. Capper, standing by the blackboard with a pointer in his hand, glanced across at Temple, over his spectacles.

" What is the matter, Temple ? Why do you not open the cupboard and take out the map ? " he inquired.

" The handle's jammed, or somethin', sir," answered Temple. " I can't get it to turn."

" What ? What ? Nonsense," said Mr. Capper, testily. " Please bring the map at once, Temple ! The lesson is being delayed, Temple ! Do not waste time."

Cecil Reginald made another effort to turn the door-handle. Then he put both hands to it, and put his beef into it. Then, at last, it began to turn, slowly.

Inside that map-cupboard, Billy Bunter's fat hands grasped his end of the door-handle, desperately resisting. As Temple turned it to the right, to open it, Bunter strove to keep it well to the left, to keep it shut. But now that Cecil Reginald had both hands to the task, he was slowly but surely gaining the upper hand.

Dabney, and Fry, and the rest of the Fourth, watched Temple curiously. His face was pink with exertion as he strove with the door-handle on the map-cupboard. It was quite an unusual occurrence, and seemed inexplicable. Mr. Capper watched him impatiently. Perhaps he suspected Temple of wasting time, owing to lack of keenness on that interesting and important subject, geography. It was not uncommon for little Mr. Capper's leg to be pulled in his form-room.

"Temple!" rapped Mr. Capper.

"Oh! Yes, sir!" gasped Temple.

"You are wasting the time of the form. Open that cupboard immediately and bring here the large map of Europe."

"Oh! Yes, sir! It's moving now, sir. It—it seems stiff, somehow."

Temple, with a double-handed wrench, got that handle turned at last. Then he pulled.

But the door did not open. This was more inexplicable than ever: for the door, being now unlatched, certainly should have come open at a pull. But it did not.

The reason was simple: but invisible. Braced to resist the pull, with both hands clutching the door-handle, inside the map-cupboard, was a fat Owl, holding the door shut.

Bunter held on desperately.

It had not occurred to the fat Owl, when he had taken refuge in the form-room cupboard, that something there might be required in the lesson. If the Fourth had been doing Latin, or English Verse, or history, it would have been all right for Bunter. It was just his ill-luck that they were going to do geography, for which a large map was required. But Billy Bunter dared not be discovered—if he could help it! He did not want to be marched away to his own form-room with Mr. Capper's hand on his collar. Very much indeed he didn't!

So desperate was Bunter's hold on the door-handle, that Temple's pull from outside failed to shift the door. He pulled, and pulled, and dragged, and dragged, growing pinker and pinker: but the door did not stir.

"Temple!" Mr. Capper's voice was getting angry. "Temple! What does this mean? Why do you not open that cupboard, Temple?"

"Oh, gad! I—I mean, it—it won't come open, sir," spluttered Temple. "I—I don't know what's the matter with it, but it won't——"

"Nonsense!"

" It's jammed somehow, sir—something seems to be holding it inside——"

" Absurd ! "

" By gum ! " murmured Fry to Dabney. " There can't be anything wrong with that door, you know. Is old Temple larking with Capper ? "

" Oh, rather," grinned Dabney.

" Bring that map at once, Temple ! " exclaimed Mr. Capper. " I will not allow the time of the form to be wasted in this manner. At once ! "

Temple wrenched. The door yielded, about half an inch, at that wrench. But it was only for a split second. It jammed shut again.

" Oh, crikey ! " gasped Temple, taken quite aback, by that peculiar phenomenon. " I—I can't make it out——"

Mr. Capper, frowning, strode across the form-room. He pushed Cecil Reginald aside, and grasped the door-handle of the cupboard himself.

" Stand back, Temple ! I will open the door ! I am quite assured that there is no difficulty in the matter.

" But really, sir—— ! " gasped Temple.

" Nonsense ! "

Mr. Capper grasped and pulled. He had little doubt that Temple had been wasting time. But his expression changed, as he pulled at the door. It did not come open.

" Bless my soul ! " ejaculated Mr. Capper.

" You—you see, sir——"

" It is extraordinary," said Mr. Capper. " There was nothing amiss with the door yesterday. However, I shall get it open."

Having ascertained that the handle was turned, and the latch drawn, Mr. Capper braced himself to pull. He pulled in vain. Temple watched him : the whole Fourth Form watched him. It was quite a singular episode, and a good deal more interesting than geography.

" Upon my word ! " gasped Mr. Capper. " It—it appears to be jammed somehow, Temple, as you said !

It is—is unlatched, and—and yet it does not come open !
However, I shall certainly open it."

And Mr. Capper, not to be beaten by that obstinate
door, grasped the handle with both hands, planted his
feet firmly on the floor, and tugged.

That did it !

The hapless fat Owl inside, exerting himself to the
uttermost, had been able to resist Temple. But Mr.
Capper was too much for him ! That terrific double-
handed tug by Mr. Capper wrenched the door wide
open : so suddenly that Mr. Capper, taken by surprise
by his own success, staggered back, lost his balance, and
sat down on the floor of the form-room with a resounding
bump.

"Ooooh ! " gasped Mr. Capper, as he bumped.

"Oh, gad ! " stuttered Temple, at what followed. Forth
from the map cupboard came a fat figure, with fat hands
still clinging to the door-handle—no less than William
George Bunter, of the Remove, dragged headlong out of
the cupboard by the opening door.

"Bunter ! " yelled Dabney.

"Bunter ! " roared all the Fourth.

"He—he—he was in the cupboard——! " gasped
Temple. "Holding the door shut, by gad ! Bunter——"

"That fat ass Bunter——"

"That's where he was hiding——"

"Oh, rather ! "

"Ha, ha, ha ! "

Billy Bunter blinked round him through his big spectacles.
He blinked at Mr. Capper, sitting on the floor and gazing
at him like a form-master in a dream—at Cecil Reginald
Temple—at the crowd of Fourth-formers yelling with
laughter.

"Oh, crikey ! " gasped Bunter.

"Ha, ha, ha ! "

"Bib-bub-bob-Bunter ! " stuttered Mr. Capper. "Bob-
bib-bub-Bunter ! Bob-bub-bab-Bunter was in the kik-kik-

cupboard ! It was Bob-bob-Bunter—bless my soul ! " He scrambled breathlessly up. " Boy ! Stop ! "

Bunter flew.

The Fourth-form room, and its map-cupboard, were no longer a refuge for Bunter. Bunter could have made himself quite comfortable in that refuge, with Loder's blankets and pillow, and enjoyed a happy nap while the Fourth were in form—if only that lesson hadn't been geography ! As it was, it behoved Bunter to burn the wind, before Mr. Capper grasped him.

He flew across the form-room for the door on the corridor. After him flew Mr. Capper.

" Bunter ! Stop ! I shall take you to your form-master ! Stop ! " roared Mr. Capper, as he rushed. " Do you hear me ? Bunter ! Boy ! Stop ! "

Bunter tore open the form-room door, with Mr. Capper's extended hand within six inches of his collar. He bounded into the corridor. Mr. Capper, panting, rushed out after him—in time to see a fat flying figure vanish round a corner. Billy Bunter, going strong, was on his travels again !

" Bless my soul ! " gasped Mr. Capper.

Having recovered his breath, Mr. Capper walked along to the Remove room, to apprise Mr. Quelch of the latest development in the Bunter Odyssey. He left his form yelling with laughter. The wild adventures of the fat Owl seemed serious, very serious indeed, to Billy Bunter : but so far as other fellows were concerned, they seemed to add considerably to the gaiety of existence at Greyfriars School.

CHAPTER XXXIII

HORACE KNOWS HOW

COKER of the Fifth frowned.

"It's pretty thick!" he said.

Potter and Greene looked at him over the study table.

"Cutting it like this!" said Coker, warmly.

"Well, you cut it," said Potter.

"What?"

"You cut it, old chap," said Greene.

Coker stared at them.

They were at tea, in Coker's study.

There was toast for tea. Coker had sliced the loaf, Potter had toasted the slices at the study fire, Greene had buttered them with margarine. Now the three Fifth-form men were travelling through the toast, with the assistance of jam and marmalade.

Coker had been looking thoughtful. He had been silent, since they sat down to tea. Potter and Greene hoped that he would keep it up. Silence never seemed so golden, to Potter and Greene, as when Horace Coker wasn't talking.

But that was too much to hope. Coker, after several minutes of thoughtful silence, broke it with the remark that it was pretty thick, cutting it like this: a remark which Potter and Greene naturally supposed to refer to the toast that Coker was devouring in considerable quantities. The toast was, in fact, fairly thick: Coker had a heavy hand with a bread-knife, as with everything else.

"Gone mad?" asked Coker, staring at his comrades. "Or are you trying to be funny, or what? I said it was pretty thick, cutting it like this."

"Well, who cut it?" said Potter.

"Eh! You know that as well as I do! Young Bunter——"

" What ? "

Coker had politely inquired whether his comrades had gone mad ! They almost wondered, for a moment, whether Coker had ! Not ten minutes ago, they had seen Coker cut the loaf for toast, and he certainly had cut it pretty thick. They could only blink at him.

" Young Bunter ? " repeated Potter.

" Yes ! I suppose you know that he cut it—or do you go about with your eyes shut and your ears bunged up ? " asked Coker, sarcastically.

" Bunter hasn't been here, since the day before yesterday," said Potter, blankly.

" I know that ! "

" Then what the thump do you mean, if you mean anything ? " asked Potter. " I know it's pretty thick : but you cut it yourself——"

" Not ten minutes ago," said Greene. " You cut it, and Potter toasted it, and——"

" You silly ass ! " roared Coker.

" Well, you jolly well know you did," exclaimed Greene, hotly. " Not ten minutes ago, with that bread knife——"

" You blithering cuckoo ! "

" But you did cut it—— ! " gasped Potter.

" Do you think I'm talking about the toast ? " roared Coker.

" Eh ? Aren't you ? "

" No, you fathead ! No, you ass ! "

The toast, apparently, was not, after all, the item at present on the agenda. To what else Coker could possibly be referring, Potter and Greene did not know. Neither did they want to know. However, Horace Coker proceeded to tell them.

" I said it was pretty thick, cutting it like this ! " he hooted. " Not the sort of thing that ought to happen at Greyfriars. It's two or three days now since Bunter cut it, and I say it's too thick."

N

" Oh ! " said Potter and Greene. They understood now the sense in which Coker was using the verb ' to cut '. Coker, it seemed, was interested in the amazing antics of Billy Bunter of the Remove, now the reigning topic in the school. Why Coker was interested in a matter that did not concern him, or the Fifth, in the very least, Potter and Greene, as before, did not know, and did not want to know. But, as before, Coker went on to tell them.

" That fat tick had the cheek to park himself in this study, first of all," he said. " And after he was rooted out, and the pre's got after him, he butted me in the bread-basket——"

" Ha, ha, ha ! " contributed Potter and Greene, involuntarily.

" Oh ! You think that's funny, do you ? " snorted Coker. " Well, it's too thick. Fags can't carry on like this—cutting it, dodging beaks, and butting senior men in the bread-basket. From what I hear, that young smudge bagged something from his beak's study, and he's going to be bunked when they snaffle him. Well, the sooner the better, in my opinion."

" Oh, quite," said Potter. " Pass the jam ! "

" But can they snaffle him ? " said Coker, derisively. " All the prefects are after him, and a fat lot of good they are. Wingate's an ass. He's no more able to catch a runaway fag, than to pick a good man from the Fifth for the first eleven ! But this isn't going on."

" No business of ours, is it ? " asked Potter.

" Don't be an ass, Potter ! This kind of thing won't do for Greyfriars," said Coker. " As the pre's can't do anything, I'm taking the matter in hand. That's what I've been thinking out. I've been thinking——"

" You have ? " asked Potter, as if surprised.

" Yes, I have ! What do you mean, Potter ? "

" Oh ! Nothing ! Carry on, old man."

" I'm going to hand that young sweep over to the Head, and now I've thought it out, I know how ! It's not quite so tough as the beaks and pre's seem to think—I can handle it all right."

" Know where he is ? " asked Greene.

" Nobody knows where he is, fathead, or they'd have had him before this."

" You're going to collar him without knowing where he is ? " asked Potter, blandly : with a private wink at Greene.

" Exactly ! " said Coker, calmly.

" Oh ! " said Potter and Greene.

" He was rooted out of Capper's form-room this morning," went on Coker. "Looks as if he snoozed there, as they found blankets and things in the cupboard—missing from a study in the Sixth, I hear. Capper ought to have grabbed him—but he let him get away. Mary saw him scooting up the stairs afterwards—the housemaid, you know—that fat idiot crashed into her Hoover the other day, and bottled it—well, Mary saw him scooting up—lots of fellows know. He never came down again—he's up in the attics some-where—lots of odd spots where a fellow can park himself out of sight. The pre's have been rooting after him—but have they found him ? "

Coker snorted.

" They haven't—and they won't ! But there's one thing that they haven't thought of—and I have ! " said Coker, triumphantly.

" Give it a name, old man," yawned Potter, helping himself to marmalade.

" What about food ? " asked Coker.

" This grub's all right, old bean—toast and marmalade, for tea——"

" You silly idiot ! I mean what about food for Bunter ? " hooted Coker. " A fellow can't live without food—especially a greedy little pig like Bunter, who was always snooping tuck from the studies. He can hide as long as he jolly well likes—but he will have to come out of his hide-out for food."

"They'll get him, if he shows up."

"He won't show up! I've thought all that out," explained Coker. "He will sneak out late, after everybody's gone to bed. That's what he did the first night, when he snooped a pie, and I'll bet he snooped something from a study last night, too! That's what he will do to-night, see?"

"Shouldn't wonder," assented Potter.

"And that's where I come in," said Coker. "He's somewhere up in the attics—and to get anywhere where there's grub, he will have to come down past the study landing. And that's where he's going to be collared."

"Oh!" ejaculated Potter and Greene together.

"He will leave it late, to be safe, I expect," said Coker. "He can leave it till midnight, if he likes—he's going to be bagged all the same."

"But we shall be in the dorm, if it's late," said Potter.

"Dorm at nine-forty-five, you know," remarked Greene.

"Think I'd forgotten that?" snorted Coker.

"Oh! Hadn't you?"

"No!" roared Coker. "I hadn't! Now, as I planned this thing, we three turn out of the dorm at, say, half-past ten——"

"Wha-a-at?"

"—and keep watch on the study landing, in the dark, till that fat little scoundrel comes down rooting for food——"

Potter and Greene gazed at Coker. If Horace James Coker supposed that they, George Potter and William Greene, were going to turn out of bed after lights out, and incur all possible penalties for breaking dormitory bounds, for the pleasure of standing about on a cold landing in the dark, Horace James Coker had another guess coming. They did not speak—they just gazed at him.

"But——!" went on Coker, shaking his head.

"But——!" murmured Potter.

"I fancy I'd better do it alone," said Coker. "Sorry, and all that—I'd like your company, and you're my pals : but you're rather fatheads, if you don't mind my mentioning it——"

"Oh !" gasped Potter. "Not at all."

"I mean to say, if that fat tick hears a sound, and takes the alarm, he will bolt like a rabbit, and we should have had all our trouble for nothing," explained Coker. "That's not what we want—and ten to one you fellows would bungle it. I mean, you know what you are !" added Coker, argumentatively.

"Oh ! Yes ! But——"

"No good jawing, Potter—I've got that settled," said Coker. "I'd like your company, as I've said : but this is a matter of strategy, and I'm going to handle it alone."

Coker spoke decidedly.

Potter closed one eye—the furthest from Coker—at Greene. Greene just contrived to change a chuckle into a cough.

"Sorry, and all that," said Coker. "But that's that ! You fellows stick in bed to-night, and leave it to me. I've the brains for it, you know. I'll tell you about it afterwards."

"Oh ! Do !" gasped Potter and Greene.

"Leave it at that !" said Coker.

With great cordiality, Potter and Greene left it at that. They were prepared to argue with Coker, to row with him, even to sit on his head, if he sought to drag them out of their warm beds at half-past ten. But they were more than willing to leave it at that. And it was left at that !

CHAPTER XXXIV

CAUGHT IN THE DARK

Dark and gloomy, and more than a little draughty and chilly, was the study landing, when eleven strokes boomed out from the clock-tower of Greyfriars in the misty night.

It was not only dark and gloomy. It was, in fact, as black as a hat. Horace Coker could not have seen his hand before his face, if he had had any fancy so to do.

He was feeling the draught. His fingers and toes were chilly. He was sleepy. But he was a sticker. Having set his hand to the plough, as it were, he was not going to turn back.

But it was not a pleasant vigil. It was unpleasant.

Coker was accustomed to putting in solid sleep of a night. But he had not ventured to close his eyes when the Fifth went to bed at nine-forty-five, lest he should fail to reopen them at the appointed time. Potter and Greene and the rest of the Fifth had gone to sleep. Coker, almost propping his eyes open, had remained a lone watcher of the night.

At half-past ten he had emerged.

He put on a coat over his pyjamas. He put on his socks. But he did not venture to add any further footgear—for silence was essential. In his socks, Coker crept from the dormitory, down the stair, and reached the study landing. He made no sound. And having groped his way to the oaken banisters that overlooked the well of the great staircase, Coker leaned on those banisters, and waited. He was still waiting when eleven chimed out.

His feet were getting very cold. His fingers were chilly. He nodded every now and then, but pulled himself up. He was bored and tired of the darkness, the silence, and his lonely vigil. But he was a sticker—and he stuck !

He was, at least, cheered by the reflection that he was going to do what the beaks and the Sixth-form prefects had failed to do. That fat tick, Bunter of the Remove, had evaded pursuit and capture for two or three days—setting authority at defiance, causing no end of commotion. That, in Coker's opinion, was a scandalous state of things, and he, Horace James Coker, was going to put a stop to it.

He knew how. That fat tick was absolutely certain to come scouting out for grub during the night. If he did, he had to materialise on that landing. He would not see Coker in the dark. Neither would Coker see him. But Coker would hear him—and grab !

It was as simple as that !

Coker—in the intervals of nodding drowsily—listened intently. He heard the wind that moaned over ancient roofs, and the rustle of old ivy outside windows. He heard the faint cracking of time-worn wainscot : and in fact all the faint, mysterious sounds that are heard when a building is silent in the dead of night. But he did not hear a footstep—which was what he wanted to hear. No doubt that fat tick was leaving it late, for safety.

Suddenly, Coker gave a start.

He had heard nothing—or if he had, it was so faint a sound that he could not define it. But he had a feeling that he was no longer alone in the dark.

It was rather a creepy feeling.

But Coker was not given to nerves. His practical mind did not run to ghosts or burglars. If he had heard anybody, it was Bunter : and it occurred to him that that fat tick might be creeping on tiptoe, perhaps in his socks like Coker, and that there would be no footfalls to be heard.

He listened intently, quite wide awake now.

Again the faintest of sounds—a sort of faint brushing sound, it seemed to Coker. Someone was there—on that vast landing in the dark. He was sure of that. But whoever it was, was as cautious as Coker himself—making no sound, or next to no sound.

That made Coker's task more difficult. He had counted on a footfall, not expecting this excessive caution on the part of a fat Remove tick. He had to know where the tick was, before he rushed and grabbed. If he missed him in the dark, the fat tick would bolt—and there were several staircases, and quite a number of passages, that opened from the study landing—innumerable avenues of retreat for a startled tick! A wild chase up and down passages and staircases in the dark was not Coker's programme.

He strained his ears. They were large, and the reception was good. This time he was sure that he located that faint sound.

At one spot on the landing, backing to the old oaken balustrade, was a long settee. Coker was standing within a few yards of it, as he leaned on the old oak rail. And he was as good as certain that what he had heard, was the sound of somebody sitting down, carefully and stealthily, on that settee.

This was rather a puzzle.

Bunter, when he came, might be expected to head for the nearest source of provender—the studies, or the lower stairs as the way to the pantry. It was quite unexpected for him to sit down on the settee. He was fat and lazy, no doubt, but it was hardly the time and place for him to sit down and rest.

Still, Coker could believe his ears. Someone was quite close at hand in the dark, and that someone had sat down on the settee. Why he had done so did not really matter very much—the fact was enough.

It was time for Coker to go into action.

He knew where his man was now : and he knew exactly what he was going to do.

Silent in his socks, suppressing his breathing, Coker of the Fifth moved slowly and cautiously along the oaken balustrade towards the settee.

He could not see it : but he ascertained its location suddenly, by his knee knocking against it when he reached it.

The sound of the impact was slight. But it seemed to have caught wary ears, for following it, Coker heard a sharp intake of breath in the dark. Whoever was sitting on the settee had heard him, and was startled.

Further caution was unnecessary, and might waste precious moments. Coker rushed.

A split second, and his grasp was on an unseen figure on the settee. There was no time, no chance, for that unseen figure to dodge. Coker had him !

He heard a startled gasp as his clutch closed.

" Oooooooh ! "

His clutch closed like a steel vice. Coker's hands were extensive and strong, and there was plenty of beef in his grasp.

" Got you ! " panted Coker.

He had got him—there was no mistake about that. His stout right arm was round an unseen neck, tightening like the grip of a boa-constrictor, and must have almost choked the unhappy victim. His left hand grasped an arm. Coker had got him—utterly.

" Gurrrggh ! " came in suffocated accents. " Gurrrggh ! "

The unseen figure struggled, frantically.

Coker had hardly expected that. He had not looked for resistance from a fat tick like Bunter. But he was quite ready to deal with it. That choking right arm constricted the hapless victim's neck yet more tightly : and Coker's left was like a pair of pincers on the unseen arm. He could struggle if he liked : Coker had him all right.

" Wurrrggh ! Urrrgh ! Woooooh ! " gurgled the unseen one, apparently trying to speak. " Gurrrrrrggh ! "

With unexpected strength, on the part of a fat tick, the unseen one gave grasp for grasp, and Coker, to his surprise, staggered backwards. But he did not let go—that bearlike hug never slackened. He had him, and he was keeping him.

MR. PROUT STARED AT COKER

"You silly fathead, chuck it!" panted Coker. "I've got you."

The unseen one did not chuck it. Exerting strength that was quite amazing in a fat tick, he pitched Coker off, and dragged his suffering neck free. Coker heard him panting wildly for breath.

But Coker was off only for a second. He was not giving that fat tick a chance to dodge away in the dark. He fairly hurled himself at the panting figure, and they went down on the landing together, Coker on top, with a bump and a crash. Then there was a wild and whirling struggle in the dark: in the midst of which, a door was heard to open, and a voice called:

"What is that noise? What is that disturbance? Who is that?" It was the boom of Mr. Prout, master of the Fifth. Evidently, Prout had awakened.

Coker gave a panting shout.

"This way, sir! I've caught Bunter."

"What? What?"

"Bunter, sir—I've caught Bunter! Put on a light, sir."

"Bless my soul!"

There were sounds of groping movements in the dark. Then a light flashed on, illuminating the landing. Coker, with a sinewy knee planted on a wriggling, struggling form, stared across at Prout, in a voluminous dressing-gown, and called: and Mr. Prout, with an extraordinary expression on his face, stared at Coker.

"This way, sir! I've got him!"

"Coker——"

"I've got him, sir——"

"Are you mad, Coker?"

"What——"

"What are you doing to Mr. Quelch?" roared Prout.

CHAPTER XXXV

NOT BUNTER

" Mr. Quelch ! "

Coker stuttered that name.

He had been looking at Prout. Now he looked down at his capture. It was not easy for Coker to believe his eyes, when, for the first time, he saw who it was that he had caught in the dark.

Not for a moment had he doubted, or dreamed of doubting, that it was that fat tick, Bunter of the Remove.

But it wasn't ! It was nothing like Bunter. It bore not the remotest resemblance to Bunter. Coker's sinewy knee was planted on Mr. Quelch, the master of the Remove : it was Mr. Quelch's angular, infuriated face that stared up at him—it was Quelch, Henry Samuel Quelch, who was panting and gurgling helplessly for breath, unable to speak, unable to do anything but gurgle and splutter.

Coker gazed at him.

It was Quelch ! Not Bunter, but Quelch ! If his capture had turned out to be, not Bunter, but the Emperor of Abyssinia, or the President of the United States, it could not have astonished Coker more. He could hardly believe that it was Quelch ! He almost doubted the evidence of his eyes. But it was Quelch !

" Oh ! " gasped Coker.

He released his victim. He removed his sinewy knee, which had been squeezing the last ounce of wind out of the Remove master. He staggered to his feet. He backed away. The back of his knees contacted the edge of the settee, and he sat down, rather suddenly. He sat there helplessly, staring with popping eyes.

" Quelch ! " gasped Mr. Prout. " My dear fellow— what—— ? "

" Urrrrrggh ! "

" What—what—what—— ? "

" Gurrrrggh ! "

Mr. Quelch sat up, on the floor. He gasped and gurgled for breath. Prout advanced, and gave him a hand up. Slowly and painfully, Mr. Quelch resumed the perpendicular. He leaned on the stout Prout.

" Wurrrrggh ! " he mumbled. " Urrrgh ! I—I—I—gurrggh ! "

" Coker ! What—— ? "

" Oh, crikey ! " moaned Coker.

" What are you doing out of your dormitory, Coker ? "

" I—I—I—oh, jiminy ! "

" And you, my dear Quelch—what—what—— ? "

" Urrgh ! I—I am breathless ! " Quelch was finding his voice, at last. " I—I—that insensate boy—that block-head—ooooogh ! "

" But what—— ? "

Quelch, with an effort, pulled himself together a little. The glint in his eyes, as he looked at the dismayed Coker, was positively deadly. Coker could only gaze pop-eyed at him, even yet hardly able to believe that it was Quelch.

" I—I came——" Quelch tried to speak calmly. " I came up to this landing from my study, Mr. Prout, to sit there on that settee, in the dark, to watch for that trouble-some boy Bunter, who, I have no doubt, will leave his hiding-place in search of food during the night—gurrrggh ! "

" Oh ! " gasped Coker.

It had not occurred to Coker that anyone else might have guessed Bunter's probable tactics that night ! He was not aware that his own powerful intellect was equalled by any other at Greyfriars. It dawned upon him now that Quelch had had the same idea !

" I sat on that settee," said Mr. Quelch, after another gurgle. " And when I heard a sound, I had no doubt that it was Bunter. And then—wurrrggh ! "

Quelch broke off, for another gurgle.

" And then—suddenly—that—that insensate boy—that
—that blockhead—that—that—that Coker—sprang on me
in the dark ! " gasped Quelch. " He sprang on me like—
like—like a tiger——"

" Bless my soul ! "

" Oh, crumbs ! " moaned Coker.

" Unless he is insane, I cannot understand his action !
He sprang on me in the dark——"

" I—I—I—— " babbled Coker.

" Coker ! What is the meaning of this ? " thundered
Prout. " What—— ? "

" I—I—I thought it was Bunter, sir," moaned Coker.
" I—I—I never knew Mr. Quelch was up—never dreamed—
oh, crikey—I—I—I thought it was that fat tick—I—I mean
Bunter ! I—I was watching for—for Bunter, sir, and—
and I couldn't see in the dark, and—and—and—oh, crikey ! "

" And for what reason, Coker, were you meddling in a
matter with which you have no concern ? "

Coker made no reply to that. It was not of much use
to explain to Prout that he was constitutionally incapable
of minding his own business !

" Upon my word ! " boomed Prout. " Coker—— "

" I—I never meant—I—I thought—— "

" Silence ! Mr. Quelch, I can only express my regret,
my very deep regret, that this boy of my form—what did
you say, Quelch ? "

" Gruuugggh."

" Oh ! My regret—my deepest regret—Coker, you
utterly, impenetrably stupid boy—you—you—you—— "
Words and breath seemed to fail Prout together.

" I—I—I was going to kik-kik-catch B-b-b-Bunter—— "

" Silence ! Coker, loth as I am to use the cane in a
senior form, I shall certainly do so on this occasion—— "

" Oh ! " gasped Coker.

" I shall cane you with the greatest severity—— "

" But I—I say, I—I was only—— "

" Silence ! Mr. Quelch, I express once more my deep regret. Coker, follow me downstairs immediately."

Prout swept like a thundercloud to the staircase. Coker feebly picked himself up from the settee, and limply followed him. Quelch was left still gasping and spluttering on the study landing.

Coker followed his form-master downstairs, in the lowest of spirits. Coker, so far as he could see, was in no way to blame. What had happened was unfortunate, Coker admitted that. But his intentions had been good : he had been going to deal with a matter, successfully, that had baffled beaks and prefects for whole days. It was hardly his fault that Quelch had come up quietly to the study landing with precisely the same object : still less his fault that, not being able to see like a cat in the dark, he had collared Quelch supposing him to be Bunter. But both Prout and Quelch seemed to think that Coker was to blame somehow.

Prout switched on lights, and stalked ahead, with dressing-gown billowing. Coker almost limped after him to his study.

In that study, Prout selected a cane : seldom used, but now about to get a little unaccustomed exercise. He fixed Coker with a baleful eye.

" Take off that overcoat, Coker ! "

Coker breathed very hard. He would have preferred to keep that overcoat on—not only because the night was chilly ! Pyjamas were a very poor protection against a cane—especially as Prout's whole aspect indicated that he was going to lay it on with unaccustomed vim.

Coker peeled off the overcoat, slowly.

" Now bend over that chair, Coker ! "

" I—I—I was only going to catch Bunter, sir——"

" I have told you to bend over that chair, Coker ! "

Breathing still harder, Coker bent over the chair. Up went the cane in Prout's stout right hand. Down it came —swiping !

" Oooooh ! " gasped Coker.

Seldom was a cane used in a senior form. But what followed showed that Prout had not forgotten how to handle it.

Six times that cane came down on Coker's pyjamas. Coker wriggled, squirmed, gasped, and finally roared. Prout stopped at six—though he looked very much disposed to go on. However, he laid down the cane.

" Coker ! Return to your dormitory immediately ! If you leave it again after lights out, you will be reported to Dr. Locke for a flogging ! Go."

Coker went.

Quelch was gone, when he repassed the study landing, on his way up. No doubt, after what had happened, Mr. Quelch was no longer feeling disposed to sit up keeping watch and ward for Bunter. Coker was no longer thinking of either Quelch or Bunter—he had nearer considerations to think about. He wriggled his way up the dormitory staircase, tottered to his bed, and almost collapsed into it. After which, the nocturnal silence in the Fifth-form dormitory was broken by spasmodic gasps, grunts, and ejaculations, from Coker's bed.

" Oh ! ow ! wow ! Oggh ! Wooogh ! Oh ! Ow ! "

Two fellows, in the beds on either side of Coker's woke and peered into the gloom.

" That you, Coker ? " murmured Potter.

" Wow ! "

" Been out after Bunter ? " asked Greene.

" Yow-ow ! "

" Anything happened ? "

" Woooh ! That old ass, Prout, whopped me, because I got that other old ass, Quelch, in the dark, thinking it was Bunter——"

" Ha, ha, ha ! "

" Oh ! Laugh ! " hissed Coker. " Funny, ain't it ! Six on my pyjamas—six of the best ! Ow ! wow ! Woooh ! Well, I can tell you I'm fed up ! That fat tick, Bunter, can cruise about the House every night this term, for all I care—I shan't interfere! I'm not going to do the prefects' work for them! Or the beaks', either! I shall just leave the lot of them to stew in their own juice! Wow! And," added Coker, in a sulphurous voice, "if I hear another snigger from you, I'll turn out with my bolster, and give you something to snigger about."

After which Coker did not hear another snigger from Potter or Greene: though until they fell asleep again Potter and Greene heard a succession of mumbles, moans, grunts and groans, from Coker.

O

CHAPTER XXXVI

QUELCH ON THE TRAIL

Snore!

"Hallo, hallo, hallo!" roared Bob Cherry.

Snore!

"Great pip!"

Snore!

"The great-pipfulness is terrific."

The rising-bell was ringing in the misty morning. The forms at Greyfriars were turning out at the clang of the bell. The Lower Fourth Form turned out to the surprise of their lives.

Up to a few days ago, a deep and resonant snore, to the accompaniment of the rising-bell, had not been an unaccustomed sound in the Remove dormitory. Billy Bunter seldom woke till some kindly fellow hurled a boot, or dragged off blankets. But of late, Bunter had not been seen there, and his snore had not been heard—he had been both invisible and inaudible. And now——!

Snore!

"Bunter!" gasped Harry Wharton.

"Bunter!"

"Here——!"

"In bed——!"

"Oh, my hat!"

"The esteemed and idiotic Bunter!"

Bunter's bed was no longer unoccupied. A fat head was on the pillow. Two little round eyes were clamped shut. A mouth of considerable extent was open. It was Bunter: fast asleep and snoring: his echoing snore competing, as of old, with the clang of the rising-bell.

The Remove fellows gathered round that bed, staring at Bunter. They could hardly believe their eyes or their

ears. Where Bunter had been, nobody knew : except that
he was supposed to have parked himself in remote attics.
Since then he had evidently been somewhere where there
was food. There were smears of jam on the fat face on
the pillow. Crumbs of cakes adhered to the smears of
jam. Bunter had not gone supperless to bed.

" Oh, gad ! " said Lord Mauleverer. " If a pre looked
in now——"

" Or Quelch—— ! " grinned the Bounder.

" They'd have him ! " said Bob Cherry. " Better wake
him up."

Bob hooked back the bedclothes, grasped a fat shoulder,
and shook. There was a sleepy mumble from Billy Bunter.

" Urrgh ! Leggo ! Beast ! 'Tain't rising-bell ! Leggo."

" Ha, ha, ha ! "

" Wake up, you fat ass ! " chuckled Bob.

" Beast ! Shan't ! Leave a fellow alone ! Groooh."

" Ha, ha, ha ! "

Shake ! shake ! shake ! A visit from a beak or a prefect,
at rising-bell, was not perhaps likely : but it might happen,
with beaks and prefects on the prowl for Bunter. It was
only good-natured to warn the fat Owl that Greyfriars
was astir.

" Oh ! " Billy Bunter opened his eyes, and blinked at
a crowd of staring faces. " Oh ! I say, you fellows, is
that rising-bell ? "

" It is—it are ! " said Bob.

Bunter groped for his spectacles, and jammed them on
his fat little nose. Then he put a fat leg out of bed.

" What are you doing here, you fat ass ? " asked Harry
Wharton. " Made up your mind to give yourself up ? "

" No fear ! Not till that postal order's found ! I say,
have you fellows found it yet ? " asked Bunter.

" Let's go through his pockets, and find it for him now ! "
suggested Skinner.

" Ha, ha, ha ! "

" Oh, really, Skinner ! I say, you fellows, I had to

come here to sleep," said Bunter. " It was too jolly cold up in the attics, and I had to leave Loder's blankets in old Capper's form-room, you know——"

" Ha, ha, ha ! "

" Keep it dark ! I shall be able to come back again to-night if old Quelch doesn't get wise to it ! I say, gimme my clothes—gimme me shoes, Wharton—gimme my trousers, Nugent—gimme my jacket, Toddy—I say, mind you don't drop anything out of the pockets."

Billy Bunter was generally a slow and late riser. But on this occasion he was quite brisk. Now that the school was astir, he realised that he had better get back to his hide-out in the shortest possible time.

He bundled on clothes. As he did so, a tin of sardines dropped from one pocket, and a stream of biscuits from another.

" Hallo, hallo, hallo ! Whose sardines ? " exclaimed Bob Cherry.

" Whose biscuits ? " grinned the Bounder.

" The whosefulness is terrific."

" I say, you fellows, pick those things up for me, will you ? " exclaimed Bunter, hastily. " I say, I was awfully hungry up in the attics, and when I came down to look for some grub, there was a row going on on the study landing—I heard Quelch and Prout—and I had to go back. I had to wait an awful long time before it was safe to go to the Remove studies."

" What did you want to go to the Remove studies for ? " grinned Bob.

" Well, I knew you fellows wouldn't mind, being pals," said Bunter. " If you knew how awfully hungry I was——"

" If you've been to my study——" exclaimed the Bounder.

" Oh ! I haven't, Smithy ! If you miss any sardines, or biscuits, I don't know anything about them, Smithy."

" Ha, ha, ha ! "

" You fat brigand——"

" If you're going to be mean about a spot of tuck, Smithy, I'll pay for it, when my postal order comes. I never touched the cake in your study. If it's gone, I never ate it."

" Ha, ha, ha ! "

Billy Bunter, evidently, had had supper in the Remove studies. With an eye to the future, he had packed his pockets with as much as they would hold—rather more, in fact, for as he bundled on his clothes, more and more edibles dropped from them. As he clutched up the tin of sardines, biscuits shot from one pocket, a wedge of cake from another, and a bag of bullseyes from a third. And as he clawed up biscuits and bullseyes, he shed apples, nuts, and scones.

" I say, Harry, old chap, squint into the passage and see if anybody's about, before I cut," said Bunter. " I can't stay here, you know."

" O.K." said the captain of the Remove, and he crossed to the dormitory door, opened it, and glanced out.

The next moment he jumped, at the sight of an angular figure and a frowning face down the corridor.

" Oh, my hat ! Quelch ! "

Billy Bunter gave a squeak of alarm.

" Oh, crikey ! Is the beast coming here ? What the thump is he coming here for ? He never comes here at rising-bell——"

" He's in the passage."

" Oh, lor' ! "

" The game's up, old fat man," grinned the Bounder.

" The upfulness is terrific."

" I—I—I say, Wharton, see if he's coming this way. Perhaps—perhaps he ain't coming here ! " gasped Bunter.

Harry Wharton glanced out of the doorway again. With the Remove master in the corridor, Bunter's escape from the dormitory was cut off. If Quelch was coming there—— !

Quelch, at the moment, was standing in the corridor, staring at some small object on the floor. Wharton stared at it from the door, and discerned that it was a biscuit. Then he understood. Glancing past Mr. Quelch, he spotted several more biscuits strewn along the passage, several bulls-eyes, and a chunk of cake. Quelch was following a trail!

"Oh, scissors!" gasped the captain of the Remove.

Evidently Billy Bunter, in the studies, had packed his pockets not wisely but too well! Small objects had exuded here and there on his way to the dormitory. He had left a trail behind him, which it did not need a Chingachgook to follow! And Quelch was on the trail!

"Is—is—is he coming?" gasped Bunter, as Harry Wharton turned back from the door.

"He's coming."

"I—I say, I—I'll get under the bed! The beast can't know I'm here——"

"He jolly well does—he's following a trail of biscuits——"

"Wha-a-at?"

"Ha, ha, ha!" yelled the juniors.

"Oh, crikey!"

"You were spilling the loot all the way here last night, you fat chump——"

"Ha, ha, ha!"

"Oh, lor'!"

Mr. Quelch's tread was heard in the passage now. Apparently he had made up his mind whither that trail led, and was coming on to the dormitory.

Billy Bunter stood, for a moment or two, blinking like a scared owl. But his fat wits worked, under the spur of peril. He made a jump, and backed behind the open door of the dormitory.

A moment more, and Mr. Quelch appeared in the doorway. He fixed a pair of gimlet-eyes on the crowd of Remove fellows in pyjamas.

"Bunter is here!" he rapped. "I am assured of it—he is here! Bunter, where are you? Bunter!"

Mr. Quelch strode into the dormitory, his gimlet-eyes searching for a fat figure. Behind him, the fat figure darted out from behind the door, and shot into the passage.

" Bunter ! Where are you, Bunter ? Bunter—why—what——" Mr. Quelch spun round, just in time to see the fat figure vanish. " Why—why—what—Bunter—stop —I command you to stop—Bunter—— ! " Quelch, with billowing gown, swept out of the doorway in pursuit.

" Oh, my hat ! " gasped Bob Cherry. " Poor old Bunter ! "

" Ha, ha, ha ! "

The juniors crammed the doorway, staring down the passage. Bunter, heading for the landing, was going at about 60 m.p.h. shedding biscuits, cake, apples, and all sorts of edibles from his pockets, as he careered frantically on. Behind him rushed Quelch, also going strong.

" He'll get him—— ! " said the Bounder.

" Got him ! "

" No——"

" Yes——"

" Oh, my hat ! "

" Man down ! "

" Ha, ha, ha ! "

Indubitably, Quelch would have ' got him ' : had he not stumbled, and slipped, on a tin of sardines shed by the careering Owl in his flight. But he did stumble, and he did slip : and he sat down : and before he was on his feet again, Billy Bunter had vanished.

CHAPTER XXXVII

CORNERED

" THIS cannot continue, Mr. Quelch."

" Certainly not, sir."

" The—the state of affairs is—is extraordinary ! " said Dr. Locke.

" Very ! " said Mr. Quelch.

" The boy must be found."

" I agree, sir."

" He must be found without further delay," said the Head. " It is absolutely essential, Mr. Quelch, that the boy should be found without further delay."

Mr. Quelch made no rejoinder to that.

He agreed with the Head : in principle, as it were. Obviously, the boy had to be found, and without delay. The present state of affairs was not only extraordinary : it was intolerable. Mr. Prout, in Common-room, had described it as unprecedented and unparalleled. Really, it was all that, and more. Only—the boy could not be found !

Dr. Locke's face was very grave. Quelch's was grave also, with deep annoyance mingled with its gravity. Quelch, as the missing junior's form-master, was really responsible. And he seemed quite unable to deal with this extraordinary, intolerable, unprecedented, and unparalleled state of affairs.

It was extremely annoying and disturbing to Mr. Quelch. A boy in his form, whom he had been marching to his head-master for judgment, had eluded him, and for whole days remained at large about the school : causing excitement, merriment, and general commotion. It could not go on. Yet, apparently, it had to ! For once more Billy Bunter had vanished as completely as if he had borrowed the cloak-of-darkness in the fairy tale. Somewhere within the wide walls of Greyfriars School lurked an elusive fat Owl. But where ?

"On Tuesday," resumed Dr. Locke, "this boy eluded you, Mr. Quelch ! It is now Friday morning."

Mr. Quelch did not really need that information. He had a calendar in his own study. He made no reply.

"This cannot continue !" repeated the Head.

They were in the head-master's study. It was morning break. The Head had requested Mr. Quelch to see him in his study after second school. Only too well aware that the matter to be discussed was Bunter, Quelch had come reluctantly : but he had come.

Dr. Locke sat at his writing-table, on which he gently drummed with slim fingers. Mr. Quelch sat on a chair at that table, feeling a good deal like a culprit. It was, in fact, his duty to produce Bunter. And he could not produce Bunter.

"It is extraordinary," went on the Head. "Where can the boy be ? It is very unfortunate that you did not —hem—secure him, when it transpired that he had spent the night in his own dormitory."

"Very unfortunate," agreed Mr. Quelch.

"But since then——"

"He was seen," said Mr. Quelch. "Several boys saw him running down the dormitory staircase—and Wingate caught sight of him, in the distance, at the corner of this corridor——"

"But since—— ? "

"Since then he has not been seen."

"You do not think he has quitted the House, Mr. Quelch ? "

"That is scarcely possible, sir, unobserved."

"Or escaped into the attics—— ? "

"He would have been observed, sir."

"Then it would appear that the boy is concealed some-where on the ground floor of the building ? "

" It would appear so, sir."

" He must be discovered, Mr. Quelch."

" Undoubtedly, sir."

The Head drummed on the table again. He was at a
loss. Quelch was at a loss. The fattest and most fatuous
member of the Greyfriars community had, in fact, both of
them beaten. The elusive Owl had had no chance of
getting out of the House unseen—no chance of dodging
back into the rambling attics at the top of the building
—he was somewhere among the studies and form-rooms :
but where ?

Tap !

The door opened, and Wingate of the Sixth appeared.
The Head glanced at him inquiringly : Quelch eagerly.

" Has the boy been found, Wingate ? " asked the Head.

" I am sorry, sir, no ! We have searched pretty nearly
everywhere, sir, but I can only report that we have seen
nothing of Bunter."

" Please continue the search, Wingate."

" Very well, sir."

The Greyfriars' captain retired and shut the door.

" It is really amazing, Mr. Quelch," said Dr. Locke.
" Where can the boy be ? I understand that he was seen
on one occasion in the music-room——"

" He is not there now, sir."

" And on another occasion in a junior form-room—
Mr. Capper's, I think—hidden in some recess——"

" Every form-room has been searched, sir."

" It is amazing ! " said the Head. " Is it possible, Mr.
Quelch, that he may have had the temerity, the audacity,
to conceal himself in some master's study ? "

Mr. Quelch did not reply. He did not seem to hear.
He was not looking at the Head. His eyes had suddenly
fixed on a spot on the Head's carpet. He gazed at that
spot as if it fascinated him.

Dr. Locke glanced at him, puzzled, and slightly irritated.
He was accustomed to concentrated attention from mem-

bers of his staff when he addressed them. Quelch, for
the moment, seemed to have forgotten his Chief's existence.

"Mr. Quelch——" The Head's voice had an edge
on it.

"Bless my soul!" exclaimed Mr. Quelch, his gimlet-
eyes still glued on that fascinating spot on the carpet.
"Is it possible—can it be possible—upon my word!"

"Really, Mr. Quelch——" The Head almost snapped.

Still unheeding, Mr. Quelch rose to his feet, and stepped
towards that small spot on the carpet which, after his
eyes had once fallen upon it, had riveted his attention.
He gazed down at it: and Dr. Locke, surprised and
startled, gazed at him. Quelch seemed quite inexplicable
to the Head, at that moment.

"Upon my word!" repeated Mr. Quelch, his eyes
glinting.

"Mr. Quelch!" the Head rapped. "Will you have
the goodness to explain——"

"Yes, sir!" Mr. Quelch took note of his Chief's existence
at length. "Look at this, sir—I did not observe it when I
entered the study, but now that I notice it—look——" A
lean fore-finger pointed at the spot on the carpet.

"I had not observed it at all, Mr. Quelch, and I fail
to see any reason for giving it attention now." Dr. Locke's
voice had sharpened. "Really, Mr. Quelch——"

"It is a squashed biscuit, sir."

"A—a—a biscuit?"

"On which someone has trodden," said Mr. Quelch.
"Undoubtedly a biscuit, trodden on, and trodden into
the carpet—recently. It must have been dropped since
the maids were here this morning, or it would have been
swept away."

"Undoubtedly," said the Head. "I understand from
Mrs. Kebble that the vacuum-sweeper is out of action,
owing to some accident, and indeed I think she mentioned
that a young man is coming from Courtfield this morning
to repair it. But the carpet must have been attended to

by other means, I imagine. If you are sure, Mr. Quelch, that that is a biscuit——"

" It is—or was—a biscuit, sir."

" Then it must have been dropped here, Mr. Quelch——"

" And recently, sir——"

Dr. Locke rose to his feet. There was a trace of excitement now in his scholarly face. He knew what was in the Remove master's mind.

" Mr. Quelch! You mentioned that you traced that troublesome boy, Bunter, this morning, by edible articles—particularly biscuits—which he had dropped——"

" Precisely, sir."

" And now——"

" Now, sir—— ! " breathed Mr. Quelch.

" Bless my soul ! " said the Head.

The same thought was in both minds. It was one more spot of ' sign ' in the trail of the vanished Owl. And this time it was in the Head's study ! Bunter had vanished—somewhere—among the apartments on the ground floor : almost innumerable apartments, without leaving a clue—till the gimlet-eyes spotted that section of a squashed biscuit !

" He has been here ! " breathed the Head.

" He has been here ! " repeated Mr. Quelch, like an echo.

" In this study ! " said the Head.

" In this study ! " echoed Quelch.

" His Head-master's study—what audacity—what effrontery—what temerity ! His Head-master's study——"

" His Head-master's study," assented Quelch, still understudying Echo.

" Mr. Quelch ! Can—can—can the boy still be here ? " Dr. Locke almost gasped. " Is—is—is it possible—is it conceivable—that the wretched boy may be, at this very moment, concealed in this very study ? "

Mr. Quelch's jaw squared.

" That, sir, is what I propose immediately to ascertain," he said, grimly.

" Pray do so, Mr. Quelch, without delay ! "

Mr. Quelch proceeded to do so without delay. He ducked a tall head to glance under the writing-table. He ducked it lower to glance under a settee by the window. He circumnavigated a screen—he looked behind a book-case. Then he twirled away a high-backed arm-chair that stood in a corner—— And then—— !

" Oh, crikey ! "

" Bunter ! " almost shouted Mr. Quelch.

" Bunter ! " thundered the Head.

" Oh, lor' ! "

Sitting in the angle of the wall, hitherto hidden by the arm-chair, was a fat figure, crumpled in that confined space : and a pair of little round eyes blinked through a pair of big spectacles, in terror, at the two masters, as they gazed at the elusive Owl of the Remove—cornered at last !

CHAPTER XXXVIII

STERN JUDGMENT

Dr. Locke sat at his writing-table, his brow stern and severe, his eyes fixed on a fat grubby face that confronted him across the table.

Billy Bunter stood before his head-master, with his fat knees knocking together.

Mr. Quelch stood at Bunter's elbow. The fat Owl was to be given no chance to dodge again. At the first sign of dodging, Quelch's steely grip was ready to close on him like a vice.

Bunter's game was up !

For three days—three whole days—had the fat Owl of the Remove dodged beaks, eluded prefects, postponed the head-master's judgment. For three days and nights had his amazing antics lasted. But finis was written, at last, to the exciting Odyssey of the fat and fatuous Owl. Odysseus, after his wanderings, landed in his native isle, whence he had started : Bunter, after his, landed in his head-master's study, whence he also had started ! The long-eluded judgment was now to be pronounced : and it remained only for Bunter to hear the words of doom !

" Bunter ! " The Head's voice was deep.

" Oh, dear ! Yes, sir," mumbled Bunter, with a longing blink at the door.

" For several days, Bunter, you have made it impossible for me to deal with you, by escaping and eluding authority. Now that you stand before me at last, I shall deal with you without delay."

" I—I—I——"

" Mr. Quelch has acquainted me with all the circumstances. On Tuesday this week you abstracted a postal order from his study——"

"I—I thought it was mine, sir," moaned Bunter. "It —it was on my letter, sir, and it was open, and—and I thought Mr. Quelch might have taken it out, sir——"

"Nonsense!"

"I—I mean, I—I thought it might have dropped out, and Mr. Quelch picked it up and put it with the letter——"

"Mr. Quelch was prepared to believe that you might have made so stupid, so absurd, an error, Bunter, making allowance for your stupidity——"

"Oh, really, sir——"

"—if you had returned the postal order——"

"Certainly," said Mr. Quelch. "But——"

"But," said the Head, "you did not return it, Bunter. You admitted to Mr. Quelch, at the door of this study, that it was in your possession, but instead of returning it, you took to flight——"

"I—I didn't, sir!" gasped Bunter. "I—I mean, I— I never meant—oh, lor'——"

"You told me it was in your study?" rapped Mr. Quelch.

"That—that was only a—a—a figure of speech, sir——"

"What?"

"I—I—I meant that it was lost, sir—— That's why I couldn't cash it, sir."

"Upon my word!"

"Having admitted this, you failed to return it," said the Head. "The case is clear, Bunter."

"Quite clear," said Mr. Quelch.

"But—but—but I—I didn't—I hadn't—I—I wasn't!" howled Bunter. "I—I only told Mr. Quelch that to—to get away, sir——"

"What?"

"He had hold of my shoulder, sir," wailed Bunter. "I—I'd have told him anything to make him leggo, sir!"

"Bless my soul!"

"I—I hope you can take my word, sir——!"

The Head gazed at Bunter. In the circumstances, he

was not likely to take his word ! The hapless fat Owl had, in fact, tied himself up hopelessly in the net of his own prevarications. If there was any truth spotted about among his innumerable fibs, the Head was unable to sort it out.

" If you do not tell me the truth, Bunter——! " said Dr. Locke, at last.

" Oh, yes, sir. I always do, sir ! You can ask Mr. Quelch," groaned the fat Owl. " He knows, sir."

" Mr. Quelch tells me that you are the most untruthful boy in his form, Bunter," said the Head, grimly.

" Oh ! Dud-dud-does he, sir ? "

" He does, Bunter ! And I can form my own judgment by what you are saying now," said Dr. Locke. " I cannot believe your assertion that the postal order was lost, Bunter, after your admission to your form-master. Obviously it was your intention to cash it——"

" Oh ! No, sir. It—it was all a mistake ! The—the fact is, sir, that I—I—I never had it at all——"

" You never had it at all ! Did you say that you never had it at all, Bunter ? " ejaculated the Head.

" Yes, sir ! No, sir ! It—it was all a mistake ! I—I never took it at all, sir—it—it wasn't there when I went to Mr. Quelch's study——"

" It was not there ? " repeated the Head, almost dazedly.

" Nunno, sir ! If—if it was, I I never saw it—I—I—I don't know anything about it, sir," moaned Bunter. " N-n-not a thing, sir ! "

" You do not know anything about it, Bunter ? You have just stated that you could not cash it because it was lost."

" Yes, sir ! I couldn't cash it when it was lost, could I, sir ? " gasped Bunter. " There was a jacket in my lining, sir——"

" What ? "

" I mean a lining in my jacket, sir——"

" What does this boy mean, Mr. Quelch ? "

" I hardly know, sir."

" I—I—I mean, a pole in the hocket, sir," stammered Bunter. The fat Owl was a little confused. " That is, I mean, a hole in the pocket—that's how it was lost, sir, —so I—I couldn't cash it, could I, sir ? I—I—I'd forgotten all about that hole in the pocket of my lining, sir——"

" You have admitted that the postal order was in your hands, Bunter——"

" Oh, no, sir ! It wasn't——"

" You have admitted it ! " thundered Dr. Locke.

" But I haven't, sir," wailed Bunter. " It wasn't in my hands, sir ! It wasn't really ! I—I should have been afraid of—of dropping it somewhere, sir ! It—it ,was in my pocket, sir."

" Grant me patience ! " exclaimed Dr. Locke. " When I say in your hands, Bunter, I mean in your possession."

" Oh ! Do you, sir ? "

Dr. Locke drew a deep, deep breath. For a moment, there was silence in the study, and Bunter blinked at his head-master, then at his form-master, and then at his head-master again.

" C-c-can I go now, sir ? " he ventured.

" What ? What did you say, Bunter ? " ejaculated Dr. Locke.

" C-can I—I go now, sir ? "

" Upon my word ! Bunter, you are so untruthful a boy, that it is futile to question you, or to hear a word you say. You have abstracted a postal order for one pound from your form-master's study. If you return it immediately, some credence may be given to your extraordinary explanation that you took it by mistake. If you do not return it, and at once, you will be expelled from this school for pilfering. Now——"

" Oh, jiminy ! "

" That is my decision, Bunter ! Either you return the postal order taken from Mr. Quelch's study, or you leave the school to-day."

P

" Ooooooooooh ! "

" For the last time, Bunter——"

" Oh, crikey ! "

" If you have nothing to say, Bunter——"

" Oh ! Yes, sir ! " howled Bunter. " It wasn't me, sir ! I never cashed it because it was lost through the pole in the hocket—I mean the jacket in the lining—and I never took it from Mr. Quelch's study at all—it wasn't there when I went to the study, and—I—I—I never went to the study, sir—never went near it, and—and—and——"

" That will do, Bunter."

" Oh ! Thank you, sir ! Can I—I go now ? "

" You may go to your dormitory and pack your box. You will do so under Mr. Quelch's charge. You will then——"

Tap !

It was a tap at the study door. Dr. Locke glanced round : Mr. Quelch glanced round : Billy Bunter blinked round : as the door opened, revealing the trim figure and rosy cheeks of Mary the housemaid.

CHAPTER XXXIX

LIGHT AT LAST

" If you please, sir—— ! " said Mary.

" What—what—— ? "

Mary stepped into the study.

Dr. Locke breathed a little hard. Mr. Quelch knitted his brows. Really, it was not a suitable moment for Mary to interrupt. Both the masters gazed at her expressively. Billy Bunter gave her an uninterested blink. Unperturbed, Mary came in.

" What—what is it, Mary ? " asked the Head, somewhat testily. " I am busy—you are interrupting me—— "

" Yes, sir," said Mary. " It's Mr. Quelch, sir—— "

" What ? what ? "

" I have been to Mr. Quelch's study, sir," said Mary, " but he was not there. So I came here, sir."

" Really—— ! " said the Head.

" If you desire to speak to me, Mary, you should wait till I am disengaged," said Mr. Quelch. " At the moment—— "

" Yes, sir," said Mary, stolidly. " Mrs. Kebble said that I had better see you at once about it, sir, as it's very important, she said, one of the young gentlemen, sir, being in trouble about it."

" Eh ? "

" What ? "

Mary's remarks were so much Greek to the Head and Mr. Quelch. True, they were well acquainted with the tongue of Demosthenes, Euripides, and Sophocles. But Mary's meaning was beyond them.

" I fail to see—— ! " said Mr. Quelch.

" Kindly explain yourself, Mary," said the Head.

" Yes, sir ! It's about the Hoover, sir—— "

" The—the—the Hoover ! " repeated Mr. Quelch.

" Yes, sir."

" You mean the—the vacuum-sweeper——— ? "

" Yes, sir."

" In the name of all that is absurd," exclaimed Mr. Quelch, " are you interrupting Dr. Locke in order to tell me something about sweeping carpets, Mary ? "

" Yes, sir."

" Then kindly tell me some other time, if it be necessary to tell me at all," exclaimed Mr. Quelch.

" Mrs. Kebble said it was important, sir, because Master Bunter was suspected, sir," said Mary, calmly.

This was doubly-Greek to the two masters. But it dawned upon them that Mary's unexpected visit to the head-master's study had something to do with the charge under which the fate of Bunter now hung in the balance.

" Bless my soul ! " said Dr. Locke. " Do you know anything about the occurrence in Mr. Quelch's study on Tuesday, Mary ? "

" Yes, sir. Everyone has been talking about it, sir," answered Mary, placidly. " We all know about the postal order being missing, sir, and Master Bunter hiding away, and——"

" Yes ! Yes ! No doubt ! No doubt ! But you have implied that you know something of the actual occurrence——"

" Yes, sir ! "

" Then kindly tell me at once what you know of the matter, and you may speak to Mr. Quelch later about the vacuum-sweeper."

" But that's it, sir," said Mary. " It's about the Hoover. The young man came from Courtfield this morning to repair the Hoover, sir. It was put out of order by Master Bunter falling on it——"

" Yes, yes, yes ! That is all immaterial, Mary. Kindly keep to the point."

" That is the point, sir," said Mary. " I was using the Hoover in Mr. Quelch's study that day, sir. That is how it happened."

" How it happened ? " repeated the Head, blankly.

" Yes, sir."

" How what happened ? " gasped Mr. Quelch.

" I mean, that is how it must have happened, sir," said Mary, " and it would have been found out the same evening, if Master Bunter had not fallen on the Hoover and damaged the motor, sir. Because after the Hoover has been done with for the day, sir, I empty the dust-bag. But the Hoover being out of order, I did not empty the dust-bag as usual, sir, but just left it, when I wheeled the Hoover away, and went to tell Mrs. Kebble what had happened."

Dr. Locke looked at Mr. Quelch. Mr. Quelch looked at Dr. Locke. They were wise gentlemen with oceans of knowledge : and if Mary had been speaking in Latin or Greek, French or German, or even Anglo-Saxon, they would have understood her without difficulty. But what she might possibly be meaning now, was a mystery to both of them. She meant something—they grasped that much, and what she meant, had something to do with Bunter and the missing postal order. But the rest was dim mystery.

" If you will try to make yourself clear, Mary——! " said Dr. Locke, with the gentle patience he had learned in forty years as a schoolmaster.

" Yes, sir. The young man came from Courtfield this morning, sir——"

" Never mind the young man from Courtfield——"

" But he has just finished repairing the Hoover, sir——"

" Never mind the Hoover now, Mary."

" And of course, sir, as he was putting the Hoover in order, he emptied the dust-bag——"

" Never mind the—the dust-bag——"

" And everything I had swept up in Mr. Quelch's study

was in it, sir," explained Mary. "Everything I swept up
in Mr. Quelch's study on Tuesday, sir——"

"No doubt ! No doubt ! But——"

"And when he found the postal order in it, sir——"

"What ? "

"WHAT ? "

"——he handed it to Mrs. Kebble, sir——" pursued
Mary.

"He—he found——"

"——a—a—a postal order—— ! "

"Yes, sir, in the dust-bag of the Hoover, sir," said Mary.
"That was what I came to tell Mr. Quelch, sir, as Mrs.
Kebble said it was important, as the postal order was
missing, sir, and Master Bunter was supposed——"

"Bless my soul ! " said the Head.

"Upon my word ! " said Mr. Quelch.

"Oh, crikey ! " gasped Billy Bunter.

Three pairs of eyes, and one pair of spectacles, were
fixed quite eagerly on the placid face of Mary.

"Mary ! " exclaimed the Head. "Do I understand you
to say that a—a postal order was found in the dust-bag
of the vacuum-sweeper, after it had been used in Mr.
Quelch's study ? "

"Yes, sir."

"Where is it now ? "

"Here, sir."

From a pocket of her apron, Mary produced a crumpled,
dusty strip of paper. She laid it on the Head's writing-
table.

Dr. Locke gazed at it. Mr. Quelch gazed at it. Billy
Bunter gazed at it with eyes that nearly popped through
his spectacles.

It was a postal order for a pound.

"Oh, jiminy ! " gasped Bunter.

"I did not notice it in sweeping up the study, sir,"
went on Mary's placid voice. "I think it was very likely
under Mr. Quelch's table, sir, among bits of waste-paper

near the waste-paper basket. If it hadn't been, I think I should have seen it, sir. But if it was under the table among bits of paper, I shouldn't see it, and it would go into the Hoover with the rest——"

" Oh ! Yes ! Quite ! "

Billy Bunter knew now where he had dropped that postal order through the hole in his pocket !

" Mr. Quelch ! Kindly examine the postal order," said Dr. Locke. " No doubt it is the one that is missing——"

" No doubt, sir, from what Mary tells us."

Mr. Quelch kindly examined the postal order. It was intact, the counterfoil still attached, and plainly marked with the office of issue, Friardale, and the date. Mr. Quelch nodded.

" Yes, sir ! This is the missing postal order, undoubtedly ! That incredibly stupid boy must have dropped it in my study, though I hardly see how he could have dropped it under the table——"

Bunter could have enlightened his form-master on that point !

" But it is certainly the postal order," said Mr. Quelch, " and its discovery in the dust-bag of the Hoover does undoubtedly bear out Bunter's statement that he had lost it——"

" Undoubtedly," agreed the Head.

" Oh, gum ! " breathed Bunter.

" Mary, I am much obliged to you," said the Head. " Thank you, Mary, for coming and telling me this ! " The Head was too courteous to add that, had Mary produced the postal order from the pocket of her apron at the start, it would have saved a lot of time

" Yes, sir," said Mary.

Mary faded out of the study. Dr. Locke and Mr. Quelch looked at one another, and then looked at Billy Bunter. Billy Bunter blinked at them, uneasily but hopefully.

" Mr. Quelch," said the Head, at last, " in view of this

confirmation of Bunter's statement that the postal order was lost, I think we may give credence to his extraordinary explanation that he did actually take it from your study by mistake——"

" I think so, sir ! Making allowance for the boy's stupidity——"

" His very unusual stupidity—— ! " assented the Head.

" His almost impenetrable obtuseness——" said Mr. Quelch.

" Bunter ! In view of this, you are exonerated," said Dr. Locke. " I shall overlook—and your form-master will kindly overlook—your extraordinary conduct during the past few days. You may go ! "

It was not necessary for the Head to speak twice ! The words were hardly out of his mouth when Billy Bunter was out of the study !

CHAPTER XL

ALL RIGHT—EXCEPT——

" Bunter ! "

  " Billy Bunter ! "

  " The esteemed and ridiculous Bunter ! "

  " That ass—— ! "

  " That chump—— ! "

  " Bunter ! "

It was quite a roar.

Break was almost over. Many Remove fellows, in the quad, were thinking, or talking, of Bunter. The fugitive Owl was still front-page news at Greyfriars. But they certainly were not expecting to see him !

Now they saw him !

A fat figure rolled out of the House. A big pair of spectacles flashed back the rays of the sun. Billy Bunter, supposed up to that moment to be hidden so deep that beaks and prefects could not get track of him, having apparently, as Fisher T. Fish expressed it, got into a hole and pulled it in after him, rolled out into full view of the whole school, as large as life.

Remove fellows, and other fellows, crowded up from all sides. Bunter grinned at them as they crowded up. The Owl of the Remove was the cynosure of all eyes.

  " Bunter ! " exclaimed Harry Wharton.

  " Bunter ! " exclaimed Frank Nugent.

  " Bunter ! " yelled Bob Cherry.

  " The absurd and preposterous Bunter ! " ejaculated Hurree Jamset Ram Singh.

  " Bunter ! " roared Johnny Bull.

  " That fat tick Bunter ! " exclaimed Coker of the Fifth.

  " Bunter, you fat ass ! " exclaimed the Bounder. " What are you doing here ? "

"Cut before Quelch spots you!" grinned Skinner.

"Look out," said Squiff.   "Wingate's in the quad——"

"Hook it, Bunter——"

"Look out for Loder——"

"Blow away, Bunter."

"They'll get you!"

Billy Bunter did not hook it. He did not blow away. He did not cut. He grinned cheerfully at the encircling crowd. Bunter was no longer on the run!

"I say, you fellows," he squeaked. "It's all right! I've just been with the Head."

"Oh!" exclaimed Harry Wharton. "Did they get you?"

"That beast Quelch did! You see, I'd dodged into the Head's study——"

"Oh, my hat!"

"I thought I was pretty safe, in the corner behind the arm-chair, but Quelch rooted me out," said Bunter, "and I can tell you that the Head was jawing me like billy-o, when it all came out, and——"

"Bunked?" asked the Bounder.

"No, I jolly well ain't."

"Then what—— ?" asked Harry Wharton

Bunter chuckled. Evidently, he was in cheery spirits. His beaming fat countenance indicated that his trials and tribulations were over—that the wicked had ceased from troubling, and the weary Owl was at rest! Once more he could venture forth into the light of day, regardless of prefects, indifferent to beaks.

"You see, it's all right," said Bunter. "They've found it."

"Who's found what?" asked Bob.

"That postal order!" trilled Bunter, triumphantly.

"What?"

"I told you it was lost, you know——"

"You did!" grunted Johnny Bull.

"You didn't believe me, Bull?" said Bunter, accusingly.

" I didn't ! " agreed Johnny.

" The truefulness of your idiotic remarks is not always terrific, my esteemed fat Bunter," remarked Hurree Jamset Ram Singh, with a shake of his dusky head.

" Oh, really, Inky——"

" You don't mean to say that you were telling the truth about it, Bunter," exclaimed the Bounder.

" I jolly well was ! " roared Bunter.

" Well ! " said Smithy. " Wonders will never cease ! "

" Ha, ha, ha ! "

" So they've found that missing postal order ? " asked Skinner.

" Yes ; they jolly well have."

" And which of your pockets did they find it in ? "

" Beast ! "

" Well, I'm jolly glad they've found it, if they have," said Harry Wharton. " But where did they find it, Bunter ? "

" In the Hoover."

" In the whatter ? " ejaculated Peter Todd.

" The Hoover—that vacuum-sweeper, or suction-sweeper, or whatever it is—in the dust-bag," said Bunter. " It must have dropped from my pocket while I was crumpled up under Quelch's table, keeping doggo while that old ass Prout was there, you know. As far as I can make out, Mary was hoovering the study afterwards, and the blessed thing took it in along with other bits of paper and things under Quelch's table. And they found it in the dust-bag this morning ! "

" Well, my hat ! "

" And has Quelch got it now ? " asked Johnny Bull.

" He jolly well has ! "

" Then you really had lost it ? "

" I told you I had ! " hooted Bunter.

" Yes, I know that ! But it seems that you really had, although you said you had ! "

" Ha, ha, ha ! "

" Oh, really, Bull ! "

" So you're not going to be bunked, after all ? " asked Hobson of the Shell.

" No jolly fear ! "

" Pity ! " remarked Skinner.

" Ha, ha, ha ! "

" Gratters, old fat man," said Harry Wharton, laughing.

" The gratterfulness is terrific."

" Terrific and preposterous ! " said Bob Cherry.   " We're not going to lose our Bunter.   There would have been a lot of dry eyes if we had !   But gratters all the same."

" It's all right now," said Bunter.   He gave the Famous Five a reproachful blink.   " You fellows doubted my word ! You needn't deny it—you did ! "

" Guilty, my lord ! "

" Another time, perhaps you'll believe me ! " said Bunter, loftily.

" Perhaps ! " said Bob.

" The perhapsfulness is terrific."

" Not likely ! " said Johnny Bull, shaking his head.

" Ha, ha, ha ! "

" Oh, really, you fellows !   I say, it's all right now— right as rain," said Bunter.   " Quite all right—except——"

" Except what ? "

" Well, you see, as that postal order wasn't mind after all, and as my Uncle Carter isn't sending me a postal order till next week, according to his letter, I'm still stony, and——"

" Hallo, hallo, hallo !   There goes the bell ! "

" Never mind the bell for a minute !   I say, you fellows, I told you that I'm expecting a postal order——"

" There's the bell——"

" Blow the bell !   Don't walk off while a fellow's talking to you !   I say, you fellows, who's going to lend me a quid till my postal order comes ? "

There was no reply to that question.   The bell was ringing for third school, and the fellows headed for the form-rooms. No doubt they were glad to see Bunter at the end of his trials and tribulations : restored to the arms of the Remove, as it were. But nobody, it seemed, was prepared to lend him a pound till his postal order came ! They passed by Bunter's question like the idle wind which they regarded not.

" I say, you fellows," howled Bunter.

But the fellows were gone ! And Billy Bunter, with a snort, rolled after them to the Remove form-room : once more to sit and absorb knowledge under a gimlet-eye, and still expecting a postal order !

THE END